BANDS OF GOLD

This Large Print Book carries the
Seal of Approval of N.A.V.H.

BANDS OF GOLD

ANGELA BENSON

THORNDIKE PRESS

An Imprint of Thomson Gale, a part of The Thomson Corporation

Detroit • New York • San Francisco • New Haven, Conn. • Waterville, Maine • London

Copyright © 1994 by Angela Benson.

Thomson Gale is part of The Thomson Corporation.

Thomson and Star Logo and Thorndike are trademarks and Gale is a registered trademark used herein under license.

Thorndike Press® Large Print African-American.

The text of this Large Print edition is unabridged.

Other aspects of the book may vary from the original edition.

Set in 16 pt. Plantin.

LIBRARY OF CONGRESS CATALOGING-IN-PUBLICATION DATA

Benson, Angela.
  Bands of gold / by Angela Benson.
    p. cm. — (Thorndike Press large print African-American)
  ISBN 0-7862-9175-3 (hardcover : alk. paper) 1. African American yuppies
  — Fiction. 2. Large type books. I. Title.
  PS3552.E5476585B36 2006
  813'.54—dc22
                                               2006029083

U.S. Hardcover:
ISBN 13: 978-0-7862-9175-5
ISBN 10: 0-7862-9175-3

Published in 2006 by arrangement with Harlequin Books S.A.

Printed in the United States of America on permanent paper
10 9 8 7 6 5 4 3 2 1

BANDS OF GOLD

CHAPTER 1

"They're pressuring me to change my mind." Christina sat in her office on the forty-first floor of Boston's John Hancock Towers, twirling the cord of the telephone handset as she spoke.

"Don't let them decide for you. It's your life."

"I know, Mom, but they have some good points. Maybe I should reconsider." Christina wrapped the telephone cord around her lower arm.

"Look, Christina," Louise began. "This is your mama talking."

Christina smiled. She knew what was coming.

"I've known you a lot longer than those people you work with and I'm telling you to do what you think is right. Go with your instincts. You know what I want, but it's not my decision. You do what's best for you. I'm with you either way. Got that?"

"I've got it," Christina answered. "Have I told you lately that you're a great mom?"

"You have, but I never get tired of hearing it," Louise replied.

"You're the greatest, Mom. Really." As Christina unwrapped the phone cord from her arm, she looked at her watch. Standing up, she said, "I have to hang up now. Walter's waiting. Wish me luck."

"You don't need it, but good luck. Let me know how things turn out."

"Okay, Mom," Christina agreed. She hung up the phone and walked out of her office.

Since her promotion to senior engineer in charge of new accounts, Christina had made the walk to Walter's office many times. Walter loved to talk; at least, he loved talking to her. He had become her self-appointed mentor, and he always wanted to know what she was doing. He had been a lot of help when she was first promoted and she appreciated that, but sometimes she felt that Walter went overboard in his concern.

"I don't want you to go," Walter began, as soon as she entered his office.

"I know, Walter, and I'm glad that you like having me around, but I have to go," Christina responded. She sat in the visitor's chair closest to his massive oak desk.

"No, you don't have to leave. You can stay

here." Walter got up from his desk and took a seat next to her.

"We've been through this before. I'm going."

Trying another tactic, he asked, "What will it take to make you stay?"

"It's not about the money. You know that," she answered, shaking her head.

"I'm not talking about money. I'm talking about OPTIMA."

Christina leaned forward slightly in her chair. She had heard about OPTIMA. The high-visibility project could skyrocket the career of some lucky manager. "What about OPTIMA?"

Walter moved back in his chair and steepled his fingers across the bridge of his nose. "The board has agreed that OPTIMA is yours if you stay."

"You can't be serious. That would mean a two-step promotion for me. That's unheard of at Communications Limited."

"There's a first time for everything." Walter took her hand in his. "We want to keep you here, Christina."

Christina withdrew her hand. "You make it sound as though I'm defecting to an enemy camp. I'm only transferring to the Atlanta office."

Walter sat back in his chair. "Going to

Atlanta is almost as bad as defection."

"It is not. How can you say that?" Christina stood up and walked towards the wall of windows that faced Copley Square. She saw specks of milling bodies that looked more like ants than people.

Walter spoke to her back. "You know you've done good work — no, outstanding work — in the seven years you've been here. Some people, me included, are looking for you to occupy a VP seat some day. The quickest way to that seat is to stay in Boston. Atlanta may as well be another company."

Christina turned to face him. "I know what you're saying is true." She knew she was on the fast track at CL. She knew she was a good engineer. She had showcased her abilities on three high-profile projects. Things were going according to plan . . . maybe even better than planned. "OPTIMA could get me the VP seat a few years early, but Atlanta is something that I have to do."

"You're allowed to change your mind, you know." Walter stood up and shoved his hands into his pants pockets. "One phone call and OPTIMA is yours."

"Walter . . ."

He interrupted, "Which do you want,

Christina, a direct path to a vice presidency, or a detour to Atlanta?"

Fifty-four-year-old Walter Thomas sat facing the windows, looking out but not seeing anything. He had been at Communications Limited, affectionately called CL by its employees, for some twenty-five years. When he had started, CL was a small, start-up operation. Today, it was a multibillion-dollar business with offices in twenty major cities across the country. Boston was its headquarters, and headquarters was where things happened. Why couldn't he get Christina to see that? He knew that he hadn't changed her mind. She still planned to go to Atlanta.

Young people, he thought. You couldn't reason with them when they got their minds set. What was Christina thinking about? Didn't she see the opportunity before her? Most engineers in her position would trade their right arm for a shot at OPTIMA.

Walter knew his reaction to Christina's planned move was as much personal as it was professional. He had watched her mature into a fine engineer. She reminded him of himself at her age. Because he considered her his protégée, he couldn't let her make the move to Atlanta, a move that could effectively stall her career.

"If I can't convince her to stay, I know someone who can," he said aloud. He turned around in his chair and dialed Rosalind's number.

Christina arrived at Mr. Chen's restaurant a few minutes late. She knew that Rosalind Jones would already be there. She gave the maître d' her name and followed him to Rosalind's table. Though she had been in the restaurant more times than she could count, she still felt awkward during the walk to the table. The back lacquered walls, the flower arrangements, the tuxedoed waiters and the spotlight-studded ceiling made a perfect picture. Too perfect. She always got the feeling that her slip was showing and that everyone noticed. Never had her slip showed, yet each time she came to this restaurant she felt the same way. It was just one of her little insecurities.

Rosalind looked up and saw her. Christina smiled. Rosalind Jones and Walter Thomas were old friends. They began their careers at CL around the same time and had achieved comparable levels of success. Both were vice presidents. Her rise to that post occurred before the Women's Movement, before the age of women "having it all." Rosalind had a job, a career, but she didn't have a husband or children.

As soon as the maître d' seated her, Christina began, "Why do I get the feeling this isn't a casual lunch?"

Rosalind laughed. "You're right, it's not. Walter has assigned me to the 'Christina project.' My job is to make you see the error of your ways and stay here in Boston."

Christina frowned. "I knew Walter had a hand in this." She was getting tired of explaining herself. "I'm hungry, so let's order before you get started."

"Fair enough," Rosalind consented.

After the women quickly placed their orders, Rosalind asked, "Why are you so hell-bent on going to Atlanta?"

Christina picked up her napkin and placed it in her lap. "As I told Walter, it's time. I've always wanted to move south. I grew up in Alabama and I went to college in Atlanta. I'm ready to go back."

"That's a strictly personal reason, Christina. Don't you see that it would be better for your career if you stayed here with OP-TIMA?"

Christina rearranged her napkin in her lap. She was determined not to get upset. "I agree that OPTIMA is a great project, but ORION has its good points as well." ORION was the primary software project assigned to the Atlanta staff.

"How can you say that? ORION is in chaos. The Board just ousted Paul Bechtel. The guy practically ruined that project. Why do you want to step into the middle of that? OPTIMA is fresh, new. It would be yours from day one."

"I don't share your view of ORION, Rosalind. I consider it a challenge. I've been putting together a plan to turn the project around. It can still be successful for CL. I can make it successful."

"I don't doubt your ability at all, but I wonder at your judgment. Why do you want to go with ORION, whose chances of success are slim, when you can have OPTIMA, whose chances of success are great? The real question, Christina, is which you want more — a move to Atlanta, or a shot at the vice presidency?"

Christina sat back in her chair and clasped her hands in her lap. "I didn't know they were mutually exclusive. Are they?"

"All the data indicate your best bet is to stay here in Boston. You know the saying, 'Out of sight, out of mind.' Atlanta is definitely out of sight."

The arrival of their food interrupted the conversation.

As soon as the waiter left, Christina leaned

forward and placed her hands palms down on the table. "Listen, Rosalind, I appreciate what you and Walter are trying to do, but I know what I want."

Rosalind shook her head. "I hope you do, Christina, because I'd hate to see you throw away your career."

Christina pondered Rosalind's and Walter's comments as she did the dinner dishes later that night. When she finished, she turned off the lights in the kitchen and went to her bedroom. She sat down on the side of the bed and removed a small black leather notebook from her nightstand. Turning to the page entitled "Personal Goals," she began to read. A few minutes later, she picked up the phone and dialed her mother's number. No answer. She hung up and dialed another number.

"Marshall's Nursery," her mother answered.

"Mom, it's me." Christina still held the black leather notebook.

"Christina, how are you, honey?"

"Great, Mom," Christian answered. She placed the notebook back in the nightstand. "I know what I'm going to do."

■ ■ ■ ■

One year later

Christina and Louise arrived at Boston's Four Seasons Hotel for the Communications Limited Annual Awards Ceremony at seven o'clock. Since Christina was the guest of honor, she and Louise sat at the head of the table.

As soon as dessert was served, Walter moved to the podium. The tinkling of fork against glass got everyone's attention and he began.

"This evening we're honoring one of our own, Christina Marshall. She's being honored for her work on ORION. This time last year few of us were optimistic about the success of ORION. Gross mismanagement had the project behind schedule and out of focus. Christina changed all of that.

"Her success is no surprise. Stellar performance has marked each of her eight years here at CL, from her first assignment as associate engineer, to her job as project engineer, then senior engineer, and now managing engineer for ORION."

Walter turned to Christina. "Ladies and gentlemen, Christina Marshall."

Christina made the short walk to the podium amid a swell of applause. She wondered again at her wisdom in wearing the form-fitting blue sequined gown. Her first thought had been that it hugged her full breasts a bit too snugly, but Louise had convinced her that that wasn't the case. Now, making the trip to the podium, she was unsure again. Maybe the dress was too tight. Maybe she shouldn't have worn her hair up, exposing her long neck and smooth shoulders. Maybe . . .

Christina shook off the negative thoughts. She held her head high and stood tall, naked shoulder and neck be damned. Tonight was her night and she was going to enjoy it.

She viewed the award as confirmation of her instincts. She had been right to go to Atlanta. It had been a tough year, but all the hard work had paid off. The success of ORION had put her back on the fast track. "Thank you, Walter. Thanks to the board for this recognition. I share it with my staff in Atlanta. They worked tirelessly for the past year and the success of ORION is the result. We in Atlanta accept this award as a symbol of the faith that CL has in our operation. We will continue to serve CL with the professionalism and excellence that inspired this award. Thank you."

Another round of applause followed as Christina returned to her seat.

Rosalind took the podium next. "It's no secret that some of us were convinced that Christina shouldn't take the ORION position. We thought OPTIMA was the better project for her. Though she proved us wrong on the first point, we still think that she's the best person for OPTIMA. So, effective the first of next month, Christina Marshall is the new district manager for OPTIMA."

Louise smiled at Christina and squeezed her hand with joy. "I knew you'd make the right decision. Now you have OPTIMA *and* Atlanta. You have everything you wanted."

Christina returned pressure to her mother's hand. "Yes, Mom, everything I wanted." Even as she spoke the words, Christina knew they weren't true. She didn't have everything she wanted. Not yet.

CHAPTER 2

Christina looked at the clock on the micro-wave above the oven. Good timing. It was almost seven. Liza should be arriving any minute now, she thought, as she put her special green bean casserole in the oven.

It has been several years since she'd seen her old friend. She sighed over the fact that it had taken OPTIMA to bring them back together. She had her fingers crossed that Liza would take the job as one of her project managers. It would be good to have a girlfriend again. As if on cue, the doorbell rang.

"It's so good to see you again, Liza. Has it really been three years?" Christina asked, after they had shared hugs.

"Three long years," Liza said. "The last time we saw each other was the night we celebrated our promotions to senior engineer."

"Yes," Christina said. "A combination

celebration and going-away party."

"You were lucky. You got to stay in Boston, but I had to move to Forth Worth."

"At the time, I didn't see myself as the lucky one. I would have given anything for a move back south."

"Yeah," Liza said. "And look what happened when you did move south. Congrats again on your promotion to district manager and your success with ORION. I'm sorry I couldn't make the banquet."

Christina waved her hands to dismiss Liza's apology. "Don't even think about it. You sent a card. I understand. Now tell me what you've been up to."

Christina led Liza to the family room, where they seated themselves on identical facing blue leather couches. They began to catch up on all that had happened while they'd been apart.

"You're getting married!" Christina practically shrieked at her friend's news. "I didn't even know you were seeing anyone. When did this happen?"

"You knew I was seeing someone, Christina. I told you. Remember? His name's Robert. I met him at a Professional Accountants meeting."

"Oh, yes, I do recall something about your going to some meeting to meet men."

Liza placed one hand on her hip and shook her finger at Christina. "I didn't go to meet men. I have a real interest in accounting."

Christina laughed. "Sure you do, Liza. Anyway, I'm not knocking it. Maybe I should try it. It worked well for you."

Christina got up from the couch. "I want to hear all about this guy of yours. How about something to drink first? This is an occasion for wine. Which do you prefer, white or red?"

"White."

"Two white wines coming up."

When Christina went to prepare the drinks, Liza got up and walked around the room. She was seated in front of the fireplace when Christina returned.

Taking a sip, Liza began her story. "You remember how much I hated Fort Worth when I first got there? After the first month, I was sure that going there was the biggest mistake of my life. Then I met Robert." Liza faced Christina. "He changed my life. It's hard to explain."

That single statement touched Christina in a secret place. For the first time, she was envious of Liza. To cover her feelings, she remarked in jest, "So, he was your knight in shining armor. He rescued you from the boredom of Forth Worth."

"No," Liza corrected, her voice soft, almost serene. "It wasn't like that. It may have started like that, but Robert and I had to work hard for our love."

"What do you mean?" Christina asked, now serious.

"From the beginning I liked him a lot. He was such fun to be with. We had common interests — I loved a good party, we found the same things funny. The laughter attracted me first. Then his cooking."

Christina was surprised. "He cooks?"

Liza nodded. "The man is a master chef. He started cooking for me after our second date. He said that I didn't eat right and he made it his business to see that I did. I liked that. It showed that he cared, and it felt good to have someone care." Liza's voice wavered as she said the last. She got up, swirling her drink around in her glass. Her eyes focused intently on Varnette P. Honeywood's *Jackie's Song,* hanging on the wall above the television, but it seemed her thoughts were miles away.

"What is it, Liza?" Christina asked.

Liza looked at Christina then. She smiled a smile that didn't quite reach her eyes. "He had problems with my weight at first."

"Oh," was the only comment Christina

22

could make. She knew how the weight comments could kill a budding relationship. Obviously, though, Liza and Robert had gotten past them.

"He had this picture of the woman he would marry. She was a size 5 or 7 or 9. You know that I'm none of those."

Christina looked at her friend's two-hundred pound frame and understood how she must have felt. Though Liza was an attractive, well-proportioned woman with soft features, Christina knew that sometimes men only saw the weight. Christina had first-hand experience with that herself. She had been Liza's weight before and knew it was hell getting a relationship started and even tougher keeping it going. One could work through it, though. Liza and Robert were proof of that. "How did you two deal with it?"

"I fought for him. In the past, I would have backed out of the relationship to keep from getting hurt. This time I couldn't do that. Robert had become too important to me. It was too close to call for a while, but once Robert admitted to himself that he loved me, we knew we had it made." Liza smiled and lifted her glass in a toast. "Here's to women who fight for what they want."

"I'm for all that," Christina agreed, lifting

her glass. "So, what about sex?" The question rushed out. If she had taken time to think about it, she would never have asked it.

"What about it?"

It was too late for Christina to take it back now. "That's what I'm asking you."

"Of course, we've made love. We're good together. What more can I say?"

Christina placed her glass on the table and rose from her seat. Though she wanted to have this conversation, she was beginning to feel uncomfortable. Vulnerable. "I don't quite know how to ask this, but I need to know."

"Just ask. It's obviously important to you. If I don't want to answer it, I won't."

The next words rushed out of Christina's mouth. "Was it hard to take your clothes off the first time?"

Liza didn't answer immediately. She took a deep breath and nodded in a way that made Christina think that the question brought unhappy memories. "It was a little difficult the first time. I knew that Robert cared for me, but I didn't know how he'd respond to the whole me, naked. His response . . . well, let's call it enthusiastic. After the first time, it was no longer an issue." Liza's expression brightened and she looked directly at Christina. "Why do you ask?"

Christina turned away. "It scares me, Liza. That's the reason, or at least that's one of the reasons, I haven't allowed anybody to get close to me. I'm afraid of the rejection. I've lost a lot of weight, but I still don't have a model's body and I don't know if I could handle rejection if it came at an intimate moment like that."

Surprised, Liza sat on the couch and placed her glass on the cocktail table. "Are you telling me you're still a virgin?" When Christina didn't answer, Liza continued, "What about you and Bruce?"

Christina took a seat on the couch facing Liza. "Nothing happened. We came close a few times. I just couldn't go through with it. I had mixed feelings. I liked being close, but I feared his reaction to my naked body and I was scared to death of becoming pregnant. There was no way I was going to get pregnant and have to quit school. My worst nightmare is being an unwed mother. I saw the problems my mom faced, and I don't want to face them. Neither do I want to put my children through them."

"There's such a thing as birth control," Liza reasoned.

Christina picked up her glass and ran her

finger around its rim. "Yes, but nothing is a hundred percent effective. Anyway, with Bruce, fear of pregnancy wasn't the only hindrance. I wasn't sure I loved him. So, I couldn't make love with him."

"My, my," Liza clasped her hands together. "A thirty-year-old virgin. I'll bet there aren't many of you around."

"You'd lose your money. The June issue of *Cosmopolitan* had a survey that showed there are a large group of us."

Liza began shaking her head. "I don't see how you made it through college."

"In the words of my mother, I kept my dress down and my legs closed."

Laughing, Liza admonished, "Christina, you're awful."

"It's true, though now it's like a bad habit that I can't break."

"I've never heard virginity called a bad habit before."

"You know what I mean," Christina said. She drank the last of her wine and leaned back on the couch. "Once you get used to keeping men at arm's length, you find yourself doing it automatically, even when you don't want to. Now that I've waited so long, I find more reasons I shouldn't — my body, my age, AIDS. You name it."

"All people have insecurities, Christina,

but they don't let those insecurities stop them from pursuing relationships. You shouldn't let yours stop you, either."

Intellectually, she knew Liza was right, but emotionally, she wasn't sure she was ready for that kind of advice. "It's so easy to fill my life with other things — the house, work — so that I don't have to think about how much I'm missing or how much I want a real relationship, marriage, and children."

"You can have all of that, if you're willing to work for it. You've got to get outside yourself and take a risk. Being vulnerable is the foundation of any relationship."

Christina knew there was truth in Liza's words, but it was too much for her to think about right now. To lighten the conversation, she asked, "Are you sure I can't have a relationship that's guaranteed not to hurt? I'm so used to formulas and equations that I should be able to create the perfect relationship."

Liza shook her head. "Sorry, my friend, it doesn't work that way. Everybody gets hurt. Some more than others. As they say, 'No pain, No gain.' "

"You must be getting tired, Liza. Isn't that an exercise slogan?"

Liza laughed. "What do you expect this late at night? You have to catch me in the morning for something original."

"I'll remember that." Christina stood up. "My famous green bean casserole should be ready about now. Are you hungry?"

Liza stood, too. "I thought you'd never ask. Lead the way."

The women ate a relaxed dinner as Liza talked more about her wedding plans. After dinner, Christina gave Liza the grand tour of her home. They ended up in the guest bedroom where Liza would sleep. The blue-patterned curtains and comforter were warm and suited the night and the night's conversation.

"You have a very comfortable and inviting home, Christina. I hope Robert and I can find something as good. We really want to buy a house. How long have you been here?"

"Seven months now. It seems longer, though," Christina answered.

"How so?"

"There's a lot of work to do when you live in a house. Yard work and housework. And there's not that much time left when you're working twelve- and fifteen-hour days. It might be easier for you and Robert, since there will be two of you."

Liza didn't agree. "That won't help. We're both going to be very busy when we first move here. Maybe we should wait a while before we buy?"

"That's what I did. When I first moved back, I lived in an apartment in midtown, so I'd be close to work. I was working close to twenty-four-hour days then."

Liza sat on the edge of the bed and pulled off her shoes. "Why such long hours? I know there was a lot of work, but that much time is a bit extreme, even for you."

"I was determined to make a success of this move," Christina said, leaning against the chest nearest the door. "Walter and Rosalind were dead set against it. They didn't think it was a wise career move. I wanted to prove them wrong."

"Well, you definitely did that," Liza stated.

"So I did," Christina said. She *had* proved Rosalind and Walter wrong, but she still hadn't achieved her primary goal. Talking with Liza tonight made her realize that all the more.

"It seems like you're settling in for the duration."

"In a way, I am," Christina said. "I never considered Boston home. It was a stopover on my way back to Atlanta. Now that I'm here, I want to establish roots, settle down, build a future." Christina knew she sounded like she was on a soapbox. "Sound crazy?"

"Not at all. That's the way I feel. I want

Robert and me to establish roots, settle down, build a future."

"You're lucky," Christina said. "You've already found that special person to share the future with you."

Christina and Liza rushed to the office the next morning. It was about a thirty-minute drive, in rush-hour traffic, from Christina's house to the midtown office of Communications Limited. Christina took Liza on a tour of the facility, introduced her to the staff, and then took her to lunch with the people who would be reporting to her. After lunch they went back to Christina's office.

"It's going to be at least four months before I can make the move," Liza said. "With my current project, the wedding and the honeymoon, four months is probably optimistic."

"We'll work that out. I'm just glad you want the job. Your delayed start won't present much of a problem if Jackson Duncan can start immediately. The first six to nine months will be planning anyway, and Jackson will handle that. You'll handle the implementation."

"Has he accepted the job?" Liza asked.

Christina shook her head. She was interviewing Jackson Duncan for the other project manager position on her staff. "He'll be in tomorrow."

"I've heard only good things about his work. And though he has the reputation of being a ladies' man, I hope he takes the job."

"His reputation doesn't bother me," Christina said. "I'm only interested in what he'll do in the office. And I have a feeling that he's going to accept the job. Walter hinted that he'd recommended Jackson take it. And you know how Walter recommends."

Liza laughed. "I see what you mean." She looked at her watch. "The limo should be here to take me to the airport. I'd better go down now."

Christina rode the elevator to the lobby with her. "It's been good seeing you again, Liza. Thanks for the talk last night."

"Remember what I told you — don't let your insecurities stop you from going after what you want. You don't let it happen in your professional life, so don't let it happen in your personal life. Go after what you want."

After giving Christina a short hug, Liza got into the limo. Christina watched as the car pulled away. "Go after what you want," Christina spoke softly to herself. "Maybe I should do that."

"Excuse me, Miss Marshall." A security

guard interrupted her thoughts. "Do you need any help?"

"No," Christina said. "I'm fine."

Christina returned to her office. She tried to review the paperwork on Jackson Duncan, but her mind still focused on her conversation with Liza last night. Since she wasn't accomplishing anything, she placed the Jackson Duncan file in her briefcase and left for the day.

Once home, Christina went directly to her bedroom and removed the small black leather notebook from her nightstand. She sat on the floor beside the bed, turned to the page entitled "Personal Goals," and began to read. The list read:

1. Move to Atlanta
2. Get established in job
3. Buy house
4. Get established in community
5. Make friends
6. Fall in love
7. Get married
8. Have 3 children

Of the eight entries, Christina had already accomplished the first three. The Outstanding Manager Award for her work on ORION indicated her success. Now she was a district manager and OPTIMA was her project. Not bad for one year.

She was working on numbers 4 and 5. Numbers 6, 7, and 8 were dearest to her heart. What Christina really wanted, and she was embarrassed to think it even to herself, was to be in love. She wanted to share her life with a special man. Not exactly modern or progressive thinking, but her thinking nonetheless.

As she sat on the floor beside her bed, she began to make a list of things she could do and places she could go to meet eligible men. Liza would be proud of her for making a move. Yes, making the list was the first step; acting on it would follow. Though she was afraid, she knew she had to start somewhere.

After finishing her list, Christina ate a light dinner and started on the Jackson Duncan file. He was twenty-eight and had been at CL for six years, and a managing engineer for two. Both years were spent on special projects for the president of CL. Quite impressive, Christina thought with a smile. According to his last manager, his arrogance was outweighed only by his effectiveness. Jackson Duncan was the stereotypical CL executive. His career path led directly to senior management.

He may be just what we need to get OPTIMA off the drawing board, she thought. The interview tomorrow should prove interesting.

It was nine-thirty in the evening. Jackson Duncan sat at the bar in the Georgian Hotel on Peachtree Street in Atlanta and thought about Christina Marshall. He had read her file on the flight in from Los Angeles. The file only confirmed what his friend, Walter Thomas, had already told him. Christina Marshall was a no-nonsense, get-the-job-done type. Her accomplishments impressed him, especially her work on ORION. The chance to work on OPTIMA with her convinced him that Atlanta wouldn't be a bad move.

OPTIMA was a career-making project, and Christina Marshall had Boston's attention. They would be watching her every move, which was fine with Jackson. He welcomed the attention. He knew that success with OPTIMA was key to a promotion and a district manager slot back in Boston. It was already agreed. He just had to bide his time with OPTIMA until a suitable position in Boston came open.

His thoughts came back to Christina Marshall. In some ways, his career followed hers. The lady must really be something, he thought. The interview tomorrow should prove interesting.

As Jackson finished his drink, he noticed an attractive black-haired woman with long legs sitting alone across from him. Before he could turn away, she looked up and smiled at him. Jackson recognized that smile. Why the hell not, he thought. He ordered another drink and walked over to meet the smiling lady.

CHAPTER 3

Jackson checked his appearance in the mirrored lobby walls. Not bad, he thought, for a guy who'd gotten only three hours of sleep. Mona, the black-haired woman from the bar, had kept him busy for over half the night. Not that he was complaining. No, work like that didn't cause a man to complain. Mona had been just the right kind of woman. She'd wanted only a good time for one night, no strings. And she'd been prepared. Jackson wondered if her name was really Mona.

The long, shapely legs and bouncing breasts of a woman crossing the street to the building interrupted his thoughts. He watched intently as the woman walked up the steps and through the lobby doors. He decided, as she entered the lobby door, that if she made eye contact with him, he would introduce himself. The woman didn't look his way. Obviously, she was in a hurry. Probably late for some meeting.

Jackson looked at his watch. Nine-fifteen. His interview with Christina Marshall was scheduled for nine o'clock. He checked with the lobby desk again. He didn't like waiting. And it was worse waiting today. He was hyped up about this assignment. Finally, a middle-aged woman, most like a secretary, walked up to him.

"Mr. Duncan, I'm sorry you had to wait. Miss Marshall can see you now."

Jackson followed the woman back to Christina Marshall's office.

When Jackson entered the office, he was surprised to see the woman he had watched crossing the street. She sat at the desk with the phone to her ear.

"Look, George," she was saying, "something is wrong with the car. Cars don't stop on the interstate for no reason at all."

The woman looked up and motioned Jackson to a chair in front of her desk. She went back to her conversation as he took a seat.

Jackson used the opportunity to get a good look at Christina Marshall. For some reason, he had never imagined how she looked. Until now, he had thought of her in sexless terms as an executive much like himself. This Christina Marshall was a lot different from him — in all the right places. She was a knockout in a nontraditional way. She was tall, about five foot ten. She wasn't overweight, but neither could she be called slim. He liked her fullness, the roundness of her shape, especially her breasts. The breasts he had noticed as she'd crossed the street were no longer bouncing, but they looked as soft as pillows. He wondered how it would feel to rest his head on them. His gaze moved from her breasts to her strong, inviting neck and on to her face. Her face was hard to describe, but Jackson liked it. It was delicate, yet it had strength. The full lips were colored with coral lipstick that accentuated her honey-brown complexion. He imagined kissing away every speck of the color. As he was thinking of the words to describe her silken black hair, Jackson realized he was having a physical reaction to Miss Marshall that could prove embarrassing to them both.

To stop staring at her and to stop the rush of blood to his groin, he got up and pretended interest in the art hanging on her office walls. It was no use. He could no more stop his mind from thinking about her than he could stop his body from responding. Giving her a glance and pointing toward the door, Jackson left her office for an emergency run to the bathroom.

He couldn't believe what was happening to him. He hadn't had such an immediate physical reaction to a woman since he was fourteen years old. *You are here to work with her on OPTIMA while you wait for your promotion,* he reminded himself. *Starting something with Miss Marshall would be a mistake.*

Finished in the bathroom, Jackson made his way back to Christina's office. *If Mona is any indication, there are plenty of women here in Atlanta,* he reminded himself. *So stay away from the boss.*

"I can't talk about this any longer, George," Christina said. "Call me after you repair the car."

Christina placed the receiver on the hook. She was glad she had been on the phone when Jackson arrived. She couldn't believe he was the man she had noticed briefly in the lobby. She had thought him appealing and she had known that he had been watching her. That knowledge boosted her self-confidence. Remembering her conversation with Liza about going after what she wanted, she had considered making eye contact with the man and giving him a smile. Yet, she had checked herself with the reminder that she was late for an appointment. Besides, she knew nothing about the man. Anyway, she didn't want to start considering every man she met a possible prospect. She wasn't that desperate. Yet.

She admitted she'd been shaken when the man had walked into her office. She had intentionally kept the conversation with George going longer than necessary. She needed the time to compose herself. For a moment she had wondered if her mind was playing tricks on her, but no, that was Jackson Duncan. Her secretary guarded her door with a warriorlike force. Jackson Duncan would be the only man to walk through it.

None of her research prepared her for meeting Jackson Duncan in the flesh. He was a very attractive man, from the close-cropped wavy black hair to . . . His reentry into the room stopped her thoughts. As he strode purposefully toward her, she came around her desk and extended her hand.

"Please forgive the delay. My car broke down this morning. That was my mechanic on the phone. Can we start over, Mr. Duncan?"

He took her hand and squeezed it briefly before letting it go. "No need for that, Miss Marshall. And, the name is Jackson."

"Jackson it is, then. I'm Christina. Would you like to sit over there?" She pointed to a sitting area with two wing chairs and a small table.

"That's fine with me," Jackson answered.

After they were seated, she asked, "So, what do you think of Atlanta so far?"

"I could get to love it here. It's a beautiful city. Beautiful, and inviting."

Christina felt Jackson was talking about more than the city, but she didn't dare inquire. Using her most professional tone, she asked him about the work he had done as managing engineer. He gave her details of his two most recent projects. Although she already knew about them from her research, she wanted his description of his contribution.

He spoke with animation. Christina knew from the cadence of his voice and the twinkle in his eyes that he enjoyed his work very much. He wasn't selfish in his praise. He noted the contribution of others without downplaying his own.

"Did they brief you on OPTIMA and your role should you decide to accept the position?"

"I talked with Walter Thomas about it and Rosalind flew out to LA to convince me to take the job. I'd like to get your view,

41

though. Walter and Rosalind tend to give only enough information to get you to do what they want you to do."

Christina found his observation amusing and accurate, but she didn't comment on it. "OPTIMA is aimed at manufacturing facilities. We plan to write the software for each customization to meet the specific needs of individual customers without massive rewriting. Because of your previous assignments, I'd want you to lead the planning effort. This project has been on the drawing board for two years now. It's time it became a reality. Your job would be to get it off the drawing board, to get the specifications into the hands of Liza Randall. Liza will be on board in about six months, and she'll be in charge of implementation."

"How would my role change during that phase?" Jackson asked.

Christina was impressed with the question. Jackson Duncan looked ahead. "I envision more planning. By the time Liza comes on board, we should have our first customers identified. You would interface with those customers to assure that our implementation met all their needs. It might be more accurate to describe your job as planning and deployment and Liza's as development and implementation."

He seemed to be deep in thought.

"Do you have any other questions?" she asked.

Jackson didn't hesitate. "How do you describe your management style?"

Christina smiled. "You mean, of course, am I going to give you the space to do your job, or will I overmanage you."

She thought she saw respect flash in his eyes. "Yes, that's what I meant," Jackson answered.

Christina described her management style and gave her expectations for how the two of them would work together. They agreed to meet weekly to assess project status.

"When do I start?" Jackson asked.

Christina stood. "Two weeks from Monday, if possible."

Jackson got up. "Sounds good to me."

"Now that the hard part is over, why don't I show you around the place? I'd like you to meet and talk with a few members of the staff before you leave today."

Christina took Jackson to lunch at Montclair's on Peachtree, the place of choice for midtown executives for lunch. While they ate, Jackson gave his first impressions of the project and the people.

Christina smiled. "I'm glad we meet with

43

your approval."

Jackson put his fork down and looked at Christina. "Don't get me wrong, that wasn't a negative comment. I'm genuinely pleased with all the people I've met. I didn't mean that I didn't expect to find good people. I'm only giving my impression of the staff."

"You'll learn, Jackson, that I have very thick skin. You'll have to try hard to insult me."

Jackson smiled then. "I'll remember that."

How did the man get such a wonderful smile? Christina wondered. His smile made you want to smile back. She hoped she wasn't grinning at him like an idiot.

After lunch Christina left Jackson with one of the senior engineers and went back to her office. The lunch rattled her. There was something about the way Jackson looked at her. She had stopped herself from covering her breasts a couple of times. Yet it was nothing he did. It was how he made her feel.

When he laughed, something tingled down her spine. When he accidentally bumped against her arm, she felt every hair stand on end. It was electric. And his smile. When he smiled, she felt at home. There were times during the lunch when she felt as if she had a huge grin on her face. She had to pinch herself under the table to get control of her emotions.

"God, Christina. Listen to yourself think. You sound like some moonstruck teenager. Jackson Duncan is only a man — nothing more, nothing less." If you say that enough, maybe you'll believe it, she thought.

Christina forced herself to stop thinking about him as she read the latest OPTIMA report. At the end of every paragraph, she saw his smile.

Jackson was just as deeply affected by lunch with Christina. His only memory was the sway of her hips as she'd walked away, leaving him to talk with the senior engineer.

A man could get hooked on a woman like Christina, he thought. But it wouldn't be him. He had seen first-hand what that could do to a man. His father had been hooked — too much — on his mother. Jackson wondered if his father had felt for his mother what he himself was now feeing for Christina. He never understood the hold his mother had had over his father. He swore that no woman would ever control him the way his mother had controlled his father. Ironically, that was part of his appeal to women. They viewed his aloofness as a challenge. Each woman felt that she would be the woman to change him. Jackson had

45

proved them all wrong. That was why he didn't understand his reaction to Christina.

Jackson stopped Christina as she entered her office his second week on the job. "I need to talk to you for a few minutes."

"Sure, Jackson, come on in. Have a seat." Christina settled into a chair. "What's on your mind?"

At that moment Christina's breasts were on Jackson's mind. He could see the tops of them as she leaned forward to speak to him. Did she realize how she looked in that red silk blouse? "I may have to go to Boston. The OPTIMA transition team is dragging its feet. I have people here who are ready to work, and I can't get Boston to turn over all the plans."

Christina dropped her pencil on the desk. "I was afraid this would happen. Do what you have to do and keep me posted. If you don't get some cooperation by the end of the week, let me know."

Jackson flashed a smile. "Thanks, boss. I'm going to give it one more day before I make the trip."

His smile was contagious. "It's good having you on board, Jackson. Have you found a place to live yet?"

"Thanks and no. I'm living in a furnished

apartment now."

"Feel free to take some time off to get settled if you need it," Christina offered.

"I'll remember that," Jackson replied and left the office.

Jackson Duncan had arrived at CL-Atlanta and every woman on the staff knew it. Christina noticed that the women always had something to say to Jackson. And Jackson always had time to listen. There was always a smile or a laugh involved and Christina noticed a touch or two. There was a visible electric charge between Jackson and any woman with whom he spoke. Christina began to wonder if the man had enough work to do. She certainly didn't have time to flirt with every man in the office. How, then, did Jackson find time to flirt with every woman?

With shock, Christina realized she was jealous. Jackson wasn't flirting with every woman in the office. He was flirting with every woman except her. In the short time he was on staff, he didn't even engage in light banter with her. For him, everything was strictly business.

Jackson stopped by Christina's office Friday morning. "It wasn't necessary for me to make the trip to Boston. The transition team released the plans Wednesday. Our guys are working with them now. We should have some results in the next two weeks."

"That's good news. Do you have an estimate for the staff you're going to need?"

"I've worked up some numbers for you, but they won't be ready until late this afternoon. Can we postpone our regular status meeting until then?"

Christina checked her calendar. "Four-thirty okay?"

"Four-thirty it is."

Christina didn't get out of her meeting until six. Jackson was waiting in her office when she got there.

"I'm sorry I'm so late, Jackson," she said with a smile. Her heart took a leap to see him looking so incredibly handsome in a blue Armani suit. "I didn't expect you to wait, but I'm glad you did."

"I wanted to go over these numbers with you while they were fresh in my mind." His real reason for waiting was that he wanted to get one final look at her to last him the weekend.

"Give me a second to recover from that meeting. We were there for five hours. It was a killer." Christina closed her eyes and leaned back in her chair. She began to turn her head from left to right as if to remove tension.

She looked so sexy sitting there with her eyes closed and her lips slightly parted. Jackson had often resisted unbidden thoughts of her like this. But for some reason he couldn't stop them. Something about Christina Marshall made her image fill his every thought. With that in mind, Jackson moved behind her chair and began to slightly massage her neck and shoulders.

It startled Christina at first, and she knew she should stop him, but she said nothing since it felt so good and she needed it so badly.

Jackson stopped and Christina opened her eyes. He had moved and now stood in front of her. His face reflected naked hunger.

Something inside Christina responded to that hunger and she wanted to reach out and touch him. As she moved to do just that, her phone rang. She looked at Jackson and she looked at the phone. She answered the phone.

When she had finished her call, Jackson showed her the numbers. He had projections through the next year. She gave him the go-ahead for the additional staff.

As Jackson gathered his papers, he casually asked, "It's late. How about getting a bite to eat?"

Christina didn't answer immediately. The question took her by surprise. She knew that Jackson and other members of the staff ate dinner together when they worked late. She had gone with them once or twice, but Jackson made her uncomfortable, so she had stopped going. "Tonight's not a good night. Maybe another night." That was a good answer, she thought.

Jackson wasn't fooled. She wanted to pretend that nothing had happened between them, and he wasn't going to allow it. Not tonight. "We can't deny what almost happened, Christina."

She lowered her eyelids to hide her surprise. "I don't know what you're talking about."

Jackson faced her. "You do know what I'm talking about. I'm talking about what almost happened before your phone rang a while ago."

Christina turned away. "Mr. Duncan . . ." she started.

Jackson spoke to her back. "I'm attracted to you, Christina, and you're attracted to me. If your phone had not rung, you would have kissed me."

Christina didn't deny it, but she didn't admit it, either. She turned around to face

50

him. "You seem pretty confident of that."

"God, Christina, the tension between us is so strong that you can practically see it."

"I'm not saying you're right, Jackson. But even if you are, there can never be anything between us."

"Why? Because we work together? I had the same reservations, but —"

Christina interrupted him. "We don't just work together, Jackson, I'm your boss. You report to me. A less trusting person might suspect the motivation behind your interest."

Jackson rubbed his hand across his head. "Christina, I am very attracted to you. I am attracted to your smile, your eyes, the way you move, the way you handle business. And I think you feel the same way. I am not using you to further my career. Do you think I need to do that at this stage in my career?"

No, she didn't really think that, but she couldn't think of anything else to say. "Don't act so surprised. It wouldn't be the first time that it's happened."

"You mean something like that happened to you before?" he asked.

He was getting it all wrong. "Not to me, Jackson. I'm talking about in general."

"Generalities don't interest me. I'm interested in you and me."

"It's not that simple. I'm your boss. That's a complication."

"It doesn't have to be. Your position doesn't threaten me and I don't need to use you to get ahead. We both know that I'm already established here." He grinned. "And, as for you being the boss, there are benefits to a woman taking charge."

She rolled her eyes. "Be serious, Jackson."

"I don't want to be serious. I don't want *you* to be serious. I only want to see if what we feel is real." He took her hand and pulled her to him. Looking into her eyes, he asked, "Aren't you even the tiniest bit curious about it yourself? Don't you want to know?"

God help her, she did want to know. Jackson captivated her. He was so handsome, and he showed such sincerity. Being close to him felt good. She relaxed in his arms, then spoke so softly he had to lean closer to hear. "You know what they say about curiosity, don't you?"

"Tell me, Christina," he whispered. He was so close she could feel his breath on her face.

Christina abruptly stepped out of his arms and looked him square in the face. "Curiosity killed the cat."

Jackson stared at her. Then he laughed. Without saying anything else, he gathered his papers and walked toward the door. He turned back to face her. "You know what I think about that, Christina?"

When she didn't respond, he told her anyway. "A cat has nine lives, so a little curiosity won't really matter. Will it?" Without waiting for a response, he opened the door and was gone.

CHAPTER 4

Christina sat at her desk and rested her face in her hands. Curiosity killed the cat. Real good, Christina. That was a sparkling retort. Admit that Jackson has you rattled. He was right on every count. You're attracted to him and it's taking all of your energy to fight that attraction. And, yes, you would have kissed him if the phone had not rung.

She lifted her head from her hands. What am I going to do? she wondered. She knew that she shouldn't even consider a personal relationship with Jackson since he worked for her, but she was doing just that.

Maybe I met Jackson at a vulnerable time, she reasoned. Only a few nights ago I was pouring out my heart to Liza about marriage and a family, then along comes Jackson Duncan, everything a woman could want in a man. Well, almost everything, she argued with herself; your ideal man doesn't usually work for you. Except for that minor — no, major — point, Jackson Duncan would be a godsend. He was attractive, yes, but that was only part of his appeal. There was something about him, his self-confidence, maybe, that made her think he could handle anything. It instilled a sense of trust. It made her think Jackson would take care of her love if she ever gave it to him.

"I'm not too sure how easily Mr. Duncan would give his love, though," she said aloud. "Sometimes I think he carries as much baggage as I do in that area."

Christina got up from her desk and walked over to the window. She knew she should go home, but she didn't want to face an empty house this weekend. She needed to talk to someone.

I know what I'll do, she mused, I'll take a trip this weekend. And I know just the place.

She packed her briefcase and left the office feeling better than she had felt since Jackson Duncan had come to Atlanta.

Jackson began unpacking boxes in his new apartment that night. The confrontation with Christina had energized him. Now he knew how she felt. She felt the attraction, but she resisted it. He understood her apprehension, given their professional relationship. He had apprehensions, too, but he detected in Christina a fear that had nothing to do with their working relationship. All that talk about the job was a smokescreen. He was sure of it. What was she afraid of?

Maybe something happened in the past. Some guy she worked with probably mistreated her. Now I have to pay, he thought. I hate that women do that. One man does wrong, and the next man who's interested pays the price. Sometimes it makes a guy contemplate celibacy. Why even bother?

We bother because we need women. "Can't live with 'em, can't live without 'em" applies to women, too. It's hard to find a good woman. When a man finds one, he'll take all the bull that she dishes out because he knows she's worth it. Too many women are looking for someone to take care of them, financially and emotionally. That burden is too big for any man. A strong woman with her own goals and her own identity is a treasure more than worth the wait and the hassle.

"Hold on there, Jackson," he chided himself. "You're thinking like a man ready to settle down. That's not you. You're going to be in Atlanta at most two years, and then it's back to Boston with a promotion. Now concentrate on unpacking those boxes before you get yourself in trouble."

It was a five-hour drive to Mobile in her recently serviced car. Christina's first choice had been to visit her mother in Selma, but Louise was going to the Nursery Owners' Convention in Memphis. Mobile was her second choice. Christina had promised herself that she would "see the South" this year. She planned to do it in a series of weekend trips. Among other cities, she had already visited Asheville, Savannah, and Birmingham. Mobile seemed a reasonable next place.

The drive down was uneventful. She arrived at the Malaga Inn in downtown Mobile a littler after one in the morning.

After a good night's sleep, Christina faced Saturday morning, late Saturday morning, with excited anticipation. She decided to take an escorted tour to get an overview of the historic downtown area and then to visit the battleship. The tour bus was one of those open air buses patterned after the nineteenth-century horse-drawn trolleys. She took an empty seat about midway the bus. There were quite a few people on board, three older couples, four couples about her age, and about two groups of two together. She was the only person alone.

Though she regularly traveled alone, sometimes she envied the couples and friends traveling together. She had tried vacationing with girlfriends before, but it had never worked out. You needed to be pretty good friends with somebody for it to work.

Christina's attention was drawn to the front of the bus as a tall, dark man got on. She watched him as he moved down the aisle to take a seat. As he passed her, she averted her eyes so as not to make eye contact. When she realized what she had done, she cursed herself. Damn, she thought, I could have smiled at him. He's alone; I'm alone. We could have shared this tour together. At least I would have had someone to talk with.

The tour went down Dauphin Street, circling the park at Bienville Square before stopping at Horst House on Conti Street. After getting off the bus, Christina consulted her tourbook. A deep voice interrupted her.

"An amazing restoration job, wouldn't you agree?" It was the man from the bus.

"I was thinking the same thing. I can't imagine anyone ever living here, though," she said with a nervous laugh. "It's too formal."

"I prefer a place that's a bit more casual myself," he said, "but it is impressive."

"Like fine art. You enjoy looking at it in a museum, but you would never be comfortable with it in your home."

"Yes, that's it exactly."

Christina walked over to get a closer look at an odd-looking object that may have been a vase, but it contained no flowers. The man followed her.

"Do you have any idea what it is?" he asked.

God, the thing is ugly. She frowned. "No, I don't. It's kind of . . . interesting looking."

He smiled. "It *is* ugly, isn't it?"

She returned his smile. At least he was honest enough to speak his mind.

"I'm Reggie Stevens," he said, extending his hand to her.

She shook it. "Christina Marshall."

"Nice to meet you, Christina. How about me following you around for the rest of this tour? Maybe you can teach me something about history and art appreciation."

She saw the kidding in his eyes, so she laughed. "I don't know about my teaching you anything. It may be a case of the blind leading the blind, but you're welcome to follow me around."

He bent at the waist in an exaggerated bow. "Thank you, madam. After you."

Christina and Reggie spent the rest of the

tour together. He was funny, and she enjoyed his company. From Oklahoma City, he was in town for an interview with International Paper. Having never been to Mobile before, he had come in early to see the city.

When the tour ended, Reggie asked, "What are your plans for the rest of the day?"

She pulled her tourbook from her purse. "I'm going to Battleship Park. What about you?"

"I was planning to visit there myself. Mind if I tag along?"

Christina hesitated. She was sure she wanted his company, but she wasn't sure if that was wise. A woman alone could never be too careful.

Reggie jumped in before she could answer. "We can take separate cars. That way, you can dump me if I begin to bore you," he said with a smile.

She considered his request. He's a pleasant man and we won't be traveling together, she reasoned. Oh, what the hell? "Sure, it ought to be fun."

They drove to Battleship Park in separate cars, with Christina leading the way. She wanted to take the harbor tour of Mobile Bay.

"I'm sorry, the last tour was at one-thirty," the reservationist said.

"I thought the last tour was at three-thirty," Christina responded, her disappointment obvious. "I'm sure I read that somewhere."

"You probably got our schedules mixed up. We only have the three-thirty tour in June, July, and August."

"I hate that I missed it." She looked at Reggie, who hadn't said a word. "I really wanted to go out on the water."

"Maybe we could do it tomorrow."

Christina noticed with a grin that he had said, "we." So he was planning to spend time with her tomorrow. She liked that.

Reggie turned to the reservationist. "What's tomorrow's schedule?"

"We have tours at eleven and one-thirty. We also have a dinner cruise tonight at seven. You'd probably enjoy that more. You don't get the narrated tour, but it's pretty out there at night. Couples enjoy it. There's plenty of food and good music. You can even dance if you like."

"Sounds like it might be fun." Turning to Christina, he asked, "What do you say?"

Christina still wondered at the reservationist's assumption that she and Reggie were a couple. She liked the thought of being part of a couple. Jackson's smile registered in her brain. She pushed the thought aside. "Okay, let's do it." She turned to the reservationist. "How much is it?"

The reservationist told them the price and they paid. Reggie offered to pay for Christina, but she declined with a polite smile.

Reggie checked his watch. "We don't have to be back until six-thirty. That gives us three hours. Let's get started."

The tour of the battleship took ninety minutes. Reggie had spent two years in Navy ROTC, so he had first-hand information about ships that made the tour more enjoyable.

"You weren't lying when you said you were planning to come here, were you?" Christina asked.

His eyes widened in surprise. "No, I had planned to come. Did you think I was lying?"

"I didn't exactly think of it as lying," she said, not wanting to hurt his feelings. "I thought of it more as a pick-up line."

He laughed. "I might have used one if you'd said you were going somewhere else, but fate was on my side and I didn't have to."

She lifted a questioning brow. "You think it was fate, do you?"

"Of course. How else can I explain an attractive woman like you on a tour bus *alone*, in Mobile, of all places, at the same time that I am in Mobile on that same tour bus? The gods must be watching out for me."

"I take that to mean you've enjoyed my company."

He took her hand and led her toward the submarine. "That's the understatement of the year."

"I'm starving," Christina said, after the tour of the submarine. "What time is it?"

Reggie turned his wrist so he could see his watch. "It's about six. We still have some time before the cruise. Can you hold out, or would you like to get something to drink?"

"I'd better get something to drink." She looked around. "Where can we go?"

"I remember a snack bar near the entrance." He took her hand and led her to it.

They took a seat after getting their drinks. Reggie told her about his upbringing. She had a warm feeling as she listened to the stories of his happy clan.

"Do you have a close family?" he asked.

"It's only my mom and me. We're very close. Over the years we've become friends as well as mother and daughter. She's one special lady."

"That's the way I feel about my mom. My dad's also a good guy. They've been married for forty-two years. That's good in anybody's book."

Christina envied Reggie his parents. Not that her mom wasn't fantastic, but she missed having a father. The more she thought about having a family of her own, the more she thought about her father. How she wished she could have known him. "I can't even imagine a marriage lasting that long. I'm only . . ." She stopped before revealing her age.

Reggie laughed. "You can tell me your age. I promise not to hold it against you." He raised his right hand. "Scout's honor. To make it easy for you, I'm thirty-seven."

"I'm thirty."

"I would have guessed that you were younger."

"Flattery will get you everywhere. Now, back to your parents. I can't imagine being with someone that long. Their marriage is older than I am. What's their secret?"

"I wonder at that myself sometimes. I think the key is openness. They don't keep secrets from each other. They talk about everything."

"Ummm . . ." Christina wondered what sharing your life with someone for forty-two years would be like. She hoped she'd get to experience it. Maybe with someone like Jackson. Christina felt her face flush. Now where did that come from?

Reggie pushed aside his drink cup. "We'd better start making our way back to the boat now." He stood up and helped her with her chair.

Christina welcomed the short walk. She needed the time to clear her mind of thoughts of Jackson.

They heard the music before they saw the boat. There was already a crowd. Reggie found a table near the crowded dance floor.

Before they took a seat, he asked, "Is this okay?"

She nodded and took the chair he was holding for her. She searched for the buffet table; she was starved.

"Would you rather eat or dance first?"

Christina moved her gaze to him. "Food first."

They made their way to the food and helped themselves to generous servings. They didn't talk much as they ate. Christina took the opportunity to observe Reggie more closely. She liked him. He was easy to talk to, and he liked to laugh. Strong and confident like Jackson, but much more open. Christina shook her head at the comparison. Why was she thinking about Jackson?

"Something wrong?" Reggie asked.

His voice brought her attention back to him. "I was thinking about the fun we've had today. It's been a real pleasure, an unexpected, but welcome pleasure."

"You talk like the night is over. Not yet, Cinderella. How about a dance?"

"I'd like that."

It had been a while since Christina had been out dancing, and she was enjoying herself. The music was good, and Reggie was a smooth dancer.

They danced for a long while, then took a walk on the top deck away from the dancers. They held hands but didn't speak as they watched the Mobile city lights shine in the distance. Christina liked the sense of togetherness she was feeling. It's been too long, she thought. She had almost forgotten what it felt like to be with a man like this. It was definitely something she could get used to.

The night passed quickly, and soon the cruise was over. They walked hand-in-hand to Christina's car. Reggie hadn't kissed her all night, though he'd had many opportunities. Well, if he doesn't kiss me, I'll kiss him, she decided.

She didn't need to worry. When they got to her car, Reggie leaned over and kissed her. A short, sweet kiss on the lips. He pulled back and looked into her eyes. "I think something special is happening."

Christina started to speak, but Reggie put a finger to her lips. "You don't have to say anything. I'm not rushing you. I'm only telling you what I'm feeling. Will I see you tomorrow?"

Christina wasn't sure what was happening, but she liked it. "I'm leaving early in the afternoon."

"Why don't I meet you for breakfast?"

She nodded as he ushered her into her car. She rolled down the window to say a final goodnight. He leaned in and gave her another kiss. "Sweet dreams," he said, and walked to his car.

He followed her to her hotel and waited in his car until she was safely in the lobby. Without any attempt at further conversation, he drove away.

Christina had sweet dreams that night. She dreamed of her and Reggie. At some point in the dream, Reggie began to look a lot like Jackson.

Jackson considered it a stroke of luck that the Atlanta chapter of his fraternity was having a picnic this Saturday afternoon. He had finished unpacking this morning and had called a fraternity brother who was a friend of a friend. He hoped to meet some interesting people, maybe some women to take his mind off Christina. After rethinking the situation last night, he decided it would be best for him and Christina if he didn't pursue her. If she'd been a little more receptive, he might have gone through with it. If he had been looking for a long-term relationship, he might have gone through with it. Since neither was the case, he was going to leave it alone.

"Hey, man, you must be Jackson." A smiling light-skinned man in an Omega T-shirt with the name "Maddog" written across the front was speaking to him. "I'm Ellis."

Jackson gave the fraternity handshake. "How did you know who I was, man? I didn't describe myself when we talked this morning."

"Maybe I'm psychic," Ellis joked. "Really, man, I called Tom in LA last night and he told me your line name." Ellis pointed to the name "MackDaddy" printed on Jackson's T-shirt.

Jackson laughed. "What else did Tom tell you about me? I haven't talked to him since I've been here."

Ellis turned away when someone called his name. He turned back to Jackson. "They're here. Let's get this meeting over so we can party. The women will be here in a couple of hours and we need to have the business finished then."

Jackson followed Ellis over to the other guys. They had a large chapter. Over two hundred on the roll, and nearly seventy-five at this meeting. Once again his fraternity affiliation was helping him settle into a new area.

As Ellis had said, the women started to arrive a couple of hours later. There were wives, girlfriends, and female friends. There were mostly couples, but that didn't bother Jackson; he liked going out alone. Usually a wife or girlfriend knew someone they would love to fix him up with. He took it all in stride. Today was no different.

"I know you'll like her," Betty was saying. Betty was Ellis's wife and she was talking about Angela, one of her sorority sisters.

"What makes you think an Omega man would be interested in an AKA woman?" he teased. "Omega men want Delta women."

"Please! Delta women are out. Ellis and I are the perfect example of what a good match you'd make with Angela. Are you free tomorrow night? We can have a few people over. A smaller group in a more intimate setting."

"Tomorrow's great. I appreciate your hospitality."

"Hey, it's my pleasure. Besides, I want to make sure that you meet Angela before one of these other women introduces you to one of their single girlfriends. AKA women watch out for each other." She laughed and was starting to say more when someone called her name. "Ellis will call you with directions. See you tomorrow. Again, welcome to Atlanta."

Jackson watched Betty as she rushed away. Ellis has done well for himself, he thought.

Jackson enjoyed the picnic. He ended up with three dinner invites, not counting tomorrow with Ellis and Betty, and at least fifteen "we must get together"s. With a little effort, he'd keep so busy that he wouldn't have time to think about Christina.

"I want to keep in touch with you, Christina," Reggie said over breakfast at the Malaga the next morning. "Maybe come to Atlanta. I've been through the airport a few times, but never a real visit."

"I'd like that, Reggie. You'd love the city, and I'd enjoy being your guide."

He reached his hand across the table and

rested it atop hers. "Seeing the city wouldn't be my reason for coming. I'd be coming to see you."

Christina liked his directness. The feel of his hand against hers wasn't so bad, either. "I know, and it pleases me."

He removed his hand and continued eating. "Now that that's settled, what do you want to do for the rest of the morning?"

Christina checked out of her hotel and packed her car, and they drove down Spring Hill Avenue to the University of South Alabama. They strolled the campus.

"It's about time I get on the road for home," she said sometime later.

"I've been dreading those words, but I know you have to go. Let's head back for the cars."

As they made their way to the cars, Christina thought about the kisses they'd shared last night and felt her cheeks burn at the memory.

Today's kiss was more intense than last night's, holding a promise of future kisses and caresses. She liked the feel and the smell of him. And she liked his taste. Too soon she was in her car and Reggie was waving after her. His "I'll call you" seemed much more than a polite gesture.

Christina stopped to gas up a few miles outside Montgomery. While at the station, she called to see if her mother was home.

"I got back early," her mother said. "Why don't you stop over on your way back? You can drive to Atlanta Monday morning."

"Sounds like a good idea, Mom. I'll do that. Look for me in about an hour."

Exactly sixty-six minutes later Christina pulled into the driveway of her mother's house. She hadn't grown up in this house, so she'd never thought of the place as home. It was simply her mother's house, but she felt safe and comfortable here. The absence of the Ford Bronco in the driveway told Christina that her mother was out. She shook her head as she thought of her mother in the Bronco. Louise had bought a small Chevy truck when she'd first opened the nursery. Last year she'd gotten rid of her truck and gotten the Bronco. She'd said a lot about needing the Bronco for deliveries, but Christina could tell by the way Louise drove and by the way she cared for the car that it was her toy. It was unlike Louise to splurge on herself, and Christina was glad that she had.

Christina got out of her car and walked to the back of the house. She reached under the azalea pot on the back porch for the key. It was there. Small towns, she thought, as she opened the back door.

As soon as she walked into the kitchen, she heard Louise pull up out front. She went to open the door for her mother, and saw Louise taking packages from the back seat of the Bronco. My mom is a beautiful woman, she thought. She could easily pass for forty.

For as long as Christina could remember, people had asked if she and Louise were sisters. It had bothered her during her teen years, especially since she was taller than her mom even then, but as she'd grown older and more confident, it hadn't mattered as much. She'd never thought of Louise as anything but mom. As she looked at her today, she was reminded that Louise was so much more than just her mother. She was an attractive and desirable woman. There had been a couple men in Louise's life over the years. Christina wondered why there had never been anyone special.

Louise was also a successful business-woman. She had worked as a nurse for almost thirty years before taking early retirement two years ago to open the nursery.

That risk had proved profitable. The nursery had been operating in the black for the last year. Business was so good that she now had three full-time workers and was thinking about expanding. Yes, Louise was much more than just her mother.

Coming out of her reverie, Christina asked from the doorway, "Need any help?"

Louise looked up. "Hello, sweetheart. I thought I'd get back before you got here. I went to the post office and stopped off to get us a bite to eat. I hope you're hungry."

"I'm always hungry for the Colonel, Mom. You know that." Christina took the barrel of Kentucky Fried Chicken. "Let me help you. You take the mail and I'll take the food."

"How was your drive?" Louise asked, as they walked back into the house.

"Uneventful about sums it up."

"I don't like the idea of your traveling up and down the road by yourself. It's too dangerous."

"Mom . . ."

Louise held up her hand. "I know what you're going to say. You're a grown woman. You can take care of yourself."

"That's right. I *am* a grown woman and I *can* take care of myself. Besides, I'm careful. I don't take risks. I always make sure I have a tank of gas. I keep my car serviced and I have the single woman's substitute for a husband, Triple-A."

"Yes, but do you have to do so much traveling alone? Why don't you go with friends? That would be safer."

Christina placed the bucket of chicken on the table. "I know that, but I can't always wait until someone else is free. I don't want to wait. It makes me feel that I can't live my life. Do you understand what I mean?"

Louise looked at Christina. "Sometimes I forget how independent you are."

Christina smiled. "I'm like my mother."

Louise gave a small laugh. "Sometimes I forget that, too. So, how was Mobile?"

"I'm going to tell you about Mobile and the latest happenings in Atlanta, but first let's eat and talk about Memphis."

Louise took potato salad from the refrigerator and plates from the cabinet. She talked about the conference while they ate. She planned to take a Thanksgiving cruise with some people she had met at the conference.

"How can you plan a cruise with people you've known less than two days? Mom, you're the one who needs to be careful."

"It's safe enough. The Nursery Owners of Greater New Orleans are planning the trip.

75

They plan something every year."

Christina retreated. "That's more like it."

"I met a couple there that had recently opened their second nursery. It made me rethink my position. Maybe I should expand. What do you think?"

"You want to expand. I know you can make a go of a second shop. Give your attorney a call next week and see what he says."

"I was thinking of doing exactly that. It'd be fun to have another shop. A lot of work, but a lot of fun."

Christina envied her mom's sense of purpose, her excitement with her work and her life. "I hope I find as much fulfillment in my life as you've found in yours. How do you do it, Mom? Tell your daughter your secret."

"There's no secret, sweetheart. Life is what you make it. Aren't you fulfilled?"

Christina sighed. "I thought I was. As long as I was planning for what I wanted, I felt that I was on track. I knew what I wanted and I was going after it. I felt good, but now that I have what I planned for, I feel there ought to be more. I feel like I've won a prize that I worked hard for only to question whether it was really worth it."

"Are we talking about something more

than work, darling?" Louise asked gently.

Christina got up from the table and rinsed off her plate. When she was done, she leaned back against the sink. "God, Mom, sometimes I feel that work is all I have. It used to be enough, but it's not anymore."

"What's happened to change everything?"

Christina thought about Liza's upcoming wedding. "The work hasn't changed, so I must have changed. I don't know, Mom. I only know that I'm very discontented right now."

"You do know, Christina," her mother said.

Christina heard the challenge in her mother's voice. She moved away from the sink and crossed her arms. "What's that supposed to mean, Mother?"

"Don't 'Mother' me. You know why you're discontented. You just won't voice it."

"I don't know what you are talking about."

Louise shrugged. "If you say so. How about some dessert? I have chocolate cake in the fridge."

Christina wouldn't let it go. "I don't want cake, Mother. I want to know what you're talking about."

"All right, Christina, if you won't say it, I will. You're lonely, sweetheart. Now don't get insulted. It's not like I've said you have bad breath. A lot of people are lonely. It's a curable malady."

Christina uncrossed her arms and dropped them to her sides. She knew her mother was right. "I'm not lonely, Mother. I'm alone, but I'm not lonely. There's a difference."

"I know, Christina. You've been alone a long time, but now you're lonely. To be alone is to be happy to be by yourself; being lonely is being unhappy to be by yourself."

Christina didn't speak immediately. Finally, she asked, "Has it been that obvious, Mom?"

CHAPTER 5

"It's obvious to me because I'm your mother and I know when something isn't right with you."

Christina returned to her seat at the table. "How long have you known that something was wrong?"

"I've seen it coming for a while, Christina. It had to happen.

"You had to realize that the job wasn't enough." Louise took her daughter's hand. "Christina, sweetheart, you need to build a life for yourself apart from that job. You need to make friends."

Christina jerked her hand away and stood up. "You mean male friends, Mother?"

"You said it, I didn't."

"For your information, Mother —" she practically sneered the word "mother" "— I met someone, a male, this weekend."

"I hope he was a nice man, dear, but that's not really the issue, is it? We're talking about you and how you feel about your life."

Christina looked at her mother and her heart filled with all the love she had always felt. Leave it to Mom to stick to the subject. Christina had learned early how to avoid painful discussions. Her mother caught on and stopped it at home. In the outside world, Christina could control her interactions with people, but at home, Louise always made her face her fears. It was a pain in the butt sometimes, but Christina loved her mother for it because she knew that her mother did it out of love.

Christina gave in. "You win, Mom. You always do." She ran both hands through her hair and threw her head back. "God, where do I start?"

Christina started with her response to the news of Liza's wedding and ended with a description of her weekend with Reggie.

"I'm glad that you're opening your eyes to your surroundings and finding people that interest you, but I think you could have been a bit more cautious. What do you really know about this man?"

"Not again. I was careful, Mom. I've never been much of a risk taker, but I have to learn to follow my instincts more." She pulled out a chair and sat directly in front of her. Taking her mom's hand in hers, she said, "I'm going to need your support."

Louise squeezed her daughter's hand. "You know I'm here for you. What do you want me to do?"

"That's just it. I don't know." Christina stood up again. "I'm having so many new emotions. I feel like a teenager who needs guidance in dating. I'm a thirty year-old professionally competent woman who handles multimillion-dollar projects, but I can't seem to get a handle on this man-woman thing."

"It's only natural, Christina. You learn how to deal with men by dealing with men. You've never really dated, so you don't have much experience."

Christina thought about that awhile. How she wished her father was here. "It feels strange to want a husband and a family. A part of me feels I should be content with what I have, but another part of me would seriously consider chucking it all to be a housewife and mother. I feel like a heretic and a traitor for thinking that way."

"There's nothing wrong with your feelings," Louise said. "Women have choices. You can choose to have a career, or you can choose to have a family, or you can choose to have both. The only responsibility you have is to yourself. You've got to decide what you want and go after that. You can't let other people's expectations dictate your life."

"I know you're right, but these thoughts make me feel like a weakling. It's disgusting."

"Growing pains are natural. Don't think for a minute that needing people makes you weak. Your strength is shown in your doing what makes you happy."

Christina sat down again. "How did you do it, Mom? You're happy and fulfilled, but you don't have a man. You never really did in all the time that I was growing up."

Louise looked away from her daughter. "There's not a special man in my life and there hasn't been for a long time." She turned back to face Christina. "I had you, Christina, and you made the difference. You filled spaces, provided love, and provided a way for me to show my love. Though there was no special man, there was an outlet for my love and that outlet was you."

Christina knew a daughter's love and a lover's love were two totally different experiences. "Was it enough?"

"I made it enough. As you got older, I developed other interests. Now that you're gone, I have the nursery."

"You love the nursery, Mom, but the

nursery can't love back."

Louise nodded. "I know. I've been doing some thinking of my own lately. I wonder if I didn't do us both a disservice by not having an intimate relationship. At the time it seemed the right decision to make, but as I look at you and me now, I wonder if it was."

Christina paused before she spoke. "Do you ever think about him?"

"Who?"

"You know who, Mother. My father. Do you ever think about him?"

Louise was silent for a minute. "At times. It still hurts. All this time and it still hurts. I loved him and I still miss him." Louise took a napkin from the table and wiped away the tears that had quickened in her eyes.

"I don't want to make you sad, but I need to talk about him. Is that okay?"

Louise nodded.

Christina got up again and walked around the room. She got anxious when she thought about her father. "I've been thinking about him lately. Tell me about how you met and what happened."

Louise paused for a moment before speaking. "I met him the summer after my freshman year at Alabama A&M. I was working as a nurse's aide at the hospital in Bottoms. I went to a voter registration rally with one of my girlfriends. Thomas Evans was the speaker. His electrifying speech inspired me to become a volunteer voter registrar. I met your father at the orientation for registrars. I remember my girlfriend nudging me when she first saw him looking at me. He was gorgeous. A tall, bulky man. So handsome. All the women thought him attractive and smart. I had no interest in him because I thought he was conceited. My lack of interest attracted him to me. I think. He asked me out for over a month before I agreed to go out with him.

"I fell in love with him the night of our first date," Louise said, as if in her memories. "He was so much more than what I thought. He had character, substance. I remember the fervor and strength of his thoughts, his plans. I knew that night that I wanted to spend the rest of my life with him. It was love at first sight, but not the kind of sight that had to do with your eyes. I saw inside to the man that he really was, and I loved that man. I've never felt that way again."

Christina had heard the story many times before, but it warmed her heart to hear it again. If only she had known her father. "When did you know he felt the same way about you?"

Louise gave a teary smile "He told me that first night. When we said goodnight, he told me that he loved me and that he wanted to marry me. I couldn't say anything, but I knew he meant it. Does this make sense to you Christina?"

"It makes a lot of sense. Go on."

"After that first night, we were practically inseparable. Your grandparents thought he was going to move in. They fell in love with him as fast as I did."

"How did you make it after he died?"

"It almost killed me. He never knew about my pregnancy. It was such a fluke. At a time when young men were dying in riots, Christian died of pneumonia. He had come to visit during Thanksgiving vacation. We made love the first time during that visit. He wanted to wait, but I didn't." Louise paused. "I got my way and I got you."

Christina wiped at the tears in her eyes. She nodded to signal her mother to continue.

"I don't know how I made it. I didn't realize I was pregnant until February. Fear was my first emotion. But your grandmother really came through for me. It took all of my courage to tell her. She held me while I cried, and told me that she loved me. She even told your grandfather for me. If he was angry, I never knew it. He supported me just like your grandmother did. How I wish you had known them longer!"

Christina went to her mother and held her. Through her tears, she said, "Me, too. I was so young when they died. I wish I had known my father. I miss him so much sometimes."

"He would have loved you so much. I named you Christina so you would always have him with you." Louise pulled away so she could see her daughter's face. "I love you, Christina, and I've never regretted having you. You made the suffering bearable. Knowing that I would always have a part of Christian with me kept me going. Even through the deaths of your grandparents."

"I love you, too, Mom, and I know that you love me and that Big Mama and Big Daddy loved me. What about my other grandparents?"

"Big Mama and Big Daddy decided it best that we not tell them. Christian was dead. Your grandparents and I were your family, and after they died, you and I were a family."

Christina wanted to ask more questions. But she saw something that looked like fear in her mother's eyes. She didn't know the reason for the fear, but she felt that the time for questions had passed. She reached for her mother again and they held each other as they cried.

Jackson called his father early Sunday morning as he always did on the first Sunday of the month.

"Morning, Dad," Jackson said, right before he heard the phone drop.

"That you, Jackson?"

"Yeah, Dad, it's me. What's that noise?" Jackson heard something, maybe music in the background.

"I got some of your mother's old records on the record player. Your mamma sure could dance. She loved to dance, too."

"I know, Dad, I know."

Jackson stopped listening as his father went into his age-old storytelling. When he drank, he thought about his wife. Maybe when he thought about his wife he drank. Either way, when he thought about her, he had to talk about her. Jackson's emotions for his father went to extremes. Sometimes he was overwhelmed with love for the man that had been his father for the first fifteen years of his life. At other times, he was overcome with anger and hatred at the man who had been his father for the last thirteen years. Mostly, he felt pity for the man who had loved a woman who after twenty years of marriage decided she no longer loved him.

His feelings for Sarah (he rarely thought of her as his mother) were more definite. He hated her. He hated what she had done to his family. He hated what she had done to his father. Most of all, he hated what she had done to him. What had she really done? She had left her husband and son, showing them clearly she didn't love them. He could understand a woman leaving a man, but he couldn't understand a woman leaving her child. For that he hated her.

His dad was saying something. "Yes, I know what you mean, Dad. I have to go now. I'll talk to you soon."

His Dad mumbled "G'bye," and they hung up.

Jackson hated making the monthly phone calls. He never knew if his father would be drunk and sad or sober and depressed. Either way, his father was a lost cause. He refused to get over Sarah. Jackson had long given up trying to help him. His father didn't want help. He wanted to wallow in pity, and nothing was going to stop him.

Jackson picked up the Sunday *Journal-Constitution* in an effort to clear his head. It worked, and soon his thoughts centered on the adventures of Doonesbury and Curtis.

Jackson arrived at Ellis and Betty's around two. Betty answered the door. "Welcome. We're all out back. You're in luck, Angela's already here."

Jackson laughed. "You don't give up, do you?"

"Haven't you figured it out yet, Jackson?"

"Figured what out?"

Betty wagged her finger at him. "And you the man about town. Shame on you. Haven't you heard that matchmaking is the married woman's way of staying single forever? You get to date, albeit vicariously, without guilt. And sometimes you even get your husband's help." She winked at him and led him out to the patio.

"Hey, everybody, the guest of honor is here. Jackson Duncan, meet Michael and Jewel Taylor and Angela Ware. Mike's an Omega. Jewel and Angela are AKAs. I'll leave it to you to take the subtle hint."

Betty started to say more, but Ellis covered her mouth with his hand and the others laughed.

Angela walked over to Jackson, her eyes twinkling. "Welcome to Atlanta. I won't hold it against her," she said, referring to

Betty, "if you won't. Deal?" She extended her hand.

He took her hand. "Deal." He dropped her hand and gestured toward Betty. "Is she always like this?"

"No. Betty is in rare form today. You really impressed her at the picnic. She thought you were a good guy. Your response to that introduction proved it."

Jackson assessed Angela. She was an attractive woman, tall, brown-skinned, slim, with a sexy voice and legs that were pretty but not as full as Christina's. Wrong thought. "When did Betty become your matchmaker? I would think you'd have men lined up around the block."

Angela gave him a half-smile. "There was probably a compliment in there somewhere, but I tell you, it's pretty hard to find."

"I apologize. I only meant that you're a very attractive woman and I wouldn't think you'd need the services of a matchmaker."

"That's better," Angela responded. "Betty and I were college roommates. We've always watched out for each other. I introduced her to Ellis. She's trying to return the favor."

Jackson was about to comment again on Betty and her matchmaking, but Angela spoke first. "Excuse me, I see Jewel and Betty heading into the house. If I don't help,

I'm dead meat." She winked and was gone.

Jackson watched her walk away, thinking he'd have to thank Betty for introducing him to Angela.

"Get over here, Jackson," Ellis called. "I have a feeling you're going to need the counsel of married men to make it through this afternoon."

Mike and Jackson watched as Ellis plopped the steaks on the grill. "You have a nice spread here, Ellis," Jackson commented. "How long have you lived here?"

Ellis looked up from the grill. "Thanks, man. Betty found this place about four years ago when there was still a family living here. She decided then that we would own it. When it came on the market two years ago, we got it."

"Betty is something else," Michael commented. "Jewel is getting to be a lot like her. We're looking for a house now and yours is the standard. God, I hope we find something before the year 2007."

Jackson listened as Mike and Ellis exchanged funny stories about their wives. It was obvious that both men were deeply in love. Jackson felt left out and a little envious.

"When will the monsters be back?" Mike was asking.

Again Ellis laughed. "You call mine monsters, but I bet your tune will change in about six months. E.J. and Anne will be back tonight. Betty's parents took them for the weekend. For Betty and me, it's been a honeymoon around here. We spend as much time in bed as possible. Unfortunately, for most of that time, we're asleep."

"Sure, man," Jackson said with sarcasm.

Ellis threw another steak on the grill. "I wish. Wait until you have a working wife and two toddlers. Any break from the kids is a time to catch up on sleep. Not that we didn't have some fun. A man takes what he can get."

"The times at my house have only gotten better," Mike said. "Jewel has this new surge of passion since she found out about the baby. It's great."

"You'd better enjoy it while you can," Ellis advised. "And prepare yourself for that dry period that's going to start sometime in her ninth month and last until the baby is about six weeks old."

"You guys are something else," Jackson said. "Do your wives have any idea what you're talking about out here?"

Mike and Ellis chuckled. Mike answered, "Jewel gives guidelines on what I can and can't say."

Ellis pointed his spatula toward the house. "What do you think they're doing in there? You can bet a month's pay they aren't discussing the best way to make potato salad."

Mike pointed to Jackson. "I'd bet my pay that they're discussing you, big boy. By now, they're probably deciding how many children you and Angela should have."

"He *is* cute," Angela agreed. He was more than cute, but she'd never tell that to Betty and Jewel. They moved into overdrive when they learned she was attracted to someone.

"Cute? Honey, that is one fine man. If only I weren't married," Betty chimed in.

Jewel spoke next. "You'd better jump on that one quick, Ange. The women are going to be out for that man."

"Ellis says he has some executive engineering position at Communications Limited downtown," Betty offered.

"I haven't heard of Communications Limited," Jewel said.

"Ellis says their offices are in the Peterson Building. Anyway, Ellis says it's a good company and Jackson has a good position."

Jewel and Betty looked at Angela.

"Why are you two looking at me like that?" Angela asked.

Jewel and Betty looked at each other. They shrugged their shoulders, then each grabbed a casserole dish and headed for the patio. Betty spoke, "If you don't know, girlfriend, we can't help you."

Mike and Jewel were standing. "We hate to eat and run, but we promised Jewel's parents we'd stop by tonight."

Ellis stood. "It's okay, man. Now is not the time to irritate the grandparents-to-be. They make the best babysitters."

Betty punched him in the leg. "Ellis, you're so bad."

Mike extended his hand to Jackson. "It was nice meeting you, man. You'll have to go out on the course with Ellis and me sometime. I could use the competition."

"Thanks, man. I'd like that. Give me a tee-off time and I'm there."

Jackson noticed Jewel whisper something to Angela before saying goodbye to everyone else. While Ellis walked Mike and Jewel out, Betty began clearing away the food. She declined Angela and Jackson's offer to help.

Angela smiled and Jackson noticed she had a very pretty smile. "If Ellis is not back in ten minutes," she said, "we can safely assume that he and Betty are giving us some time to get to know each other better."

"It really doesn't bother you, does it?"

"This matchmaking stuff?"

Jackson nodded.

"Not really. They're my friends. They're trying to be helpful. Like I said before, if you can handle it, so can I. How does it make you feel?"

"At first it was funny, but I'm beginning to think they're serious."

Angela laughed. "They are, but don't get too scared. We haven't set a wedding date yet. Let's talk about something else. How do you like Atlanta so far?"

Jackson gave Angela his first impressions of the city and found that they shared common interests and viewpoints. Angela was easy to talk to, and before long they were talking like old friends.

"You'll have to visit Auburn Avenue and the AU Center. They're pretty close to your apartment building."

"Soon, too." Jackson decided to flirt. "Will I need a guide?"

Angela went along with him. "I think you might."

Ellis and Betty walked out of the house and joined them. "What are you two talking about?"

"Angela was telling me of some sites I

need to see. I think she volunteered to be my guide."

Betty nodded approval then asked, "Is she taking you to Stone Mountain?"

"I hadn't thought about Stone Mountain," Angela said.

"Everybody has to see the Laser Light Show," Ellis added.

"Laser Light Show?" Jackson asked.

"A fireworks display only with lasers," Betty explained. "You'll like it."

"Sounds like fun," Jackson said. He looked at Angela. "What do you think, tour guide?"

"That could be our first outing. Since we're right here at Stone Mountain, we could even do that tonight. That is," she looked at the three of them, "if you guys are up for it?"

"I'm game," Jackson said. Looking at Betty and Ellis, he asked, "How about you two?"

Ellis opened his mouth to answer, but Betty beat him to it. "We can't tonight. My folks are bringing the kids back any minute now. Why don't you two go on, though?"

"Sounds like a plan to me." Jackson winked at Betty, then turned to Angela. "Ready to go guide?"

The ride to Stone Mountain Park took

about fifteen minutes. After they entered the main gate to the park, Jackson said, "You give good directions. How long have you been a guide?"

Angela smiled and directed him to the parking lot nearest Memorial Lawn. "We got here at the right time. The show started at nine-thirty, but as you can see, people are already getting in place. I'm glad Betty thought of this."

Jackson studied her for a long moment. "I'm glad, too." She *is* attractive, he thought, even if her build is not like Christina's.

"Shall I get the blanket so we can get seated?" he asked, needing to remove Christina from his thoughts.

"Yes, we'd better stake out a spot. Thanks to Betty, we can have cider and cheese while we wait."

Jackson grabbed the blanket and Angela took the picnic basket. She picked a spot and they spread the picnic blanket. Jackson opened the basket and poured them both a glass of cider.

Neither spoke for a while. They looked at the people around them as they nursed their drinks. Jackson saw a man and woman in their early thirties with a child. He assumed they were a family. The child, a red-haired boy, carried a blue balloon on a string and had what appeared to be chocolate ice cream smeared around his mouth. Attractive family, he thought. His gaze went to a couple seated not far from them. They were young, early twenties. They shared an intense embrace, kissing as if they couldn't get enough of each other. Young love, Jackson thought. He turned to see Angela looking at the same couple.

"Ain't love grand?" he commented, finishing off his cider.

"Nothing like it. At that age or ours."

"Have you ever been in love, Angela?"

She laughed. "Many times. How about you?"

Jackson answered seriously. "Never."

"Not even as a teenager?"

He shook his head.

"That's sad, Jackson, and a little hard to believe."

An image of Christina flashed in his mind. "It's true."

"I bet you've broken a lot of hearts, though."

He raised his right hand. "I plead the fifth." Lowering his hand, he said, "Tell me more about Angela."

"What do you want to know about her?"

Jackson rubbed his chin, pretending to think hard. "Well, I already know she's beautiful, she's smart, she has a good sense of humor, she gives great directions, she has close friends, and she has a sexy voice." He snapped his fingers. That's it, he thought. "I knew your voice sounded familiar. You're on the radio, aren't you?"

Angela unfolded her legs and stretched them out on the blanket. "Don't pretend Betty didn't tell you. She tells everybody. She used to introduce me as her friend Angela who's on the radio station WAOK."

Jackson leaned back on his elbows and laughed. "That sounds like Betty, but I swear she didn't tell me."

"Good. It really bothers me when she does that. We've had more than a few heated discussions about it. Maybe she finally understands. I'm glad she didn't tell you."

"You're such a good sport about the matchmaking. Why is this a problem?"

Angela brushed a nonexistent spec from her slacks. "I like to keep my personal and professional lives separate. Once people find out that I'm in radio, they turn into groupies and want the inside scoop on some artist. That can get old real fast."

"I understand the need to keep your work life separate, but I find it impossible to do in reality." He was thinking about Christina.

"It works, but you need a strict set of

guidelines and you have to follow them religiously."

He could use all the help he could get. "For example?"

"I don't date anyone that I work with. Nothing but problems."

"Is that conclusion based on experience?"

"No. I've come close a couple of times, but it was never worth the risk. If the personal relationship doesn't work, what happens to the professional relationship? If the personal relationship does work, what happens to professional competition? My career is very important to me and I don't want to jeopardize it."

Let's go fishing, Jackson thought. "What if your attraction to the person was strong and you thought it might be the real thing?"

"That's never been the case. In each situation, for me at least, the chance of something lasting was never really high, so why risk it? There are plenty of other men out there."

And there's plenty of women. The problem is that all women are *not* created equal. "You've thought a lot about it."

Angela crossed her ankles, then inclined her head toward him. "I have. I don't know how it is for men, but I've found that professional women have to be above reproach,

and sex with coworkers falls in the reproach-
ful category. It's the old 'she slept her way
to the top' story."

"That's archaic thinking."

"Haven't you noticed that this country
still holds a somewhat archaic view of
women? And it's worse for black women."
She looked around. "The show's about to
start. Get ready to enjoy it."

"I'm ready," Jackson said. His thoughts
went back to Christina. If she would risk it,
he would pursue a relationship with her,
but she had made her intentions clear. He
looked at Angela as she watched the show.
She was good people. He liked her and
thought that she liked him. Maybe Angela
was the person he needed to keep his mind
off Christina.

When the show ended, Jackson drove Angela to her home in Decatur.

He walked her to the door. "When's our
next outing?"

"Are you serious about my being your
guide?"

"Very serious. How about it?"

"Let me think about it. I'll call you early
in the week and we can make plans."

"Are you really going to call, or are you
letting me down easy?" he teased.

"Somehow, Jackson Duncan, I don't think you've ever been turned down." She reached up and gave him a quick kiss. "Goodnight." She entered the house before he could say or do anything more.

When Jackson got home, he pulled out his briefcase and began to prepare for work. It only brought back thoughts of Christina. He wondered how he was going to approach her, given what had happened Friday. What did she expect him to do? What did she want him to do?

His thoughts turned to Angela. She was going to help him forget Christina. Well, maybe "forget" was too strong a word. The most he hoped for was that Angela would keep him distracted so he wouldn't think about Christina as much.

Angela was almost right when she had said that he had never been turned down before. His record had been perfect until Friday with Christina. God, he loved a challenge. Could he do the right thing and leave Christina alone, or would he follow his emotions? Only time would tell.

CHAPTER 6

The offices at CL were dark when Christina arrived Monday morning. She switched on the lights in her secretary's office and proceeded to her own office. She was more tired than usual. Leaving her mom's house at three o'clock in the morning had seemed like a good idea since she couldn't sleep, but now her body was rebelling.

She looked at her watch. Seven o'clock. That was actually late for her; she was usually in by six. She used the time to catch up on reading, go over her schedule for the day, and prepare for any meetings. Today she had to plan for the afternoon staff meeting. She liked getting together with her people on Mondays to make sure the week started right and to identify any issues that need her intervention. The meetings worked well. She had tried Monday morning meetings, but they didn't give the staff any time to wrap up the loose ends that invariably cropped up late Friday. She and Jackson met on Fridays, she remembered. A heated flush graced her cheeks as she recalled their last meeting.

Christina headed straight for the couch. Once she would have considered an office like hers extravagant. Now, she realized it was only functional. Since she spent so much time there, she needed the space and comfort.

Christina sat down, slipped off her black pumps, opened her briefcase, and began to read. She yawned and wished she had some tea. In forty-five minutes Penny, her secretary, would bring her morning tea. She yawned again and closed her eyes. She didn't know when she slipped into sleep.

She woke up when the door opened. She didn't bother to open her eyes or make a comment. It must be seven forty-five, she thought. Penny would place the tea on the desk and quietly leave the room. If she didn't hear Christina moving around by eight o'clock, she'd come back to check on her. Christina waited to hear Penny do her task and leave. When it seemed to be taking a long time, she called to her. "Penny, what are you doing?" A masculine voice answered, "Penny's not here yet. It's only seven-thirty."

Christina opened her eyes and quickly sat upright. A tall, gray-haired man stood near her desk. If she had met him under other circumstances, she would have thought him distinguished looking. In the present circumstances, she thought he looked a bit misplaced, even weird. There was a haunting look in his eyes, too.

Christina stood up as he walked from the desk where he was standing toward the couch. "Excuse me. Are you looking for someone?" she asked.

The man hesitated a second, then extended his hand. "Paul Bechtel."

The name sounded familiar to Christina, but she couldn't place it. The man must have concluded as much from the look on her face. He said, "This used to be my office." He looked around the room. "Though it's changed a lot since I was last here."

Now she remembered. Paul Bechtel was district manager for ORION before her. She never knew the details, but he had been fired before her arrival. She assumed it had had to do with the state of the product then.

"Mr. Bechtel." She shook his hand. "I'm Christina Marshall." She slipped on her shoes and went to stand behind her desk. "What can I do to help you this morning?"

Bechtel said nothing and merely looked at

Christina. She was beginning to get nervous. What was he doing here? How did he get in? Before she could say anything else, Penny walked in with the tea.

Penny saw Christina first. "Good morning, Christina. How was your weekend?" Then she saw Bechtel. She stopped in her tracks. "Mr. Bechtel . . . what brings you here?"

Christina saw Bechtel smile for the first time. "You haven't changed at all, have you, Penny?" He walked toward her. "I've been feeling homesick for the place and thought I'd drop by." He looked at Christina. "Sorry if I frightened you, Ms. Marshall. I only wanted to see the old place." With that, he walked past Penny out the door.

Christina realized she'd been holding her breath. She let it go. Looking at Penny, she said, "That was spooky."

"What?" Penny placed the tea on the table. "Oh. Mr. Bechtel being here?"

Christina wrapped her arms around herself. "Yes, it was spooky waking up and finding him standing here. The way he looked at me was eerie. How did he get in here, anyway?"

"I really don't know," Penny said. "He doesn't have a badge, but one of the security guards may have remembered him and let him in."

"Well, they shouldn't do that. Check with security. I need to know who let him in. We can't have unauthorized people roaming around our office. There's a lot of proprietary work going on in here."

"I'll call them," Penny said. "Is there anything else you need?"

Christina was still thinking about Bechtel. Remembering his comment about Penny not being in until seven forty-five, she asked, "Did you bring Bechtel tea every morning, too, or was it coffee?"

Penny shook her head. "I didn't work for Bechtel. Doris was his secretary." Doris now worked for Jackson.

Christina opened her mouth to ask another question when the phone rang. "I'll take it," she said to Penny. Penny nodded and left the office.

Christina sat and talked with Walter in Boston. She brought him up to date with the schedules. Before hanging up, she thought about Paul Bechtel. She told Walter about the incident this morning.

"Bechtel is an idiot. Don't worry about him. Be sure you tell security not to let him in the building again. Damn it. That man never should have been allowed in. What kind of security do you have down there, anyway?"

Christina wanted to find out more about Bechtel, but sensing Walter's irritation, she decided not to pursue that at this time. "I'm checking with them now. I'll have some answers before the end of the day. Don't worry."

With that they hung up. Christina sat for a while thinking about the morning. Jackson interrupted her thoughts when he burst into the office.

"Look what just arrived for you." He was carrying a bouquet of pink roses. "You must have an admirer." He placed the flowers on her desk.

"Where did you get these?" Christina asked. She wondered if they were a gift from Jackson himself. Maybe a peace offering.

"They came when Penny was in your office earlier. She would have brought them in, but you were on your call with Walter."

"You seem to know a lot about what I'm doing," she commented.

He touched one of the rose petals. "So, who are they from?"

Christina lifted a brow. "You didn't read the card?"

Jackson clutched at his heart. "You wound me. I only deliver; I don't read."

Christina didn't open the card. She waited for Jackson to speak.

Finally he said, "I think we should clear the air concerning Friday."

Christina didn't comment.

Jackson continued, "I was out of line. Will you accept my apology?"

Christina felt a little hurt. What was he really saying here? "No apology needed. I haven't even thought about it."

Was that a twitch she detected? No, it must not have been, because now Jackson was smiling. "Good," he said. "Now I can get back to work." He walked to the door. Looking over his shoulder as he walked out, he said, "Don't forget to read the card."

Jackson walked from Christina's office to his own, greeting everyone he met with a smile. Inside he was seething. He walked into his office and slammed his fist on his desk. On Friday she had wanted to pretend nothing was happening, and this morning when he'd played it that way, she'd actually looked hurt. What in the hell was going on here? Jackson sat at his desk.

She recovered quickly enough, he thought. I haven't even thought about it, she says. I know she's lying and she knows she's lying, but we're both going to pretend that the whole incident was nothing. Well, it was something to me.

Reggie was also something to him. So he'd lied about reading the card. Who the hell was Reggie, anyway? Was this somebody she'd been dating for a while? Or was it somebody new? He wondered if it was serious. It probably was. Somehow, he couldn't imagine Christina in a casual affair. She was much too rigid for that.

Jackson wondered what had happened to his control. Christina Marshall was doing a number on him and he doubted she even knew it. This weekend he had figured it all out. The conversation with Angela removed any doubts he'd had. Christina Marshall was off limits. He could deal with that. She wasn't really his type anyway. He liked his women a lot less stuffy than Miss Christina Marshall. Someone more like Angela. Yes, Angela. Thinking of her, Jackson dialed her number.

"I know you said you'd call, but I couldn't wait. When's our next outing?" he asked.

Angela laughed softly. "You're impossible. I haven't had time to make plans yet."

"If you don't think of something, I will. That's a threat."

She went along with his teasing. "And what will you think of?"

"How about lunch, for starters?"

"If it's tomorrow, you have a date."

"I'm flexible. Tomorrow it is."

Jackson hung up the phone feeling better. He liked Angela a lot and he looked forward to spending more time with her. If anybody could keep his mind off Christina, Angela could.

I was out of line, he'd said. Christina drummed her fingers on her desk. So, was that what it was? I'm glad I didn't give in to the moment. Then where would I be? Would he have come in here and said that making love to me had been out of line? Men, ha!

Christina remembered the flowers. She opened the attached card and read it. "I miss you already," it read. It was signed, "Reggie." Christina smiled as she thought about her weekend. She'd had fun with Reggie. She checked the time and decided it wasn't too early to call Oklahoma City. Reggie answered on the second ring.

"I love the roses," she said.

"It's good to hear your voice, Ms. Marshall. It means that you remember me."

The smile she heard in his voice made her feel giddy. "How could I forget you, Mr. Stevens? It's not everyday a girl gets picked up on a tour bus in Mobile."

Reggie laughed at that. "I didn't pick you up."

She teased. "What do you call it, then?"

"I call it two people meeting each other, liking each other, and spending time with each other. How about that?"

"A rose by any other name . . ."

He took that opening to change the subject. "You like the roses?"

"They're beautiful." She rubbed a petal between her thumb and forefinger.

"Like you."

Christina beamed. She wondered if he could hear it in her voice. "Thank you, Mr. Stevens."

She heard him smile again. "When can I come visit?" he asked.

She hesitated before answering. "Reggie, I don't want to rush into anything."

"I'm not rushing you, but I want to see you again." He paused. "Soon."

"Let's take it slow for the time being."

"You can call the shots," he conceded. "For now."

They talked a while longer and Reggie promised to call again before the end of the week. Christina hung up with her confidence restored. At least Reggie didn't say he had been out of line the past weekend.

■ ■ ■ ■

The staff meeting started promptly at two. Jackson watched Christina. She was good at what she did. She ran her team like an army general, but the troops treated her like a benevolent dictator. They did what she told them to do because they felt she had their best interest at heart. Even though Jackson didn't know a lot about Christina, he felt she was good people. He didn't know her favorite color, although he guessed it was blue, since she wore the color often. He didn't know her political inclination. He didn't know how she felt about the death penalty, but he would bet his life that she was honest, trustworthy, and dependable. He wanted to get to know her. To see more of her soft side. To share her goals and dreams, even her fears. He looked at this woman and he knew somewhere deep inside himself that they connected. He couldn't explain it, but he knew it as sure as he knew his name. He felt that she knew it, too.

"Jackson," Christina was speaking to him now. "I need to talk to you after the meeting."

Jackson nodded. When everyone else had left, Christina said, "We have to go to

Boston in two weeks."

That got his full attention. "What's going on?"

"Walter has called a summit."

"How long will we be there?" he asked.

"Two days, Thursday and Friday. Penny has the dates. She's getting the information to Doris. You, Liza and I will meet Thursday morning. Later that afternoon we'll meet with Walter and Rosalind. They expect the meetings to last through Friday. Will that be a problem for you?"

"No, I can arrange it. There's plenty of time to adjust my schedule."

"Good. That's all I had. Is there anything you need to tell me?"

"If you have a few minutes."

"Sure, take a seat." She pointed to the two wing chairs where they'd had their initial interview. "Is there a problem?"

They each took a chair. "No, there's no problem. I just wanted to tell you how much I'm enjoying working on OPTIMA with you. I remember our interview, and I have to say that you've been true to your word. You've given me the freedom to do my job and you've supported me all the way."

"It's been good working with you, too, Jackson. I can tell that you're in your element here. You know that Walter and Rosalind are working hard to get you back to Boston. It'll be a great career move for you, but I'm really glad you're here and I'm going to hate to see you go."

Jackson looked at her for a few minutes, thinking of the things they hadn't said. They were doing a good job of pretending Friday had never happened. He stood up. "That was all I wanted."

Jackson left and Christina remained seated. She hated and loved being alone with Jackson. She loved it because she felt so at home with him. She felt as though she could take off her shoes, get comfortable, and be herself. She hated it because she had to fight the urge to give in to that feeling. She had to keep it strictly professional with Jackson or she'd be lost. She had mixed emotions about the trip to Boston. She knew she, Jackson, and Liza needed to meet, but she also knew the trip held the potential for her and Jackson to get to know each other in a semisocial setting. She was a little afraid of that.

I'll worry about it later, she thought. For now, I'm going to concentrate on the work that has to be done.

While the staff meeting was going on in Christina's office, Penny and Doris had a meeting of their own at Penny's desk.

"I would have sworn that something was going to happen between the two of them," Doris was saying. "The electricity between them was practically scorching everything in its path."

"When I left Friday, he was in her office," Penny added.

"I would love to have been a fly on the wall for that," Doris said.

"Well, he did look a little put out at the roses she got."

Doris was encouraged. She leaned closer to Penny. "Tell me more."

"She got flowers — pink roses — this morning."

Doris was all into it now. "Who were they from? Did you see the card?"

"Of course I saw the card, and you know I didn't read it." Penny looked insulted.

Doris didn't back down. "I know you, and that's why I asked."

Penny looked around. She whispered, "The signature on the card said 'Reggie.' "

Doris whispered, "Who's Reggie?"

"I don't know. I've never heard the name before. It's the first time she's gotten roses. At work, at least. There must be something to it."

Doris leaned in still closer. "I overheard

him talking to someone named Angela this morning."

"Maybe we misread the signs and there's nothing between them," Penny wondered aloud.

Doris didn't buy it. "It ain't over till it's over. I still say those two have something going."

Penny nodded.

Angela came for lunch Tuesday. Doris led her to Jackson's office to wait for him.

A moment later, Jackson rushed into the office. "Sorry, I'm late. I got tied up in something. How long have you been waiting?"

Angela stood up. "Don't worry about it. I haven't been here long. If today is bad for you, we can reschedule. I know how the days can get out of control."

Jackson gave her a kiss on the cheek, then smiled at her. "No, I don't want to reschedule. I do appreciate your understanding, though." Jackson looked at his watch, then back to Angela. "How much time do you have?"

"Actually, I have the rest of the day. I have a promo to record tonight, so I'm free until about seven."

"That's great. If you'll give me about

thirty minutes, I promise I'll make it up to you."

"I think I can manage that. Can a girl get a cold drink around here?"

Jackson had Doris bring in sodas for them both. Angela worked on her promo while Jackson finished his report. He was almost done when Christina entered his office.

Christina was about to speak when she saw Angela. "Excuse me. I didn't know you were busy."

Jackson stood up. Was that irritation he saw in Christina's eyes? He knew it couldn't be jealousy. Or could it? "Christina Marshall, my friend, Angela Ware." He gestured to Angela. "Angela Ware, my boss, Christina Marshall."

Angela stood and the women greeted each other.

"You're on the radio, aren't you?" Christina asked.

Angela glanced at Jackson, who shook his head. "That's me," she answered.

"You have a great voice," Christina said. They exchanged niceties, then Christina asked Jackson a few quick questions about the proposal he had prepared.

After Christina left, Angela looked askance at Jackson. "So that's your boss?"

Jackson nodded.

"She's a very attractive woman."

Jackson didn't like the way this was going. He began shuffling papers on his desk. "Yes. If that's your type."

Angela kept on. "And what type is she?"

Jackson hedged. "You know. All work, no play."

"How do you know?"

Can't we change the subject? He silently pleaded. "I never see her with anybody. She's kind of uptight."

Angela continued. "That's not the impression I got."

Jackson stopped shuffling the papers. "What did you think?"

"She came across as a very together woman, but there was also a certain warmth about her. Not exactly charismatic, but close."

"Someone you think you'd like to be friends with?"

Angela thought about it. "Yes. I think Christina and I would hit it off if we were thrown into a social situation," she answered with a smile.

Jackson winced. "I'm done here. Let's go before you decide you'd rather have lunch with Christina."

Angela took Jackson to the King Center for lunch. Since it was his first visit, they toured the memorial and the house where Martin Luther King, Jr. had grown up. Afterward, they walked up and down Auburn Avenue.

"Sometimes I wish I'd been born earlier so I'd have stronger memories of the events of the early sixties," Jackson said.

"I know what you mean," Angela responded. "It's our heritage and it should be as fresh now as it was then."

"Fresh is a good word. We have to keep it fresh so it'll always be real to us."

Angela finished his thought, "Then it'll keep its value throughout all the coming generations."

Jackson thought about his problems with his father and his nonrelationship with Christina. "If we kept it fresh, we wouldn't get sidetracked on trivial issues."

"It would keep us looking at our sameness and not at our differences."

"I wonder what Martin and Coretta's relationship was like," Jackson wondered aloud. "I wonder how he courted her. What he was looking for in a woman; what she was looking for in a man. I bet the words 'love' and 'forever' had different meanings then." Jackson was thinking about his mother and father. His mother should have known what "love" and "forever" meant.

"You sound like a man who's been hurt."

Jackson didn't want to open up yet. He played it light. "All men have been hurt at some point. It started with Adam and Eve."

Angela was direct with him. "If the conversations get too personal, Jackson, let me know and I'll back off."

"I'm sorry. I didn't want to get into it."

"Next time just say that."

Jackson stopped and tilted her face up to his. "You're a special woman, Angela."

"I know, but it's good you know it, too."

CHAPTER 7

Jackson arrived at Hartsfield International Airport an hour before his scheduled six-thirty flight Wednesday night. He had had enough bad experiences with checked luggage that checking his garment bag was not even a consideration. With his briefcase in one hand and his garment bag thrown over his shoulder, Jackson walked from the main concourse to the gate.

When he arrived, he looked around for Christina. He didn't see her, so he got his boarding pass and took a seat. He opened his briefcase and pulled out the newspaper, going straight to the comics. *Curtis* and *Doonesbury* were his favorite strips. He never missed them. He smiled as he read the day's installments.

"Must be good news."

He looked over the top of his paper. Christina smiled down at him. She wore casual blue slacks and a pink sweater. She looked like the calm after a long rain. "When did you get here?"

"I just walked up and got my boarding pass." She looked at the seats on either side of him. One held his garment bag, the other his newspaper. "Mind if I sit here?"

He removed the newspaper from the seat on his right.

Christina placed her garment bag in the seat with his and sat down.

"You don't believe in checking luggage either, I see?" He glanced toward her garment bag.

She shook her head. "Not on your life. I could tell you horror stories."

He laughed. "We could have a competition. Something like, 'Can you top this?' "

She laughed with him. "Maybe we could get the airline to give bonus frequent flyer miles to the one with the best story."

Jackson felt good sharing a joke with her. "I'm sure they'd go for that. Are you looking forward to getting back to Boston?"

"Not particularly. I never felt like I belonged there. I always knew I was only passing through."

"Passing through to where?"

"Atlanta, of course." She crossed her legs and began swinging her foot back and forth. "I'd been looking for an opportunity to get back here for the last three years. Actually, I wanted to stay in Atlanta after I graduated."

"You went to school here?"

She nodded. "Spelman and Georgia Tech."

"I can't picture you as a Spelman woman."

She stopped swinging her foot and eyed him. "I don't quite know how to take that. You'd better explain yourself."

Jackson smiled at her pretend pique. "It's nothing bad. Somewhere along the way I picked up that Spelman women were a bit — how shall I put this — bourgeois?"

"Bourgeois?" Christina laughed, uncrossing her legs. "Is that your way of saying stuck-up?"

He smiled. "I was trying to be diplomatic."

"No need to mince words. There are many different views on the Spelman woman. Like us or not, you have to admit that for the most part, we have a strong sense of self and an assertiveness that is matched only by the arrogance of the Morehouse man."

Jackson thought back to his college days. "There are times when I wish I'd gone to a black college. I thought about Morehouse, but at the time an all-male school was not my idea of a good experience."

"Spelman was a good experience for me. There's something about an environment with all women — all black women. People on the outside looking in only think of the similarities of the student population — all women, all black; but within the gates, we celebrate our differences. I was amazed at the diversity among us." She paused. "Do you understand what I'm saying?"

"I think so. At Oberlin, I could look around and see the differences, but then I also saw how much alike we all were."

They were silent for a while, then Jackson spoke. "So you fell in love with Atlanta when you were a student, and always wanted to come back?"

"That's part of it. I grew up in Selma. I really wanted to be close to home, and Atlanta was close without being too close."

"Sounds like somebody is still concerned about the apron strings. Is it Mom or Dad that's holding on too tight?"

She raised her brow. "Mom. Though I'm not sure if it's her or me who's holding on too tight."

Jackson understood that. Once again, he wished he could have been closer to his father after his mother had left. "Has the move met all your expectations?"

Christina thought before answering. Atlanta had been all she'd expected, but *she* hadn't been all she'd expected. Maybe this relationship with Reggie would work out and she could move forward with her goals. "In some cases, yes. In others, no."

"Your success at work has to be one of the yes ways. What are the no's?"

"I haven't gotten as involved in the community as I'd like. I've pretty much focused on work."

"It's only natural, given the new job and all."

"I know, but I always envisioned myself being real active in the community, in the local alumnae chapter. That hasn't been the case."

Jackson sensed that she didn't want to talk about this anymore. Maybe it was getting too personal. He looked toward the gate. Noticing a change in the flight time, he said, "We're going to be late getting out of here. They've pushed our departure time to eight-thirty."

Christina looked toward the gate. "A two-hour delay. I can't believe it." She stood up. "I'll check with the attendant."

Jackson watched her walk to the gate. He was glad she was in control again. Miss Marshall didn't like to get too personal.

Christina needed to get up. She knew something like this would happen with

Jackson. She felt too comfortable with him. Now, with this flight delay, she'd have even more time to spend with him. She couldn't keep her guard up all night. After inquiring about the delay, she walked back to her seat.

"There's a thunderstorm in Boston. They don't know when we can leave. Right now, a two-hour delay is their best guess."

"It'll be midnight before we get to our hotel."

"At least," Christina agreed.

"Are you hungry?"

Such a simple question. Christina remembered the last time Jackson had asked her to go eat with him. She hadn't gone then and she wouldn't go now. "Not really, but you go ahead."

"I hate to eat alone. Come watch me?" he pleaded.

"Who'll watch our bags?"

Jackson smiled. "It's amazing how accommodating an airline becomes in situations like this. They'll let us leave them behind the counter."

"That I don't believe."

"Let's bet, then. If they let us leave the bags, you go eat with me; if they don't, you stay here with the bags." He held out his hand. "Deal?"

She shook her head, but took his hand. "Deal."

She watched him walk over to the gate counter. He said something that she couldn't hear and the gate attendant shook his head. I knew it, she thought. Jackson flashed a smile and said something else. The next thing she knew, Jackson was placing the bags behind the counter.

Jackson looked over and beckoned her to come over to him. She got up and walked over. "What did you say to guy?" she asked.

"In my own kind and gentle way, I reminded him of a long-standing principle of customer satisfaction. Now, let's find a place to eat."

Christina wondered exactly what Jackson had said, but before she could inquire further, Jackson was leading her into an eatery.

"Any preference where we sit?" he asked.

She shook her head and he led them to a table in a corner.

They sat facing each other. She watched him while he studied the menu. He had nut-brown skin and a clear complexion. He didn't have any hair on his face. She liked that. Sometimes she felt that bearded men were hiding behind their hair. Mustaches were okay, but a clean-shaven man was best.

His shoulders were wide, giving him an aura of strength. She knew from memory that his waist was tapered and his buns tight. She smiled to herself.

"Must be a good thought?" Jackson inquired.

She was so intent on studying him that she forgot that he could study her as well. How long had he been looking at her? She felt exposed. Did he know what she was thinking? Had he seen her staring? Was she that obvious? "I was thinking about the last time I was here."

"What happened?"

She hedged. "It's one of those stories that loses something in the telling. What are you going to have?"

He looked at the menu again. "Nachos and a beer."

She laughed lightly. "You don't look like the beer type. Unless, of course, it's some expensive imported beer."

He laughed, too. "Not even close. I like good domestic beer. Are you going to get something?"

"Maybe a Coke."

"Not a Diet Coke? A woman of the nineties. You can share my nachos."

When the food arrived, Jackson coaxed Christina into sharing the nachos with him.

"They're better with beer," he said.

She raised her Coke in mock salute. "Things go better with Coke."

They continued in gentle banter while they ate. She enjoyed his company. She could tell. She had slipped off her shoes, a telltale sign. She looked at her watch. "We've been here almost two hours. I didn't think it had been that long. We'd better get back to the gate."

They got back to the gate to find the passengers boarding. The weather had cleared up in Boston. Jackson got their bags and they boarded the plane.

They got to the hotel around midnight, as Jackson had predicted. Christina checked in first. The hotel had run out of king-sized rooms, so she ended up with a suite. She waited while Jackson checked in. They needed to make plans for breakfast.

"What do you mean I don't have a room?" Jackson was asking.

"I'm sorry, sir, but your reservation wasn't guaranteed."

"There must be some mistake. Of course my reservation was guaranteed." Jackson was adamant.

"I'm sorry, sir. Under ordinary circumstances we'd be able to accommodate you, but we have a convention booked. I can try to find you a room at another hotel. It'll be difficult, though."

"By all means, make the calls. I have to have a room."

Christina walked closer. She knew what was going on. She also knew that she had a suite, but she didn't think it wise to mention that to Jackson. "Is there anything I can do to help?"

"Not unless you want to give up your room or share it with me," he joked.

Christina didn't smile.

The clerk interrupted, "I've tried two hotels with no luck. I may be able to get you at a comparable hotel a bit farther away. What do you think?"

"Do I really have a choice? Just find me a room."

Christina checked her watch. It was close to one o'clock. "Look, Jackson. It's late. I have a suite. You can take the sofa in the living area. Otherwise, you're not going to get much sleep."

Jackson looked as surprised at her offer as she felt making it. "Are you sure you don't mind? I'd owe you one."

"Sure. We'll have to flip for the shower."

The desk clerk interrupted again, "Ms. Marshall, yours is actually a two-bedroom suite with two baths. You shouldn't have any

131

problem with privacy."

Shows what you know, Christina thought. This clerk must not have seen *It Happened One Night.* "Thank you," she said.

If Jackson hadn't been so tired, he would have worried about the sleeping arrangements. But it had been a long day and a long night. All he wanted was sleep. He looked over at Christina. She had to be tired, but she looked fresh and relaxed. He admitted her offer surprised him. He guessed the sleeping arrangements bothered her, too. He noticed she had visibly relaxed when the clerk said hers was a two-bedroom suite. He yawned. "Thanks again, Christina. I probably would have been up all night had you not made your offer."

"Don't think about it. We have a busy day tomorrow and we both need a good night's sleep."

The elevator reached their floor and they got off. Christina unlocked the door to their suite. "Not bad," Jackson said, giving the place the once-over. He inspected both bedrooms and pointing to the one on the right, he said, "You take that one. It has the bigger bathroom." Jackson began to feel refreshed. He wanted to talk some before going to bed.

It was not to be. Christina picked up her bag and headed for her bedroom. "Goodnight, Jackson. See you in the morning."

Jackson stared dumbfounded at the bedroom door as Christina closed it. He stood there a few minutes before flopping down on the sofa. He yawned again. I really should to go bed, he thought. He heard Christina's shower come on. With vivid thoughts of Christina in the shower, he took himself off to bed.

Christina stepped into the shower. The water felt good against her skin. Her aching muscles and worn nerves welcomed the warm water. She thought about Jackson in the next room and wondered if he was asleep yet. He looked tired, real tired. And women were supposed to be the weaker sex. You'd think the man had been working in the fields somewhere. She smiled. Tough and aggressive in the boardroom, a baby in the bedroom. She shook her head. Jackson might be a baby in the bedroom, but she knew he wouldn't be a baby in bed.

When Christina stepped out of the shower, she looked at herself in the mirror, something she didn't often do. Her breasts were not as firm as she would have liked, and her belly could have been tighter. But

133

overall, not bad for a thirty-year-old woman who had at one time weighed more than 220 pounds. She wondered what Jackson would think of her body. Tired of looking at herself, Christina put on her nightgown. She liked the way the silk felt against her skin. There was something sensual about it. When she rubbed the fabric against her skin, she felt a tingle throughout her entire body.

Shutting off the light in the bathroom, Christina headed for bed. She settled herself under the covers and closed her eyes. She jerked her eyes open and stared at the ceiling. God, she was fantasizing about Jackson. She'd done it before, but never with him this close. He was so close she felt he knew what she was thinking. She turned over on her stomach, afraid to close her eyes again.

You are a successful, intelligent woman, not some starry-eyed schoolgirl, she told herself. Get a grip on yourself. Jackson is only a man. You've known men before.

She stopped there. That was the problem. She hadn't known, in the biblical sense, a man before. Horny at thirty. She could see the headlines now. FEMALE EXEC ATTACKS MALE EMPLOYEE. That made her smile. She didn't think she'd have to attack Jackson. He'd be more than willing to help her out. She guessed he'd be a thorough lover. God knows, he was thorough in his work. No, it wasn't the night of love that concerned her; it was the day after. She didn't want to think too closely about that.

Christina and Jackson arrived at CL headquarters at eight-thirty. The day had gotten off to a good start. Breakfast had been surprisingly easy for Christina. She and Jackson had dressed in their respective rooms with no embarrassing moments. He had been seated on the couch in the living room when she'd walked out of her bedroom. They ate breakfast in the hotel while going over the day's agenda. The awkwardness of the previous night had passed. They were back on safe ground.

They took the elevator to the fortieth-floor conference room. Liza was already there.

She stood up when Jackson and Christina walked in. "Good to see you both this morning. How was your flight?"

Christina looked at Jackson. He held up both hands. "I'm not the person to ask." He extended his hand to Liza. "It's about time we met."

Liza shook his hand. "Good to meet you, Jackson. I'm eager to get to Atlanta to work with you and Christina."

"We're ready for you to start, too," Christina said. "We have our work cut out for us." Christina looked from Liza to Jackson. "I know you two want to get to know each other a little bit, but for the sake of time, can we get started now with business and plan to have a relaxing dinner together tonight?"

"It sounds good to me," Jackson answered. "How about you, Liza?"

"Great. Robert, my fiancé, came to Boston with me. He's taking this time to get to know my parents. We had planned to take you two to dinner tonight, anyway."

They seated themselves at the conference table and started to work. As the morning progressed, Christina marveled at the way they clicked. Not that they always agreed. That was not expected with minds like theirs, but they were able to reason together to reach consensus pretty quickly. That boded well for the project.

The morning passed quickly. When it was time for lunch, Liza said, "I can't go to lunch with you. Something came up late yesterday that I have to address. I'll be back for the afternoon meeting, though."

Jackson and Christina walked to Walter's office. Christina was nostalgic as she walked the corridors. She paused to look in her old office. Someone new had moved in and the office now bore no resemblance to the place where she'd worked for over four years. Nothing stays the same, she thought.

They met Rosalind at the door to Walter's office.

"Perfect timing," Rosalind said. "Walter's waiting." She led them in.

Walter turned around in his chair. He beckoned them to seats while he finished a telephone call. After he hung up, he said, "We're having lunch in the private dining room." He looked at his watch. "We'd better get going."

Christina walked alongside Jackson and they followed Walter and Rosalind to the dining room. Though Christina had eaten there many times before, the room still overwhelmed her. It was too much, too rich. She felt out of place. She took a seat quickly. She actually hated eating here. She worried that she'd spill something on the thousand-dollar tablecloth or break one of the hundred-dollar crystal glasses.

Walter's voice brought her out of her thoughts. "So, Jackson, is Atlanta all that we told you about?"

Christina watched Jackson. "It's a good city," he answered. "The people are open and friendly." He nodded in Christina's

137

direction. "The work is great."

Christina commented, "I'm glad Jackson joined us. He's been a great asset to OPTIMA."

Walter nodded. "I knew you two would make a good team. Things will only get better when Liza gets there."

They spent the rest of lunch talking about OPTIMA. Christina listened as Jackson shared their accomplishments, his concerns, and his ideas for bringing the product to market. She loved listening to him. He was really excited about his work. Though his gestures were toned down a bit, his voice exuded excitement. There was something charismatic about Jackson. You believed him; you trusted him; you knew he could do it. And, most important, you wanted him to do well. Christina smiled at him.

Walter listened to Jackson. He and Rosalind had talked a lot about the best team to support Christina in Atlanta. He knew their recommendation of Jackson and Liza was a winning combination. He looked at Christina. She had done a hell of a job in Atlanta. The woman had a career at CL, if she wanted it. Sometimes he wondered what Christina Marshall really wanted. She was excellent at her job, but Walter had the feel-

138

ing there was something more she wanted. That something was behind her decision to move to Atlanta; he was sure of it.

At that moment, Walter noticed a soft smile cross Christina's face. It took him by surprise. The smile carried a vulnerability that he'd never before associated with her. Walter followed her gaze and saw that the smile was directed towards Jackson, who was wrapped up in a discussion with Rosalind. Walter shook his head slightly. Who would have ever thought of it? He glanced in Rosalind's direction. He wondered if she had picked up on anything. He couldn't believe it. Christina and Jackson. Of course, he didn't know anything for sure, but he'd bet something was going on. His next thought was of the effect their relationship would have on OPTIMA. He knew Christina and Jackson were consummate professionals, but intimate relationships in the workplace . . . Yes, he'd have to talk to Rosalind about this.

CHAPTER 8

Christina and Jackson got back to the hotel around seven o'clock. Jackson stopped at the desk to inquire about a room. Luckily, they had one for him.

Jackson took the key from the clerk and turned to Christina. He held the key up to her. "Looks like you've lost your roommate." He could have sworn she looked disappointed.

"I'm glad you have a room," she said. "Where is it?"

"I'm on the eleventh floor," Jackson answered. "Let's go. I can move my clothes, get settled, and be ready to meet Liza and Robert for dinner, if we hurry."

They were silent for the elevator ride up. When they got to her room, Jackson packed his bag while she waited in the living room.

"That's about it," Jackson said, walking out of the bedroom. "Thanks again for letting me stay."

"No problem. I'll see you downstairs for dinner." She checked her watch. "In exactly fifteen minutes."

"Yes. I'd better get hopping."

Christina stared at the door after Jackson left. So much for *It Happened One Night.* She wondered again if ignoring her feelings for Jackson was the right approach to take. She stopped looking at the door and dropped down on the couch. She closed her eyes and cleared her mind. Then she got up and changed for dinner.

When Christina walked into the bar, Liza and Jackson were seated with a man Christina assumed was Robert. Liza glanced around as Christina walked up.

"There you are, Christina." Liza waved her forward. "Come here, we've been waiting for you. I want you to meet Robert."

A tall, dark, bearded man held out his hand to her. "Glad to meet you. Liza has told me a lot about you." He pulled Liza to him, placed his arms around her shoulder, and squeezed.

Christina was happy for Liza — a little envious, but happy. "It's about time, Robert." Christina took his hand. "Liza sure can keep a secret."

Liza smiled and leaned into Robert. "I wasn't keeping him a secret, Christina. We just lost touch for a while."

Christina tapped Liza on the shoulder. "I'm only kidding. I'm happy for you two." She turned to Robert, "So, what do you think about moving to Atlanta?"

Robert told Christina of his plans to open a public relations office as the group moved to their table.

"Liza's lucky to have you," Christina said. "Not many men would have been agreeable to relocating with their wives."

Christina was surprised when Liza chimed in. "You're right. I *am* lucky." Liza was seated on the other side of Robert. Her hand covered his on the table.

Robert looked at Liza, smiled, then turned back to Christina. "I'm the lucky one. I'd follow this woman anywhere."

"Are there any more like him stashed away anywhere?" Christina asked Liza. "I'd like to get in line for one."

Jackson answered for Liza. "That's easy, Christina. There are plenty more like Robert. He's an Omega, and there are thousands of us around."

Liza laughed. "Can you believe the first thing they learned about each other was that they were in the same fraternity?"

"Surely they couldn't tell by looking at

each other," Christina said. "Did they bark?"

Liza laughed harder. Robert answered with mock sternness. "Omegas don't bark. It was the pin. We're both wearing frat pins."

Christina looked and sure enough they both wore frat pins. "Do you always wear yours, Jackson? I don't remember seeing it before."

"I rarely wear it to work, but I usually wear it to social functions."

"I guess that means you two don't see each other much outside of work?" Robert asked. "I thought you two ran in the same social circles."

"No," Jackson answered. "This is the first time Christina and I have been out for a social evening."

"This evening is not really social," Christina clarified. "It's business."

"If this is a business dinner, I'm leaving," Robert said. "I want to relax tonight and I want my baby to relax, too." He looked from Jackson to Christina. "How about it?"

Jackson answered first. "Sounds good to me, man. How about it, Christina?"

Christina hesitated. "What does it matter what we call the evening, business or social?"

Robert held up four tickets. "If it's social,

I have tickets to the late show at a comedy club in Cambridge. If it's business, we have to leave early because I have an early meeting."

Liza punched him softly. "When did you get the tickcts? I thought the show was sold out."

"That's me. I'm your miracle man. I pulled a few strings and got us tickets." He looked again from Christina to Jackson. "What'll it be, guys?"

Jackson looked at Christina with a silent question. They all waited for her answer. She knew she was making a bad move, but she wanted to enjoy the evening. She liked being with Robert and Liza; she liked looking at their love. It was something tangible. She could feel it and she could see it. It made her wonder what she was missing. She looked at Jackson and saw that he was still looking at her. "Which comedy club is it?"

"Jackson's a great guy," Liza said. She and Christina had taken a run to the powder room during intermission. "What's he like at work?"

"As arrogant as he is here."

Liza gave her a puzzled look.

Christina knew that look meant Liza would probe until she had the answer to her question. "There's something about that man. Don't get me wrong, we work well together, but he's so, so . . ."

Liza finished for her, "So attractive? So manly? So fine?"

Christina rolled her eyes. "That's not exactly what I was going to say, Liza."

Liza snapped the cap on her lipstick and placed it back in her purse. "You mean you don't think that's a fine brother out there?"

Christina hedged, "Sure, he's attractive."

"I hear a but in there somewhere. What's wrong with the man? He's attractive. He's fun to be with, easygoing. He has a good job. Damn, if the man were any more perfect, he'd be Robert."

Christina laughed. "You and Robert have something really special, don't you?"

Liza stood behind Christina and watched as she freshened up her makeup. "I can't explain it. We're one in every sense of the word. When relationships are good, they're real good, and right now we're real good. It gets better everyday."

"The man looks at you like he could eat you up. If I wasn't so jealous, I'd be nauseated."

Liza laughed. "Robert isn't the only man looking hungry tonight."

Christina stopped putting on her lipstick

and studied Liza's reflection in the mirror. "What do you mean by that?"

"Come on, Christina. I see the way Jackson looks at you."

Christina resumed putting on her lipstick. "I don't know what you're talking about."

Liza inclined her head. "Sure you don't. So, what's up between you?"

"There's nothing but business between us."

"Right," Liza said with obvious sarcasm. "That man was not giving you business looks out there."

"What kinds of looks was he giving me?"

"That territorial thing. 'Me, Tarzan; you, Jane. I want to jump your bones.' "

Satisfied that her face was together, Christina placed her lipstick back in her purse. "That's terrible, Liza. He's giving me no such looks," Christina lied. She knew Liza was right. Jackson had given her a few looks tonight that had almost scorched her. She just didn't think anyone else had noticed.

"If you say so." Liza let it drop. "Let's get back out there before the men think we've flushed ourselves."

Christina followed Liza out of the restroom. They made their way through the crowd back to their table. Jackson and Robert were in intense conversation when they walked up.

"Hey, what are you guys talking about?" Liza asked.

Robert looked up at her. "I was telling Jackson how great being engaged is."

Liza looked at Christina. "They're not going to tell us. Compliments like that are a sure sign."

"Now, wait a minute, Liza," Jackson said. "Robert *was* telling me how good being engaged is. He practically had me wishing *I* was engaged." He leaned closer to Liza. "Of course, there probably aren't many women like you around."

Liza slid her gaze to Christina. "I don't know about that. There are still some women out there who haven't been taken."

Jackson followed Liza's gaze to Christina.

"No telling how long they're going to remain available, though," Liza continued. "Good things are usually snapped up pretty quickly."

Still looking at Christina, Jackson said, "I hear you."

"Now who's keeping secrets?" Christina asked. "What are you and Jackson whispering about?"

Liza answered, "I was giving Jackson pointers on making art acquisitions." She leveled another look at Jackson. "Good pieces last only when they're hidden. As soon as people know where they are, they snap them up. You'd better get that piece before someone else does."

Christina sensed they were discussing more than art. "What have you found, Jackson?"

"A unique piece by a new artist. I've seen the work for a while now and it's growing on me. I made an offer to buy it once, but the artist wasn't selling."

"You should try again," Christina said. "He may have changed his mind."

Jackson studied Christina for a long second and then let his gaze go back to Liza. "Maybe I'll do just that."

Robert stretched out on the bed and watched Liza read. "How much longer are you going to be baby? I want to get some sleep."

Liza looked up from her notes. "You're nothing but a big baby yourself. You can go to sleep without me."

Robert crossed his ankles and put his arms behind his head. "I know I can sleep without you, but I don't like it. I sleep better when you're near."

Liza closed her notebook and placed it on the table next to her chair. "Are you sure you want to sleep?"

Robert didn't change his position. "Of course I want to sleep. What else could I want?"

Liza sashayed over to the bed. "Oh, I can think of a few things." She began to undress. "What did you think of Jackson and Christina?"

"I liked them. It's a real coincidence that Jackson and I are in the same fraternity. He says they have a strong chapter in Atlanta. He'll introduce us to some people."

Liza stood in her bra and panties. "What did you think of Jackson and Christina as a couple?"

Liza watched Robert as she unhooked her bra.

"I didn't think of them as a couple. I only think of us as a couple." Robert raised up and put his fingers to her nipple.

Liza moaned softly. "Couldn't you tell there was something between them?"

Robert took her nipple in his mouth. "There's too much between us. Take off those panties."

Liza pressed closer to him. "Robert, I'm serious. Don't you think they're attracted to each other?"

Robert eased his hand into her underwear. "I think I'm attracted to you."

"I know that. What about them?" Liza took his head in her hand and brought his face to hers. "What do you think?"

"I think Jackson wants to be in her panties as much as I want to be in yours." He rubbed his fingers against her wetness to make his point. "What do you think?"

"I think her panties are probably as wet as mine."

Robert looked into her eyes. His gaze never left her face as she leaned down to remove her underwear.

Naked, Liza lay down next to him, not touching. "Goodnight," she said.

Robert rolled over until he was poised over her. He began kissing her. "It's going to be a good night, all right," he said. Then he began making those words come true.

Jackson and Christina got back to their hotel a little before eleven. "The bar's open. How about a nightcap?" Jackson asked.

"Good idea," Christina answered, to Jackson's surprise. He hadn't expected her to take him up on his offer.

He led her to a booth and ordered drinks for them. "Did you have a good time tonight?"

"I did. It was good seeing Liza again. I didn't realize how much I'd missed her."

"I like them. Liza and Robert are good people." He paused. "You were different tonight."

"Different how?" she asked.

"I can't really describe it. Most of the time you're so in control, so staid. Tonight you relaxed. You were a bit like that in the airport last night, but tonight you reached another level."

"I did, did I?" Christina said. She slipped her shoes off and leaned back against the booth. "I needed to get away from the office. Even if this is business, I feel more relaxed."

"It wasn't all business," Jackson reminded her gently.

Christina closed her eyes. "No, it wasn't, was it?"

Jackson watched her sitting there. She looked good enough to eat. "How long have you known Liza?"

"We started at CL together. That makes it about eight years," Christina answered. Her eyes were still closed.

"This was your first time meeting Robert?" It was a question. Jackson didn't really care about the answer. He just wanted to keep her talking, keep her here with him. The feelings she'd awakened in him refused to be put back to sleep. He was going to have to deal with them . . . and so was she.

"Yes. I found out Liza was getting married when she came to Atlanta to interview. We lost touch the past couple of years. She was in Fort Worth. I was in Boston. We were both busy."

"Two career women. Work came first."

Christina opened one eye. "I think Liza found time for a little more than work." She closed her eye again.

"She and Robert appear to be happy together."

She opened both eyes. "They love each other. I can see it. I can feel it."

Jackson wondered at her tone. "Have you ever been in love?"

"Sad to say, but no."

But he'd bet plenty of men had fallen in love with her. He wondered how many men she'd cast her spell over. "And why is that?"

Christina shrugged her shoulders. She wasn't going to answer that. Finally, he said, "I could offer a guess or two."

"I'm probably going to regret asking this, but what's your guess?"

"It's no deep insight," he said. "You've probably always focused on your career and never taken the time to invest in a relationship. Too much time and too much energy."

"Sounds like experience talking. Have you

ever been in love?"

Jackson shook his head. Never been that unfortunate, he thought. "Never been that unfortunate," he answered.

"Your work a problem?"

"That's part of it." The smaller part.

"And what's the other part?"

"I've never met a woman I knew I could trust."

"Ah, trust."

Jackson didn't say anything. He watched Christina close her eyes again. She was a beautiful woman. A part of him believed he could trust her. He wondered what she would do if he kissed her. He knew she'd taste sweet. At that moment, she opened her eyes as if she'd heard his thoughts. She didn't move. He leaned across the table and kissed her. He was right. She was sweet.

He pulled back to look into her eyes. She leaned toward him. He took her lips again. This kiss was longer and sweeter. He moved closer and wrapped her in his arms. This time when he pulled back, she followed.

"We're acting like teenagers," he said. "Let's go upstairs."

Christina nodded. Jackson left money for the drinks and led her upstairs.

Christina couldn't think. She knew she was

in the elevator with Jackson. Correction —
she was in the elevator wrapped in Jackson's
arms. She knew she had kissed him. She
knew she liked it. She knew this was probably the wrong move to make, but she
couldn't stop herself. She wanted to be with
him. She loved being in his arms.

The elevator stopped. She looked up and
saw that it was her floor. He gave her a short
kiss and led her down the hallway. He kissed
her again at her door. Somehow, she found
her keys and opened the door. He walked
in with her, closed the door behind them,
and kissed her again. God, she loved it. He
was good at this. He must have kissed more
than a few women in his time.

"God, Christina, you taste so good," he
said between kisses. "I knew it would be
like this."

Her answer was to return his kiss.

"Ohh . . ." he moaned. "I want you,
Christina, like I've never wanted any
woman."

"Yes . . ." she answered. She was still kissing him. She couldn't get enough.

He raised his head and looked down at
her. "I want to make love with you."

She heard him, but she didn't want to
answer. She wanted him to kiss her again.
She put her hand behind his head and

pulled him closer until his mouth touched hers.

He gave her what she wanted. The kiss was electrifying. She felt it in her heart, her head, all over her body.

He pulled back again. "Let's go to bed."

Christina looked deeply into his eyes. She could love this man. "I'm sorry," she said. "I'm not ready for this."

Jackson smiled. "Yes, you are. Do you want me to show you how ready?" He kissed her again.

She responded with everything she had.

He lifted his head. "You're ready." He leaned down and kissed her again.

God, I could do this forever, Christina thought. Jackson began to unbutton her blouse. Next, he took off her bra. His large hands caressed her full breasts. Her nipples hardened as he flicked his forefinger back and forth across them. The pleasure was unbearable. He kissed her again. He started with her lips, moved down her chin, her neck, her shoulders, her breasts. When his tongue touched the tip of her nipple, her knees went weak. She'd never felt anything like this before.

Suddenly, he picked her up. He kissed her mouth again as he carried her to the bedroom. He laid her on the bed and looked down at her. He looked obsessed. His eyes were full of passion, his breathing ragged, his need obvious.

She lifted her arms to him and he came to her. He laid his full weight on her. She loved the feel of him. His hands rubbed her breasts, moving down her stomach to her panties. He passed his hand against her femininity.

He moaned. "I can't wait any longer." He stood up and began to undress.

The ringing telephone stopped him. He looked at Christina and then he looked at the phone. She sat up and answered it. He didn't move. He watched her full breasts heaving.

"Hello," she said, her eyes never leaving his face. "No, Walter, this isn't a bad time. What do you need?" She paused. "Hold on a minute, Walter, I have to get my note-book." She laid the phone down and looked at Jackson. "I have to take this," she whispered.

"I can stay," he offered.

Her head was clear now and she couldn't let what was happening between them continue. "I don't think that's such a good idea."

"Is that the way it is?" he asked, a frown settling around his mouth.

"That's the way it is," she answered.

Jackson just stared at her. He opened his mouth as if to speak, but closed it without saying a word. He buttoned his shirt and righted his clothes. "You'd better watch yourself, Miss Marshall. You're beginning to look a lot like a tease."

As he walked out of the bedroom, Christina went back to the phone. "Okay, Walter, I'm ready."

CHAPTER 9

"Your admirer again, Christina. This time red roses. He must not have wanted you to get tired of pink ones," Penny said, as she arranged the bouquet on Christina's desk.

Christina looked up from her work. The roses were a welcome surprise. Roses from Reggie had been at her house when she'd gotten back from Boston. They'd been a well-needed lift after the fiasco with Jackson. She had called to thank him and ended up talking for over three hours. By the time the conversation had ended they'd planned his visit to Atlanta.

She smiled as she reached for the card. Reggie was going overboard, she thought. She loved getting them, but she'd have to tell him to stop. Maybe. "Ugh . . ." Christina moaned, as she slumped into her chair.

"What is it? Are you ill?" Penny asked. She walked behind the desk to get closer to Christina. "What's wrong?"

Christina said nothing. She handed Penny the card. Penny read to herself. "I can't believe this. Who would send this?"

Christina tried to regain her composure. "I have no idea. Who delivered the flowers?"

"They were on your desk when I arrived this morning. I didn't see the delivery boy."

A knock at Christina's door interrupted them. "Come in," Christina said. Jackson walked through the door. It was the first time she'd seen him since the flight in from Boston.

He was talking as he walked in. "I need to talk to you before the staff meeting this afternoon. Do you have some time?"

Christina didn't answer immediately. Staff meeting. This afternoon. Oh, yes. "What do you want to talk about?"

Jackson sensed something was wrong. He looked from Penny to Christina. "Did I interrupt something?"

"No."

"Yes!"

Both women answered at the same time. The no belonged to Christina; Penny gave the yes.

Again, Jackson looked from one woman to the other. "What's the problem?"

Penny looked at Christina who said nothing. "It's the roses," Penny said.

Jackson noted the red roses on Christina's desk. "I don't get it. What's wrong with them?"

Penny handed him the card. "This came with them."

Jackson opened the card. The word "Bitch" was printed in big red letters. Jackson looked directly at Christina. "When did you get this?"

"They were here when Penny came in this morning."

"They were here in your office or out on Penny's desk?" Jackson asked.

"They were here," Christina answered.

"Did you see anybody?" Jackson asked Penny.

Penny shook her head. "I was the first one in the office this morning. I even beat Christina, which is unusual."

Christina thought about her late-night conversation with Reggie. "I did get in later than usual this morning."

"That's true," Penny said. She looked at Christina. "I saw the roses when I came in with your tea. I was surprised you weren't here."

"How long had you been here before I walked in?" Christina asked.

"I came in with the tea at seven-forty-five,

as usual. I had just walked in when you arrived."

"You didn't see anything suspicious?" Jackson asked.

Again Penny shook her head. "I saw the roses, but I didn't think much about them." She looked at Christina. "You've been getting roses regularly. I assumed these were from the same person."

Jackson focused his gaze on Christina. "Who sent the other roses?" Jackson remembered the name "Reggie," but that was all he knew.

"A friend," was Christina's only answer. "I'm sure it wasn't him." Christina spoke to Penny. "Check with security to see who was in the building this morning. Don't look so worried. No harm was done."

"If you say so, Christina," Penny said. "I'll call security."

Penny left the room. Christina spoke to Jackson, "So what did you want to talk to me about?"

"You really have no idea who could have sent the roses?"

Christina shook her head. "No idea at all. I thought they were from Reggie. I don't understand it."

That was the first time she'd spoken Reggie's name to him. "I don't understand it, either, and I don't like it."

"There's nothing we can do about it now, so let's get down to business." She asked again, "What did you want to talk about?"

Jackson wanted to inquire more about the roses, but seeing Christina seated at her desk, he realized it was time to get back to work. "The status meeting. I wanted to talk with you about it. We need to split the groups now, before Liza gets here. The people can get a head start on their new work. What do you think?"

"I've been thinking the same thing. Liza would probably prefer picking her own people, but we don't have time for that. Let me talk to her and see what she thinks."

"Sounds good to me." He started for the door. Looking at the roses, he asked, "Are you sure you're okay?"

"I'm fine." She nodded toward the roses. "I should have Penny throw those out."

"Let security get rid of them. They might lead them to the culprit."

"You're right. On your way out, ask Penny to come back in here. At least she can take them out of my sight."

Jackson left the office wondering who wanted to scare Christina. He was sure those roses were meant to scare, not to harm. He still hadn't ruled out this Reggie character. He stopped at Penny's desk. "Christina wants you to remove those roses from her office." As Penny got up to go into Christina's office, Jackson stopped her. "How often has she been getting roses?"

"She's been getting a dozen every week for about a month now. The others were pink. This is the first dozen that's been red."

"Do you think they're from the same person?"

"When I first saw them, I thought they were from the same person, but now I don't know. If he cares for Christina, why would he do this? If he didn't care for her, why would he have sent the others?"

"Maybe they're having a fight or something?" Jackson offered.

"I don't think that's it," Penny responded. "Christina was happy when she saw the roses. Like she expected they were from the same person. I don't think that's it."

Since Penny was being so open, Jackson continued, "Have you ever talked to this Reggie before?"

"I've taken calls from him a couple of times. He's a nice man."

"Okay," Jackson said. Nice man. What could you really tell from a voice over the telephone? "I'm just concerned about Christina's well-being. Don't forget to make that call to security."

"I won't," Penny said. "I'd better go remove those roses now."

Christina sat alone in her office. Penny had removed the flowers, but Christina still had the card. Who would do such a thing? She couldn't believe it. She'd heard of things like this happening in the movies, but not in real life. Somebody wanted to get to her. Why? Though she thought hard, she could come up with no answers. There was a positive side to the incident, though. Her meeting with Jackson had a focus other than their weekend fiasco. She had dreaded seeing him, unsure what affect the Boston trip would have on their relationship this morning. She was touched by his concern. She twirled the card in her fingers. Yes, she thought, there was a positive side to this nasty incident.

Christina sat in the restaurant at Hartsfield Airport. She thought of the last time she was here, the day she and Jackson had flown to Boston. They had eaten lunch in this very restaurant. She smiled thinking about it. Today she was meeting Reggie's flight. She had waited at the gate until she'd learned his flight was delayed. Now she sat in the restaurant to pass the time.

She thought about Jackson and she thought about Reggie. She wondered what would have happened if she'd slept with Jackson. She replayed the scene over and over in her mind. What if, what if, what if? She was glad she hadn't. The relationship would have been too complicated. Her best bet was to see what happens with Reggie.

She and Reggie had talked regularly since Mobile. She felt she could come to love him, but she knew she wasn't there yet. Reggie knew his feelings were more serious and told her so. She had to make him take it slowly.

She checked her watch and headed back for the gate. The flight had just touched down. Reggie would be coming out any minute now. She took a quick stop by the restroom to freshen up. She wanted to look her best.

"You look gorgeous," Reggie said, before he kissed her softly on the lips. "I've missed you."

"You have, have you? We'll have to see how much," Christina teased.

"I hope that's a challenge, because I'm going to prove to you this weekend how much I've missed you. Now, where are we going for dinner? I'm starving."

She laughed. "I thought you'd want to check into your hotel first."

"Let's eat first. Who knows? Maybe I won't have to stay in a hotel, after all."

Christina played dumb. "Oh, you have friends in the city?"

"I've got one friend that I think can be persuaded to let me bunk with her."

"It's a her, is it? Just who is this friend?"

"A very special woman. If you're good, I might introduce you. I think you'd like her. You're a lot alike."

"That's what scares me."

Reggie laughed. "Enough, woman. Let's eat."

Knowing Reggie loved southern cooking, Christina took him to the Beautiful Restaurant on Cascade. He had barbecued ribs, potato salad, collard greens, cornbread, and, for dessert, apple pie.

"God, you should be as big as a house. I would be, if I ate that much."

"I'm a growing boy," Reggie said, taking the last bite of potato salad. "I have to eat."

"Do your brothers eat like you?"

"Now that you mention it, we all have healthy appetites. So does my dad."

"You men probably kept your poor mom in the kitchen all the time."

He laughed. "Mom has a pretty good appetite herself. She loves to cook, loves to eat, and she loves feeding her family."

Christina stirred her tea idly. She wondered what Reggie's family was really like. "I'd like to met your family, especially your mother."

"You're invited to come to visit anytime you want. I know my mom would love you."

"You probably say that to all the women."

Reggie wiped his mouth with his napkin, then spoke earnestly. "That's not so. I can count on one hand the number of women I've taken home to meet Mom. That's too special."

Christina was caught off guard by his sincerity. "So, why do you think she'd like me? Are we alike in some way?"

Reggie thought for a moment. "On the exterior, you're nothing alike. My mom has never worked outside the home. She's the ultimate homemaker and caretaker. She's content that way. Now that her children are grown, she takes care of my dad and the grandkids. She's fulfilled. There is something almost serene about her. There's something about you that gives off that same sense of serenity."

"That sounds good, but I don't really understand it."

"Let me say it this way: my mom's her own woman. She chose her life and she lives it because she wants to, not because she has to. You're your own woman, too. You've just chosen a different track from my mom."

Christina wondered if Reggie had her confused with someone else. She must be putting up a good front if that was what he saw. "So, you think I'm my own woman?"

"Sure you are. Look what you've accomplished. You had to have a great deal of self-assurance and skill to accomplish what you have."

"Who do you think made the better choice, me with my career, or your mom with her family?"

Reggie stopped eating. "There's not a better-or-worse. It's what's right for the individual. You're you, and my mom's my mom. You're both doing what's right for you."

Reggie's words sounded right, but Christina wasn't sure she agreed with him. Maybe at one time work had been enough for her. But not now. She wanted more.

"You could have your own family — husband, children, career, everything," Reggie was saying. "It all depends on what you want."

Christina hoped Reggie was right, but this

conversation was making her uncomfortable. Reggie was getting too close to the truth. She decided to play it light. "So, you think I can be Superwoman?"

"Not Superwoman, but a very happy woman."

Christina didn't answer, but she thought about what he'd said for a long time.

"What are we doing tomorrow?" Reggie asked. He sat on the couch in Christina's family room.

She put the popcorn in the microwave and set the timer. "There are a couple of ways we could go. Which do you prefer, cultural or entertainment?"

"How about entertainment on Saturday and cultural on Sunday?"

"Okay. Tomorrow, we can either do the great Six Flags, Stone Mountain, White Water, or the zoo. Pick one."

"That's an easy one. Six Flags. It's been ages since I've been to an amusement park. I loved it as a kid. How about you?"

"I never went much. My mom and I went once, and I went one time with a group from school."

Reggie walked over to her and took her face in his hands. "Tomorrow will be your day as much as mine. We'll both be kids."

He kissed her, then he raised his head to look at her. He rubbed his hands down both her cheeks and smiled. "I like you, Christina Marshall. I like you a lot. Now, let's get that popcorn and get ready for this movie before I get myself in trouble."

Christina reached up and kissed Reggie again. "I like you, too, Reggie Stevens." She stepped out of his embrace and got the popcorn.

They cozied up on the couch to watch an early Robert Townsend video. The movie was Reggie's idea. Christina knew it was a ploy to get into her house, but by that time she had decided to invite him anyway.

Christina enjoyed watching the movie with Reggie more than she had imagined. Afterward, they talked for a while.

"We'd better get some sleep if we're going to tackle Six Flags tomorrow." She looked askance at Reggie. "Or, we could sleep in and go later?"

"No, way," Reggie said. "We're going to do this like real kids. What time does this place open?"

"Eight or eight-thirty," Christina answered.

"We ought to be there when the gates open, but I'll live with getting there at nine."

"You're serious about this, aren't you?"

"You'll find that I'm always serious about my fun. We'd better get ready for bed."

Christina knew Reggie hadn't forgotten he was staying in the guest room. "What do you mean by that?"

"This." He leaned over and covered her mouth with his. It was the most passionate kiss they had shared. He continued kissing her for a few minutes. "We're going to have to stop or I'm going to need a cold shower before I go to bed."

Christina punched Reggie in the chest playfully. "Oh, you . . ."

"Don't stop," Christina moaned. "It feels so good."

"Those words do things to me," Reggie responded. He was massaging Christina's feet and legs.

She closed her eyes and gave herself over to his touch. "Reggie, I ache all over. How do kids do it?"

He laughed. "You're not used to all that walking. Are you feeling any better?"

"As long as you keep doing what you're doing, I'll recover. Stop and my muscles may all lock up."

Reggie continued to massage. "It was fun, though, wasn't it?"

She opened her eyes and blessed him with

a smile. "I wouldn't have missed it for anything. I had a great time. Amusement parks weren't this much fun when I was a kid. Those rides! God, how do kids do it?"

"You didn't do too badly. I thought my eardrums would burst on that Ninja roller coaster. Other than that, you were a real trooper."

"Uhhmm," she said. "Guess what?"

"What?"

Touching her fingers to her lips, she said, "I want to kiss you, but I'm too tired. What do you think of that?"

"I think we'd better get you to bed and get some rest. Tomorrow promises to be a good day."

Jackson saw her as soon as he walked in the restaurant. She was with a man, but he saw only the back of the man's head. He thought for a moment, then decided to go over and say hello. To Angela, he said, "I see Christina over there. Let's say hi before we get a table."

Angela nodded and followed Jackson to the table. When Jackson reached the table, he saw the man's face. "Reggie? Reggie Stevens, is that you?"

Reggie looked up. "Jackson? What are you doing here?" Reggie stood and the men clapped each other on the back.

"I live in Atlanta now. What are you doing here? It's been ages since I've seen you. How's your family?"

Reggie held up his hand. "Hold a minute. Let's take it one question at a time. I'm in town visiting a friend."

"How do you two know each other?" Jackson asked Christina.

Reggie's face registered his confusion. "You know Christina?" he asked Jackson.

Christina finally spoke up. "Jackson and I work together." She included Angela in the conversation. "Angela, it's good to see you again. This is Reggie Stevens."

"Hello, Reggie," Angela said.

"I'm sorry about the way Jackson and I went on," Reggie said. "I'm glad to meet you, Angela." He looked at Jackson. "Why don't you two join us?" Including Christina in his glance, he asked, "You don't mind, do you?"

Christina shook her head. "Not at all. You and Jackson have a lot to catch up on, and I can get to know Angela better." She made the invitation again. "You two should join us."

Jackson looked at Angela. She agreed, and so did he. He realized neither Reggie nor Christina had answered his question. It didn't matter, really. It was obvious Reggie was in town to visit Christina. Reggie. Reggie was "Pink Roses" Reggie. He shot Christina a quick glance.

Reggie motioned for the waiter to bring more chairs, and soon they were all seated. "How long has it been?" Reggie asked.

"It seems like forever, man," Jackson said, getting his mind back on the conversation. "I haven't talked with your brother since his wedding."

"My mom asks him about you now and then. She adopted you back then, you know."

"Your mom was good to me." Jackson explained to Angela and Christina, "Reggie's youngest brother, William, and I went to Oberlin together. I spent many holidays at their house in Oklahoma City." He asked Reggie, "Your mom still cooking those great meals?"

"Does the sun still shine? Mom's still cooking and still loving it. She always said she liked cooking for you because you ate like one of her boys."

"Those were some special times that I spent at your house, man. You and your family will never know how much it meant to me."

Christina watched the interchange between Jackson and Reggie. Neither she nor Reggie had answered his question, but she knew by the scathing glance Jackson had sent her that he realized who Reggie was to her. She couldn't help but be satisfied with his response.

"How long have you been working with this guy?" Reggie's question brought her out of her thoughts.

"About six months now," Christina said.

"Don't be modest, Christina," Jackson said. "Reggie, I actually work for Christina. She's the boss."

Reggie looked at Christina, but his question was for Jackson. "Is she a hard taskmaster?"

"She carries a whip, but she rarely uses it."

Reggie laughed and gave Christina a quick wink. "I'll bet." He then asked Angela, "So how did you get mixed up with this character?"

Christina had wondered that herself. She silently thanked Reggie for asking the question.

Angela smiled then. "The wife of one of his fraternity brothers introduced us."

"Actually, the wife fixed us up," Jackson added. "She thinks Angela's wife material."

Angela joined in. "My friend has us married with two kids." She smiled at Jackson. "We became friends in spite of her."

Christina sneaked a glance in Jackson's direction and saw him return Angela's smile. They couldn't be considering marriage, could they?

"How did you manage to surround yourself with such beautiful women?" Reggie asked Jackson.

Jackson grinned a purely masculine grin and said, "What can I say, man? I'm lucky."

Reggie smirked. "That's an understatement. What are you two doing today?"

"Angela has been showing me the sights." He turned to Angela. "What are we doing today, guide?"

"Today's the Atlanta University Center. They're having a campus production of *Dreamgirls.* I thought we'd tour the campus and see the play." She looked from Christina to Reggie. "Why don't you come with us?"

Christina didn't want to spend Sunday with Jackson and Angela, but she knew from Reggie's expression that he wanted to do exactly that. "I was going to take Reggie to southwest Atlanta today, anyway," Christina said. "It sounds like a good idea." She turned to Reggie. "What do you think?"

Reggie looked at Jackson. "Do you think

it's a bad sign that our women don't want to be alone with us?"

Chapter 10

"I can't believe you're actually checking your garment bag," Christina said.

Reggie tipped the skycap before responding to her. "I have better things to do than carry luggage."

"Like what?" she asked.

He walked over to her, put an arm around her shoulder, and began walking. "Like this."

Christina looked up at him, but kept in step. "This only takes one arm. You could have carried your bag with the other."

Reggie squeezed her to him. "Are you being difficult?"

"No," Christina answered. "I'd just hate to see your luggage get misplaced."

Reggie stopped walking. Using both arms this time, he pulled Christina to him and gave her a long kiss. When he lifted his head, he said, "That's why I need two arms free."

Christina didn't miss a beat. "Well, I think

people are overly cautious about their luggage anyway. There's only a small chance that the airline will lose it."

Reggie threw back his head and laughed. He gave her another kiss on the nose and started walking again.

Christina was glad Reggie had suggested they walk to the gate instead of taking the train. She liked being close to him like this. There was a homey feeling about Reggie. She was comfortable with him. Comfortable, but not attracted sexually. She liked kissing him, but there were no sparks for her.

She looked up at him as they walked. He was an attractive man, fun to be with, but something was missing. He must have sensed her looking at him, because he smiled down at her.

"What are you thinking about?"

She decided to be honest. "Us."

"What a coincidence. I was thinking about us, too. What do *you* think about us?"

How do I tell this man that I don't feel anything sexual for him? "I like you, Reggie," she began. "I like you a lot."

Reggie dropped his arm from around her shoulder. "Somehow, I know a 'but' is coming."

Christina took his hand in hers. "I like

you, but I think you're going faster in this relationship than I am."

"I'm not rushing you. I admit that I haven't tried to deny or hide the way I feel about you. That's the kind of guy I am."

She brushed his knuckles with her hand. "I know that and I don't want you to change. I just want you to know where I am. I don't want either of us to get hurt."

"It's a little too late for that," he said. "If this doesn't work out between us, I'll be hurt."

"You don't sound bitter or disappointed at that."

"Why should I be? That's the way relationships are. If you're involved, you've got to be vulnerable. If you're vulnerable, you might get hurt. If the relationship works, the risk is well worth it."

With his hand still in hers, they resumed their walk to the gate. After they had gone about five feet, Reggie placed his arms around her shoulders again. Christina smiled.

Jackson arrived early for the Monday afternoon staff meeting. Christina was in her office.

"I asked, but you didn't answer," he began. "How did you meet Reggie?"

180

The question surprised and annoyed Christina. They were bringing personal matters into the office. She lifted her gaze to him. "We met in Mobile."

Jackson nodded. "Reggie is a good guy. I was relieved to know that he sent the pink roses. That means he didn't send the red ones."

"You thought Reggie sent those?"

Jackson shrugged. "You have to admit it was a reasonable conclusion."

She leaned back in her desk chair. "Maybe. It never crossed my mind that it was Reggie." *Though I did think for a moment that it might be you,* she said silently. *The roses did come right after our fiasco in Boston.*

"You and Reggie," Jackson mused aloud. "He's a good guy, but it's hard for me to picture you and him together."

"What's that supposed to mean?"

"Well," Jackson continued. "It's hard for me to envision you with him the way you were with me in Boston."

Christina gasped. She couldn't believe he'd brought up Boston.

"Have you been with him that way?" he asked.

"That's none of your business."

Jackson kept coming. "Reggie's a decent,

patient man, but I doubt even he'd put up with a stunt like the one you pulled in Boston."

"I knew this would happen," Christina commented.

"Knew what would happen?" Jackson asked.

"I knew it would create problems if we started something personal. Now here you are, bringing up personal matters in the office."

"I have to bring it up in the office. I don't see you anyplace else."

"You saw me this weekend."

"Are you saying you wanted me to bring this up in front of Reggie?"

"I mean that I wanted this office to remain a place of business and nothing else."

"You owe me an explanation, Christina. Either we meet after work to discuss this or we discuss it here. The choice is yours."

"There's nothing for us to discuss."

"You don't lie very well. Did you sleep with him?"

Christina ignored that question. "As I said before, there's nothing for us to discuss. You've started something with Angela, why are you still pestering me?"

"Jealous?"

"God, no!"

"Then why bring up Angela?"

His grin told her he still believed she was jealous. She took a deep breath. "Look, Jackson. I'm going to say this once. There's nothing between us. There has been nothing between us." Jackson started to interrupt, but she didn't let him. "Boston was a mistake. It should never have happened. It's the best proof I have that we should stay strictly professional in our dealings with each other. Nothing is going to happen between us."

"I hear your words, Christina, but I also remember how you felt in my arms in Boston. I don't want to complicate your life, but we have to deal with what's between us." He paused to let his words settle around them. "For now, I'm going to play it your way. I'm going to keep it professional. I want you to remember that this is the way you wanted it. And don't ever tease me again. A man can only take so much."

She would not be intimidated. "I guess we understand each other, then?" At Jackson's nod, she said, "Let's get to work. We need to go over the agenda for the meeting."

"Have a rough day, man?" Ellis asked.

"That's an understatement," Jackson answered.

"What's up? Work, or women?"

Jackson laughed. He was glad he'd met Ellis for drinks after work today. He needed to talk to somebody. "How did you know?"

Ellis took a swallow of his drink. "That's easy, man. What else causes us trouble? Work because we have to eat, and women because we have to sleep. What gives?"

"I think I've screwed up."

"I thought you and Angela were getting along well. If there were any problems, I'm sure Betty would know. That leaves work."

Jackson shook his head. "It's not Angela. It's Christina."

"Christina, as in your boss Christina?"

"Yeah, man, one and the same."

"I feel for you, buddy. You've managed to wrap up women and work in a single problem. How'd you get involved with your boss, anyway?"

"I'm not exactly involved with her. It's complicated."

"I bet it is. There's no way sleeping with the boss couldn't be complicated."

"I'm not sleeping with her," Jackson clarified. "I just want to really badly."

"I advise you not to go that way. There are plenty of available women without you going after your boss."

"You sound like Christina. You make the

word 'boss' sound like 'monster.' God, it's a job, a title. You'd think we were living in the Dark Ages."

"Regardless of how it sounds, you'd better be careful. You're screwing with your career. What if this relationship doesn't work? She's in a position to affect your career. And if it does work and everybody finds out, what will it do to office morale? No matter how you cut it, you can't win."

Jackson had heard all the arguments before. They didn't help. He took another swig of beer. "What if Christina is the one?"

"You've got it bad, haven't you?"

"There's something that draws me to her. I've told myself to leave her alone. She's told me to leave her alone, but I can't. I dream about this woman, man. It's like I'm obsessed."

"Damn."

"It's not that bad. She has no idea how she affects me. She knows I want her, and she knows that I know she wants me, but she's determined to keep it professional. She's doing a damn good job, too. She let her guard down when we went to Boston, but she threw it back up so fast that I thought I had dreamed the whole thing."

"What happened in Boston?" Ellis asked.

"Nothing. We came close, but she backed

down." Jackson remembered how it felt to hold Christina in his arms. Hell, he'd done nothing but think about it since it happened. The woman haunted his nights and his days. It seemed the more he tried to get over her, the more she ruled his thoughts. He was going to have to do something — soon.

"Consider yourself lucky, friend," Ellis said, interrupting Jackson's thoughts. "Leave it alone. Aren't you and Angela getting close?"

"I like Angela. If Christina weren't in the picture, more might be happening with her. But I can't get Christina out of my mind."

"Angela's a good woman, Jackson. Don't lead her on if nothing can come of it."

"We're friends," Jackson explained, but he wondered how Angela would react to his description of their relationship. "I think Angela feels the same way. I don't think she's ready to get serious."

"Make sure you're right. Angela is a friend and I'd hate to see her head get messed up in this."

"I hear you, man. I'll make sure things are on the up and up with Angela. Now, let's cut this talk. What chance do you think the Braves have this year?"

■ ■ ■ ■

"We need to talk," Jackson said. He and Angela had just finished dinner at her place and they were settling in to watch television.

"Sounds serious," was Angela's response. "What do we need to talk about?"

He pointed his finger from her to him. "Us. This relationship."

"Oh. One of those conversations."

He touched a hand to the back of her neck. "Help me out here, Angela. Be serious."

"Okay." She closed the *TV Guide* she was reading and gave him her full attention. "I'm serious."

"I like you a lot, Angela," he said, taking her hand in his. "We have a lot of fun together, but I'm not ready for anything more than that."

She blinked twice. "And you think I am?"

Jackson wasn't really sure. He knew she liked him, but he didn't know how much. "No, but we've never really talked about it and I wanted — no, needed — to get it all out. I'd like for us to be friends a long time. I don't want to screw it up by getting our signals messed up."

Angela was silent.

"So, say something," Jackson prompted. He hoped he hadn't hurt her feelings.

"Is there somebody else?" Angela asked.

"Not really," Jackson responded. His thoughts went immediately to Christina.

"Does 'not really' translate to 'not yet'?"

Jackson smiled. "How come you're so smart?"

Angela removed her hand from his. "I got the impression early on that there might be somebody else."

Jackson wondered at the signals he was sending. Angela couldn't know about his feelings for Christina, could she? "And what impression was that?"

"I thought you had a thing for Christina."

"Christina? What makes you think that?"

"Something I picked up the day you introduced us. I was more convinced after that Sunday evening we spent with her and your friend Reggie."

Jackson remembered that he'd been especially careful that day. What could Angela have seen? "I didn't show any special interest in her either time. And I know she didn't show any in me."

"Maybe that was it. You were both trying too hard not to pay attention to one another."

So much for his being careful. It was Jackson's turn to be silent.

"Am I right?" she asked. "Is there something going on between the two of you?"

"Would it matter if there were?"

"Look, Jackson, it's okay with me if we're just friends. There doesn't have to be anything romantic between us. But you've got to make up your mind which it will be. Sometimes I think you want romance, and at others I think you want a buddy. If we're going to be friends, you've got to be straight with me."

She was right. He had been trying to play it both ways, but he would stop that today. "I'm sorry, Angela. Can you forgive me? I really value your friendship."

She pursed her lips in a pout. "I don't know if you deserve forgiveness."

Jackson sighed in relief, knowing her pout was done in jest. "We can be friends, then?"

She picked up the *TV Guide* again. "Only if you let me choose what we watch tonight."

Christina received an unexpected call from Angela the next week. She was making notes from a lunch meeting she'd just attended.

"I've been thinking a lot about what you said the last time I saw you," Angela said.

Christina closed her folder. "I'm sorry,

Angela, but I don't know which thing you're talking about."

"How we can be more supportive of our colleges."

Christina remembered now. After learning Angela was a graduate of Clark College, she'd wondered aloud about what more they could do to support their schools. "What have you come up with?"

"I have a great idea for a fundraiser."

"The schools always need money. What's the idea?"

"I'd rather not get into it over the phone. Are you free tomorrow night? Maybe we could meet for dinner and I can tell you about it."

"That's a good idea." Christina flipped the pages of her appointment book. "Tomorrow night looks good. Can't you tell me more about your idea now?"

"Wait until tomorrow, when I'll have time to lay the whole idea out for you. We can meet at the Pelican Club on Peachtree. Let's say six."

"I hope my curiosity doesn't get the better of me between now and then."

Angela laughed. "It won't. I'll see you tomorrow."

"See you then," Christina said, and hung up the phone. She was curious about Angela's fundraising idea. The ringing phone got her attention.

"Christina, it's Liza. I called to get your flight schedule for the weekend. We're lining up rides."

She flipped open her appointment book again. "Right, Liza. I arrive at four o'clock. I can always take a limo, if that would be better for you."

"No, four is great. My dad would have a fit if he thought I was making people take limos. He'll be there to get you."

"Okay. I'll look for him when I get there. How are you holding up?"

"I can hardly believe I'm still functioning. Panic won't set in until the rehearsal Friday night."

"I'm so excited about it, too. I've told you before, but I'm honored that you asked me to be a bridesmaid. God, I hope I don't fall and ruin your whole wedding."

Liza laughed. "You won't, but even if you did, it wouldn't ruin this wedding. Robert is determined to get married this Saturday."

"How's he holding up?"

"If he says one more time that we should have gone to the courthouse, I'm going to bash him over the head."

Christina laughed at that. "Men! You'd think they'd understand why the ceremony is so important."

"Actually, Robert is more excited about this than he's letting on. We haven't had sex in three weeks. You'd think the man was going without food!"

"Liza!" Christina admonished. "I guess the abstinence was your idea."

"It was my suggestion. We wanted to go on a fast, I guess you could say, before the wedding. Don't be surprised if we leave immediately after the ceremony and don't come back."

Christina burst out in giggles. "Liza!"

"Robert has threatened to do that. Let's hope he's joking."

"God, I'm so envious of what you and Robert have. You're so good together. I know you'll be happy."

"Thanks, Christina. I believe we'll be happy, too. It feels so right. It's making me believe in destiny. But enough of that, I'm going to hang up now. See you Friday."

"See you Friday."

Christina left work the next day at five-thirty to make her dinner date with Angela. Angela was waiting for her when she arrived.

"Let's get a table," Angela said. "I'm starved." A hostess seated them in a booth.

192

"I don't even have to see a menu. I'll take the salad bar."

"I'm with you. Let's go for it."

Both women got up. When they had filled their plates and were seated again, Christina said, "Now tell me about this fundraising idea."

Angela took a bite of macaroni salad. "We can have a radio-thon."

"A radio-thon?" Christina repeated.

"Yes, a radio-thon. We'll do it in conjunction with a phone-a-thon. We'll plan a variety talk show format for the radio and couple it with a phone-a-thon."

"I'm familiar with phone-a-thons. Spelman has one every year, but this radio-thon idea is new. Is WAOK giving us the airtime?"

"I wish," Angela said. "We can use the Clark Atlanta University station."

"How'd you manage that?"

"One of my old professors is still in the communications department. Well," Angela continued, "I talked with him. He thought it was a good idea and has agreed to give us a twelve-hour block of airtime."

Angela gave Christina the details of her plan as they ate. Once they had agreed on the major points, Christina asked Angela about her job at the radio station.

"I started as a gofer," Angela said. "My mom thought I had lost my mind. All through college she kept telling me to get a teaching certificate, get a teaching certificate. I thought she'd die when I took the job at the radio station."

"I bet she's proud of you now, though," Christina said.

"You'd think it was her idea."

"That's mothers for you," Christina agreed. Louise had encouraged her to be a teacher or a nurse. But once she'd settled on being an engineer, Louise had supported her.

"Your mom's like that, too?"

Christina nodded. "That teaching certificate was the key to success for their generation. They just wanted us to have that security."

"In my business there is no security, but I love the work. How about you?"

A few years back, Christina would have answered a resounding yes and meant it. Things were different now. "Yes," she answered, "I like my work a lot." Which was true. Amazing that a person could tell the truth and still not be honest.

CHAPTER 11

"Thanks, Jackson," Christina said. "I'm glad you could meet with me this morning."

"It worked out well for me, too," he responded. "I'm planning a long weekend for myself."

"Good. Let's move forward with the marketing projections." She wondered what his plans were but didn't dare ask. It had been her suggestion to keep their relationship professional and she was determined to stick by it.

Jackson sat next to Christina and placed the graphs in front of her. He leaned in to talk through the findings. His eyes met hers and he shifted in his chair.

"Maybe you should use the viewgraph machine," Christina offered. "That might be more comfortable for both of us."

Although Jackson didn't ask what made her uncomfortable, he was sure he knew. He took her suggestion and used the viewgraph machine to show the charts that he had drawn up.

"All the numbers indicate that we should start first in semiconductor manufacturing. It's the growth industry for the next decade. The market now has two giants, as you can see, and hundreds of small-time players. That means the competition is fierce. They'll be open to OPTIMA."

Christina studied the charts in front of her. "The numbers look good, and as usual, your research is thorough. Let me think on this and we'll talk about it again at next Friday's meeting."

"Okay," Jackson responded. "But I don't see what there is to think about. The numbers are clear."

"To you, maybe," Christina said, without looking up from the charts. "But I need to study them for a while." She had to get firm with Jackson sometimes. He seemed to think she should fall in line with every recommendation he made without evaluating it for herself. "Now, is there anything else?"

Offhandedly, he asked, "Why did you need to move up the meeting?"

Christina looked up at him then. It was none of his business. "I'm leaving for Boston today."

"More meetings?"

"Not this time. Liza's wedding is Saturday. Why all the questions?"

"No reason. Just wondering. I knew it had to be something important." He stood up and prepared to leave. "Have a good trip." He stopped when he reached the door. Looking at Christina's wastebasket, he asked, "What's this?"

Christina wasn't looking at him. She turned around. "What's what?"

"Those." He pointed to the red roses that had been thrown in the wastebasket.

"What do they look like?" Christina had hoped the incident would pass unnoticed. She'd already called security.

"What are they doing here? Since they're in the garbage, I guess they're not from Reggie."

"You guess right. They aren't from Reggie." She could see the wheels of his mind turning.

"What did the card say this time?"

"That's none of your concern."

He asked directly, "It was like the other card, wasn't it?"

"If you really must know, yes, it was."

"Have you called security?"

"Of course. By now they expect a call."

"What do you mean by that?"

She mentally kicked herself for even opening up this conversation with Jackson. "I've been getting the roses every week since the first delivery."

"What!" Jackson exclaimed. He strode toward her. "You've been getting these roses every week?"

"Yes," Christina said. She moved from the conference table to her desk. "Don't overreact. It's probably someone I let go when I first came here."

"I'm not overreacting. How did you come up with that answer?"

Christina shrugged. "It wasn't difficult after I settled down. I just thought of people who had a reason to get back at me."

"How many people did you let go, Sherlock?" Jackson asked.

"About twenty were let go and fifty more were reassigned. Security is checking into all of them. It's only a matter of time before we uncover the culprit."

Jackson checked out the roses in the wastebasket, then turned back to Christina. "I don't like it, but I guess you're right. Have you had any other problems?"

Christina shook her head. "Only the roses."

"You still need to be careful. It bothers me that they're still coming."

"You're overreacting," she said again. "Security has it under control."

Jackson raised his brow. "You sound pretty confident of that."

She was concerned, but only a little. And there was no reason for her to tell Jackson. He was not her protector; he was her employee. "I am. Security is running a thorough investigation. I'm looking for a breakthrough any day. Now, are there any more questions?"

His eyes met hers again. "I care about you, Christina. I don't like this at all."

She felt weak at his words. She was glad he cared, but she couldn't let it go beyond that. "I appreciate your concern, but there's no need. It's under control."

"I won't stop being concerned until we find out who's sending the roses. Will you keep me posted?"

Christina nodded with impatience. "Anything else?"

Jackson looked at the wastebasket one last time. "I guess not."

Jackson yawned. He was one of the first to arrive at the church. Last night had been a late night. The bachelor party for Robert had been unreal. What a night! Jackson didn't get back to his hotel until six this morning. Sleep had been quick coming but too quick over, given that he wanted to get to the church early. Before Christina. Robert had told him that she was a bridesmaid. Jackson hadn't wanted her to know he was here until later. He had plans for Miss Christina Marshall. He looked at his watch. Eleven o'clock. One hour until the fireworks. He could hardly wait.

"It's time, ladies and gentlemen," Mrs. Tremont said, clapping her hands together. "Let's get in place. We've had the rehearsal. This is the real thing. Everybody, take your places."

Christina took her position behind Liza's younger sister, Karen. Karen turned around. "Is my hair all right, Christina?"

Christina looked at the beautiful girl. She thought Karen must be more nervous than Liza. "Your hair looks great. Don't worry."

Karen wrung her hands. "I'm so nervous. What if I trip or something? Liza will never forgive me." The girl looked terrified.

"You'll do fine. Everything's going to be perfect." Mrs. Tremont walked by and handed bouquets to them. Christina said to Karen, "You'd better turn around. We're going to be marching in any minute now."

Christina watched as Karen turned

around. The girl immediately began rocking from side to side. Christina smiled. Karen was refreshing. A bit spastic, but appealing.

Now that Christina no longer had to reassure Karen, she was getting nervous herself. Last night and today had been bittersweet. She was happy for Liza and Robert, but she felt as though life was passing her by. She thought about Reggie. She had wanted him to come with her, but his work wouldn't allow it. His presence would have helped keep Jackson out of her thoughts. Jackson was there, always looming in her thoughts. She wondered where he was today, what he was doing.

Christina looked back and saw Liza. It was the first time she had seen her in her wedding dress. She was a beautiful bride. The gown was extraordinary, with a beaded lace brocade, but it was the radiance of Liza herself that was beautiful. Liza practically beamed. She saw Christina looking at her and gave her a private wink. Christina winked back, then turned around. The music started and they began to march into the church.

The church was full. As Christina walked down the aisle, she couldn't help but imagine that it was her own wedding. She imagined her mom decorating the church with arrangements from her nursery. Christina wouldn't need a church this large, though, maybe a small chapel.

When she reached her position in the front of the church, she stopped. She didn't know if she sensed him or saw him first. She wasn't even sure it was him, but it was. Jackson was here. Her heartbeat raced and she quickly faced forward to focus on Liza and Robert. She didn't know why she was so surprised — or so excited. Robert and Jackson were fraternity brothers. Maybe they had kept in touch since their trip to Boston. Maybe Liza had invited him out of professional courtesy. Either way, Liza had known he was coming and had never mentioned it to her. Why was that?

"If there is anyone here who knows a reason why this couple should not be . . ." the minister was saying. Christina turned her head slightly and looked directly into Jackson's eyes. Again she quickly turned back. She felt his eyes piercing her back. He was challenging her!

Jackson saw her as she entered the church. She was captivating in the dusty rose gown. The neckline was cut low in the front, giving an almost teasing view of the tops of her breasts. The sway of her hips as she walked by took his breath away. This was his woman. He would not be denied.

He concentrated on her as she stood with the others at the front of the church. He was determined to make her feel his presence. It worked. He saw the ever-so-slight turn of her head. He knew the moment she saw him. In the next moment he was inside her eyes, inside her head. In that split second, he knew he had communicated with her. His feelings were verified when she jerked her gaze away from him and back to the altar.

Jackson heard nothing the minister said. All his energy went into communicating his message to Christina. Today was the day to force her hand. He hoped she wouldn't deny him or herself on this day. Yes! he thought, as he saw her head turn again. For the short moment that she met his gaze again, he thought he saw acceptance in her eyes. He knew he saw fear, but he thought he saw acceptance, too. She turned too quickly for him to be sure. Mentally, he reassured her. In his mind, he held her in his arms and addressed all her fears. He had done all he could do. It was now in her hands.

As Robert kissed the bride, Christina

watched with tears in her eyes. Tears of happiness for Robert and Liza. Tears of fear for herself. She sensed that this was the last time Jackson would pursue her. After today, it would be all professional, as she had wanted.

She still felt Jackson's eyes on her as they proceeded out of the sanctuary. She kept her eyes averted so she wouldn't see him. She needed this time to think. She knew the decision she made today could change the course of her life.

Jackson arrived first at the reception. He had purposely left the church quickly. He didn't want to be around while the wedding party took pictures. He was giving Christina time. The decision was hers: either she chose to be with him, or he'd let her go.

He saw Rosalind and Walter when they walked into the ballroom. He walked over to greet them. Extending his hand to Walter, he asked them both, "Enjoying yourself today?"

Walter answered, "Sure are. How about you?"

"Other than being a bit tired, I'm having a great time. It was a beautiful wedding. Robert looks as if he relishes the shackles of marriage."

Walter laughed at that. "I have to agree. He does look like a happy man."

"And Liza was a beautiful bride," Rosalind added.

One of the ushers walked up. "Jackson, can you give us a hand for a few minutes?" he asked.

Looking to Rosalind and Walter, Jackson said, "Excuse me. Hope you two enjoy the rest of the day."

Christina didn't know what to make of Walter and Rosalind. She had never seen them embrace before. She could see the tears falling from Rosalind's eyes. She walked over. "Is something wrong?" she asked Walter.

Walter looked up but did not take his arms from around Rosalind. He smiled, "Things have never been better."

Confused, Christina asked, "Why is Rosalind crying?"

Rosalind seemed to cry harder. Walter said, "Rosalind needs to make a trip to the powder room. Why don't you go with her?"

Walter gently pushed Rosalind away from him. He looked down into her face and said, "I'm sorry it took me so long to realize what was important."

Christina was amazed when Rosalind

leaned up and kissed Walter smack on the lips. The kiss went on forever. She couldn't stop staring at them. Finally, Rosalind pulled away. No longer crying, she beamed at Christina, "We're getting married."

Christina couldn't find any words. "Married?"

Rosalind nodded vigorously, "Married."

Christina's mouth was open, but no words came out.

"Get ahold of yourself, Christina," Walter commanded. "Rosalind and I are getting married."

"I didn't even know you were seeing each other. When did this happen?"

Rosalind took a handkerchief from Walter's pocket and wiped her eyes. "It's a long story. We'll tell you some other time. Now," Rosalind looked at Walter, "Walter and I are going home to celebrate." Looking back at Christina she said, "Give Robert and Liza my love. Tell them we'll have them over when they get back from the honeymoon."

Christina said nothing. She stared after them as they left the ballroom. She couldn't believe it — Walter and Rosalind. She wondered how long this had been going on. How could she have missed the signs? Surely there had been signs. They were gone now, but Christina continued to stare at the door, shaking her head. The next person to enter was Jackson. She turned away quickly. She wasn't ready for their confrontation. She needed time to think.

"You see, the ceremony was perfect," Christina said, as she picked up a cup of punch.

"I'm glad it's over," Karen said. "I'm still nervous."

"Want to know a secret?" Christina asked. At Karen's nod, she said, "I felt my knees knocking while we were standing at the altar."

"You may have felt yours, but I heard mine," Karen said, and they laughed.

"Excuse me," Jackson said. Christina had not heard or felt him walk up. He extended his hand to her, "Dance?"

Christina looked at his hand and then moved her gaze to meet his. She placed her cup on the table, took his hand, and followed him to the dance floor. Jackson pulled her into his arms and began to move. Neither spoke. Christina knew that after tonight they would move forward in a more intimate relationship or they would put to rest forever this sexual foreplay in which they had been indulging.

As if he could read her thoughts, Jackson

exerted pressure to her lower back in agreement. She looked up to see him looking down at her. It was all in his eyes: they contained a controlled passion. They also held a question. He wanted her, but it was her decision. Christina couldn't take her eyes from his. She was caught up in his feelings, his thoughts. She wanted to be inside him. She wanted to let him inside her. Suddenly she stopped moving. A different question was now in his eyes. In answer, she took his hand and led him to the door. She asked only one question: "Do you have a car?" When he nodded, she told him the name of her hotel. Jackson squeezed her hand and led her outside.

Neither spoke as he drove the short distance. They made the walk to the elevator without speaking. Christina pressed the button for her floor. Still they said nothing. At her floor, she led him to her door. Once there, she took the key from her purse and handed it to him. He took the key and opened the door, then led her in and closed the door behind him. They stood looking at each other. Jackson's eyes still held a question. Christina knew what he wanted. She moved to stand in the circle of his arms. His hands rested lightly on either side of her waist. The questions were gone from his eyes and all she saw now was passion. She lifted her arms to place them around his neck and leaned forward so her breasts lay against his chest. At his soft moan, she pressed harder against him. She pulled his head down to her and kissed him.

For the first few moments she wondered if he was going to make her do all the work. Then she felt him respond. His hands were now tight around her waist and her body was flush with his from breasts to thighs. His hands moved down to cup her buttocks and pull them tighter against him. She heard his moan as she felt his hardness. She pulled back from the kiss to look into his eyes. He growled. The look in his eyes now was uncontrolled passion and something that she thought was relief. He pulled her back to him and picked up where they left off. When his hands moved from her buttocks to her breasts, it was her turn to moan. She heard something that wasn't a moan from him or her. What was it? She heard it again. The phone was ringing. Jackson pulled back and looked at her. His eyes were glazed with passion, but she saw the question in them.

He finally spoke. "What's it going to be, Christina?"

CHAPTER 12

Christina looked at the phone, then back at Jackson. In answer to his question, she pulled his head back down and continued the kiss. Jackson moaned, and held her even tighter. When the phone stopped ringing, Christina pulled back. She stepped out of the circle of Jackson's arms and walked to the phone. She picked it up and dialed the front desk. "Hold all calls for this room."

She stood then to face Jackson. He opened his arms to her and she walked into them. Pressing her cheek to his chest, she held him as he held her. They stood that way for a while. When he squeezed her, she pulled back to look up at him. His mouth swooped down to possess hers. She became one with him in that kiss. It was as if everything, every nerve ending, every emotion, every thought that she had was wrapped in that kiss. Only she and Jackson and whatever this was between them existed. Nothing else mattered.

She knew the inevitable end of this evening was near. She had gone over it before in her mind. She had thought she would be apprehensive, but she wasn't. She knew it would happen and she wanted it to happen. Only the how was unknown. Would he pick her up and carry her off to bed? As if he'd heard her thought, he pulled back and gazed intently at her. No, he wasn't going to pick her up and carry her off. She was going to have to make the next move. There would be no way she could say this was his idea.

She stepped out of the circle of his arms and moved to his side. She placed her arm around his waist and leaned into him. He placed his arm around her waist then and they walked together to the bedroom. When they got to the bed, Christina moved away from Jackson and turned so her back faced him. He began to place little kisses on her neck. Christina shivered at the touch of his mouth. He made a trail of kisses down her back to the zipper that started midway her back. All the while his hands fondled her breasts through the fabric of the dress.

"God, you're so soft," she heard him say. A trail of kisses followed the zipper as he took it down her back. When the dress fell from her breasts, he squeezed her nipples. She moaned, not in pain, but in desire. The trail of kisses stopped when the zipper was fully undone at the base of her back. As the dress fell to the floor, Jackson fell to his knees behind her and pressed his face full against the base of her spine. His hands moved down her front from her breasts to her belly, caressing all the way. He then wrapped his arms around her belly and pulled her tighter against him.

Christina felt her knees buckle as his hands moved farther down her front to caress her femininity. She needed to touch him. She would die if she didn't touch him. She reached back to touch his head, but it wasn't enough. She turned to face him. When she turned around, his face was in her womanness.

Jackson was enraptured. He held the woman of his dreams in his arms. She felt so good, so soft. God, he could caress her breasts all day. All day. He would never tire of them. He longed to linger over them, to taste them, to savor them, but he could linger. He had to touch her all over. Her body was to him as a room full of toys to a kid. So much to play with, so little time to do it.

He groaned aloud when she turned and the center of her womanhood pressed against his face. He felt her wetness against his face. He had to have her now. He was already straining against his pants. He needed her. Slowly he rubbed his tongue across her nether lips. In response, she moaned and pulled his head even closer to her. He darted his tongue into her. When she trembled, he held her tighter so she wouldn't fall. She was so wet. His tongue took bolder strokes and she trembled more. He had to stop or the night would be over before it started.

He pulled his head back and looked up at her. Her head was thrown back and her breasts were thrust out. She was an Amazon. A strong woman. A beautiful woman. More than anything, he wanted to push her back onto the bed and enter her wetness. He was so taut he knew he would come immediately. Deliberately, he rose from his knees, caressing his way up her body. His hands reached her cheeks at the same time his mouth reached her lips. Passion filled her eyes. He had her full surrender. It was a powerful feeling. When he could bring himself to stop the kiss, he pushed her to the bed so that she lay on her back. There was a question in her eyes when he pulled back to stand looking at her.

"It's all right, sweetheart," he said. He began to unbutton his shirt. His jacket was already discarded. "God, you're beautiful. I could look at you all day."

Christina watched as he undressed. She felt alone and exposed, now that they weren't touching. She wanted him to touch her. She wanted to touch him. All over.

His shirt fell to the floor first. God, she wanted to bury herself in his chest. She wanted those strong arms wrapped around her. Next came his belt, then his pants. His erection was obvious in the bikini briefs. When he slid them off, he stood tall and erect. She felt her heartbeat increase. He was so big. The first inklings of fear began to surface. What if it hurt? What if she didn't please him? What if he didn't please her?

The fear he saw in her eyes surprised him. He eased himself down on the bed next to her. "What's the matter, sweetheart?" he asked.

Christina couldn't tell him she was afraid so she shook her head.

He knew there was something wrong and he set out to ease her fears. He started with light kisses all across her face while his hands caressed her body. He felt the tenseness in her. Something had changed and he had no idea what. He pulled back and asked again, "What's the matter, sweetheart? You can tell me."

Christina said the words in her mind, but no sound came out of her mouth.

"I want you, Christina," he said, "and I want you to want me. This is what you want, isn't it?"

Christina nodded.

"What's the matter, then?"

"Nothing," she said. To stop the questions, she reached up and kissed him.

Jackson didn't like the desperation he felt in her kiss. He pulled away and sat up. "We can't start this way, Christina. We shouldn't be here if you can't talk to me. I want more than one night with you."

"Oh, Jackson," Christina said. He wanted her to trust him. The decision to make love with him was much easier than that request. "I'm a virgin."

Jackson wasn't sure he heard her right. "What?"

"I'm a virgin," she repeated.

God, Jackson thought. How could this beautiful woman be untouched? He couldn't think of anything to say.

"Is that a problem?" she asked. She knew some men preferred experienced women. She hoped he wasn't one of them.

Jackson shook his head. "It's not a problem, but it is surprising. How did you manage it?"

Christina picked up a pillow in an attempt to cover her nakedness. "I don't know how to answer that."

Jackson took the pillow away. "No answer needed. It was a rhetorical question. I never expected you were a virgin, that's all."

"How does it make you feel?" she asked.

Jackson knew he had to be honest with her. "It makes me scared, actually. I wanted to please you before. Now that I know it's your first time, I feel that I have to please you." He smiled then added, "If I don't, you may decide never to have sex again, and that would be a real tragedy."

Christina relaxed at his words. She reached up and ran a finger down the side of his face. "Oh, I don't know about that. I may just decide that I don't want to have sex with you again."

Jackson could see she was teasing, and he was relieved. She was back with him. "That would be an even greater tragedy."

She lay back on the bed. "So, do you want to make it with a virgin or not?"

Jackson stared at her naked body, beautiful in its openness and precious in its purity. "I want to make love with you more than

I've ever wanted to make love to a woman. Are you sure you want your first time to be with me?"

She pulled him down to her. "More than you know, Jackson. More than you know."

Christina awoke first. Jackson woke her with his snoring. He snored loudly. She couldn't move because one of his arms was thrown across her breasts. She contented herself by studying him in his sleep. Never again would she look at him and not think of this night. Never again would she look into his eyes and not remember the passion they had held for her. Never again would she look at his lips and not remember the ways and the places they had kissed her. Never again would she look at his hands and not feel the sensations they made her body feel. As her gaze moved lower on his anatomy, she knew she'd never think of Jackson without thinking of this, her first experience of love. He made it very special.

Thoughts of the past night were having an effect on Christina. She wished Jackson would wake up, but she wasn't bold enough to wake him. Instead, she moved so her breasts were massaged by the hand that rested on her chest. Soon her nipples were erect. She looked over at Jackson. His eyes were still closed and he was still snoring. Frustrated, she focused her eyes on the ceiling and began counting sheep. Maybe she could get back to sleep. One, two, three . . .

Jackson awoke with a start. He thought he heard someone counting. He looked over and saw that Christina was the culprit. She was staring at the ceiling. He turned his head to look at the ceiling.

"What are you counting?" he asked.

She stopped and looked at him. "Jackson? I didn't know you were awake."

"What are you counting?" he asked again.

"Sheep. I've been trying to get back to sleep."

"You must not be sleepy if you're counting sheep."

"I'm not, but I couldn't get up without waking you, so I tried to get back to sleep."

Jackson looked at the arm spread across her breasts. He tweaked an already erect nipple. "I see what you mean."

She was suddenly shy. "Now that you're awake, I don't have to worry about that." She removed his arm and got up from the bed.

Jackson raised up on an elbow. "Where are you going? Come back here, it's not time to get up yet."

Christina looked back at him. "Some

things can't wait." She closed the bathroom door.

Jackson kept his eyes on the door. He thought Christina had forgotten that she was naked. He hadn't. He wanted to see her walk back to the bed. She walked out of the bathroom wrapped in a towel. "No fair," he said. "I was waiting for the view."

She sat on the bed next to him. "You've seen enough already."

"I could never see enough of you," he said, as he unknotted the towel. When she was naked, he kissed her and began again the melody they had started earlier.

Christina was lying across Jackson's chest when he woke up. He could tell by the steady rhythm of her heartbeat that she was asleep. She was exhausted and he was satisfied. She had lost control more than once during the night. He was certain that her first experience at lovemaking had been good for her. It had been for him, too. Her inexperience showed, but she had a natural passion that overcame all her inexperience.

A wave of apprehension passed over Jackson as he thought about the Monday afternoon staff meeting. How would Christina act once they were back in Atlanta? Would she regret this weekend? He didn't have the answers and he didn't want the questions to ruin what was left of the weekend, so he pushed the thoughts aside.

He slapped Christina playfully on her soft bottom. "Wake up, sleepyhead. You're going to sleep the day away."

Christina grunted but didn't open her eyes. Jackson decided to let her sleep a little longer. He gently moved her from his chest to the bed. He looked at her for a few moments, then he got up.

She was still asleep when he came back in the room forty-five minutes later. He carried a tray to the bed and placed it next to her. He gave her a soft kiss on the lips. "Wake up, sleepyhead," he said again. "I have a surprise for you."

She rolled over to face him, but she still didn't open her eyes. He tickled her nose with a rose. She shook her head to get rid of the irritant. He tickled her again. She shook her head again. He tickled. She shook. She looked so funny that he laughed. She opened her eyes then.

"What are you doing?" she asked.

He pointed to the tray, then handed her the rose. "I'm serving you breakfast in bed," he said.

She gave a smile that didn't reach her eyes. "A red rose."

Jackson remembered then. How stupid could he be? He took the rose back. "I'm sorry, Christina. I wasn't thinking."

She smiled a real smile and took the flower back. "Maybe it's a good thing. Now when I see red roses, I'll think of you."

"Are you sure you want to keep it?" He mentally kicked himself for being so inconsiderate.

"I'm sure," she answered. "It was a sweet idea." She gave him a short kiss. "Thank you."

He gave her a kiss in return. "You're welcome. Now, let's feast on this breakfast that I've prepared with my own hands."

Christina raised a brow. "Your own hands?"

He held his hands up to her. "These hands picked up the room service menu. These hands dialed the room service number. These hands opened the door for the bellhop. These hands tipped the bellhop. If that's not preparation, I don't know what is."

Christina laughed before taking a bite of the French toast. "That's one way of looking at it."

After they finished eating, Jackson slid over to Christina and pulled her into his arm. "It's never been like this for me before.

221

You were the virgin, but you made me feel like one." He took her face in his hands. "Being with you was like making love for the first time."

At her look, he felt the need to clarify. "Making love, not having sex."

"Are you saying you're in love with me?" she asked.

"I don't know much about love," he answered truthfully. "I know I've never felt this way before. I've never been with a woman the way we were together last night."

"So, you're saying you're not in love with me but you feel you made love to me. That doesn't sound right."

He pulled her closer. "I know it doesn't sound right, but I have a problem with love."

"You want to talk about it?"

He shrugged. "What's the use? It won't change anything."

"It'll help me understand you better."

He squeezed her shoulders. "It sounds stupid when I say it."

"Say it anyway."

Jackson lay back on the bed and pulled her with him so she lay across his chest. He rubbed his hand back and forth in her hair. "It goes back to my parents."

"What about your parents?" Christina asked.

He was silent a while, trying to decide what to say.

"Jackson . . ." Christina softly whispered.

He spoke slowly. "I have a lot of good memories of the three of us — my mom, my dad, and me. When I was fifteen, my mom left. She just left. One day she was there, the next she was gone. To this day I don't understand it. She said she loved my dad, she loved me, but she left us. What does that say for love?"

Christina heard his pain. "It says that your mother made a mistake, Jackson. That's all it says."

Jackson continued as if she hadn't spoken. "My dad never got over it. He's never been the same. He stopped smiling the day she left. He stopped laughing. When she left, she took all the love with her."

Christina hugged him to her. "Your dad made a mistake, too."

"You're telling me. He should have gotten on with his life. He should have showed her that he didn't need her. Instead, he flushed his life down the toilet."

"That's not the mistake I'm talking about. His mistake was not seeing that his wife hadn't taken everything. She left you. His mistake was in not seeing that you were there to receive his love and to give him love in return."

"Well, I didn't need him." Jackson spat out the words. "I went on with my life."

Christina knew Jackson wasn't ready to face how much his dad, not his mother, had hurt him, so she let it go for now. "It was only my mom and me. I never knew my father," she said.

"You didn't miss much."

There was a chill in his voice and she knew he was still thinking about his dad.

"I think I did. I don't even have those early memories that you have. I used to dream about having a dad like everybody else."

"What did your mom think about that?"

"She never really knew how much I missed him. She only talked about him when I asked questions."

"Did he die when you were young or something?"

"He died before I was born. Before he and my mom could be married. My mom was a single mother before it was fashionable." Christina gave a hollow laugh.

"Was that hard for you?" he asked.

"Teasing from kids, that's all," she answered in a quiet voice.

He hugged her closer. "That can be a lot

224

for a little kid to handle."

"I weathered it all right."

"No scars?"

Scars, yes. And a lingering emptiness that had followed her all her life. "I wouldn't go that far."

They held each other for a while. "What do you want to do today?" she asked finally.

Jackson leered at her. "I'll give you three guesses."

"You have a one-track mind, Jackson Duncan."

He nuzzled her behind her ears. "But what a track it is."

"Stop, I'm serious. We can't stay in bed all day."

"Why can't we?" he asked, his tongue in her ear.

Christina felt her resistance slip a notch. "Because it's so, so . . . decadent."

He laughed.

"Don't laugh."

He continued laughing. "Is that a virginal flush I see on your face?" He nuzzled her again. "I thought we'd gotten rid of that last night."

Christina inclined her head to give him better access. "Don't you have to check out of your hotel or something?"

He stopped nuzzling. "Damn. I had forgotten about that. I'd better get dressed and get over there." He kissed her on the nose. "Want to come with me?"

Christina shook her head. She needed time alone to get her feelings together. "You go ahead."

"Come with me," he urged. "What else do you have to do?"

She saw something akin to fear in his eyes. "I'll be here when you get back," she said. "You are coming back, aren't you?"

He grinned. "I'll be back before you know I'm gone." He got up then and began to dress. "What time are you checking out of here?"

She sat on the bed and watched him dress. "Around three. I asked for late checkout because I have a late flight, eight tonight."

"Why so late?"

"I'm having dinner with Walter and Rosalind. Business."

"Oh." Jackson momentarily stopped buttoning his shirt. "And I'm not invited?"

She didn't miss the flash of annoyance that crossed his face. She'd have to talk to him about this attitude, but not today. "Not OPTIMA business, Jackson. New project planning."

"Oh." Jackson was dressed now. He looked at his watch. "I should be back by noon."

"I'll be here when you get back," she assured him.

Christina watched Jackson leave the hotel room. As soon as he closed the door, she flopped back on the bed and thought, Oh, God, what have I done?

Jackson felt as though he could run the distance to his hotel, he had that much energy. There was something right about him and Christina. He knew she still had reservations, but he also knew that she was more involved than she wanted to admit. She was not a woman to sleep with a man when she had no feelings for him. Plus, she had been a virgin. Jackson grinned when he remembered his concern about pleasing her. She had been pleased, all right. Once she'd gotten the hang of it, which didn't take long, she had more than enjoyed it. A man likes to know that he pleases his woman, and he was sure that he had pleased Christina.

There was no doubt that she pleased him. She had been so giving and so responsive. He hated being away from her now. He found acceptance in her arms. He needed that as much as he needed air to breathe. His euphoria began to fade as he realized how quickly he had connected with her. He shook off the dark thoughts and set himself to enjoy the relationship while it lasted.

Christina met him in the lobby. When he saw her standing there in blue, all he wanted was to be back in bed with her.

"I decided to wait for you here," she said. "Let's go to one of the Harbor Islands and have a picnic."

"That's a good idea. Did you check out?"

Christina shook her head. "I'm staying another night."

All right, Jackson thought. She doesn't want this to end yet, either. Maybe. "Does your staying have anything to do with us?"

She shook her head again. "Walter and Rosalind postponed the meeting until tomorrow. Rosalind called after you left."

Jackson hoped his face didn't show his disappointment. "Must be something big, for Rosalind and Walter to cancel a meeting. What's up?"

"You'll never guess."

Jackson wasn't in the guessing mood. He was uncomfortable with Christina having meetings with Rosalind and Walter that didn't include him. "I believe you, so tell me."

"Walter and Rosalind are getting married."

Jackson turned to give her an amazed look. "I didn't know they were anything more than friends. When did this happen?"

"I have no idea when it started. They told me yesterday at the reception that they were getting married."

"You knew yesterday?"

Christina nodded.

"Why didn't you mention it before now?"

Christina shrugged. If Jackson only knew how large a role that news had played in her decision to invite him back to her hotel . . . "It slipped my mind."

"I find that hard to believe. This isn't the kind of news that slips your mind."

She lifted a brow at him. "There were other things occupying my thoughts."

Jackson smiled then. "I can see how you could have been distracted." He shook his head. He couldn't believe it. "I had no idea. Walter and Rosalind. Who'd have thought it?"

"I never would have."

"They did a pretty good job of keeping their professional and personal lives separate. They're an example for us."

Christina looked at him. "What do you mean?"

"If Walter and Rosalind can pull off a romantic relationship and a professional

relationship without any negative consequences, there's no reason why we can't do
it, too."

CHAPTER 13

Christina didn't say anything. She had been thinking the same thing since she'd found out about Rosalind and Walter. It scared her. All her reasons for not having a relationship with Jackson were crashing down around her. All her excuses were gone. She watched Jackson as he led her to the car. She liked everything about him. His looks. His height. His professionalism. His easygoing nature.

"Why so quiet?" Jackson asked, as he opened the door for her.

She slid in. She was glad that he had to walk around to his side of the car. It gave her time to think. "Things are happening so fast," she said, when he was seated next to her.

"By things, I guess you mean us?"

"Yes, I mean us. It's happening too fast."

"Getting scared?"

It was uncanny how easily he had read

her emotions. "Fear is just one of the emotions I'm feeling."

"Can you tell me about it?"

She bit her lower lip. Again, he wants me
to open up. "I don't know if I can. I can't
even explain the feelings to myself."

"Do you like what you feel when you're
with me?"

She could only stare at him. "What do you
think?"

"I want to know what you feel."

Jackson reminded her of her mother in his
ability to keep her focused. "Yes, I like the
way I feel when I'm with you."

He smiled and she thought she saw relief
in his eyes. "It feels good to hear you say
that," he said. "How are you feeling now?"

She wanted to tell him. "Honestly?"

He nodded.

"Like I could lose myself in you." Then,
to lighten the conversation, she said,
"Maybe first sex at my age damages the
brain cells."

He didn't laugh. "Do you regret it?"

She knew the answer, but she paused
before telling him. How could he think she
regretted it? He was a most gentle and
tender lover. She felt warm all over when
she thought of the night they had shared.
She covered his hand that rode on the shift

column with her own. "No, I don't regret it. It was beautiful. Thank you." She reached over and gave him a kiss on the cheek.

He didn't say anything. He just turned his hand over to enclose hers. They rode in silence.

"I want to stay with you tonight," Jackson whispered. They sat under a tree on Harbor Island. She was positioned between his legs, her head resting on his chest, his arms around her waist.

"Do you think that's wise?" she asked.

He kissed the top of her head. "Does it matter if it's wise or not?"

She lowered her head. Jackson was determined to be a part of her life. She wanted it, but she was afraid. What would happen if it didn't work? What would happen if it did?

"Do you want me to stay?" he asked.

"I do, but I don't know if I should."

"I want to and you want me to, so I will."

She raised her head and looked back at him. "It's that easy, huh?"

"That easy."

She turned back around and rested her head against his chest. "What are we doing, Jackson." She wanted to know what he wanted out of this relationship.

"We're going with the magic," he said.

"Magic?"

"That's what it is — magic. I felt it long before this weekend, and I think you did, too. I felt it the first day we met. It was almost as if we were destined to be together."

He was right. She felt it. She hadn't named it, but she had felt it.

"Am I staying tonight, or do I fly out of here?" he asked a again.

"Why do you do that?" she asked.

"Do what?"

"Force me to make my intentions clear. You either wait for me to make the first move, or you make me say what I want. Why is that?"

"We have to be open and honest with each other, Christina. There are already too many things that could play against us. We don't need to add anything more to the list."

She knew he was talking about their work. "What's going to happen when we get back?"

"What do you want to happen?"

"There you go again."

He laughed then. "All right, I'll answer that one first. When we get back, we'll continue with what we've found here. We'll see where it takes us."

"I'm scared."

"I know. I'm scared, too." He paused, then asked again, "Do you want me to stay with you tonight?"

Jackson awakened her the first time with an intense bout of lovemaking. She reveled in it, so much so that she wondered if there were something to the sex addiction concept that was being talked about. Maybe she was a sex addict.

Before Jackson left for the airport, they made plans for dinner in Atlanta. It was important that they be together their first night back. Tonight would set the pace for their relationship.

The ringing phone woke Christina the second time. Wake-up call. She dressed, had a room-service breakfast and took a taxi to the Hancock Towers.

Walter's door was open, so she walked in. He was seated at his desk. "Good morning," she said. When he looked up, she added, "And congratulations."

Walter stood up. "Good morning, and thank you, Christina. I bet we surprised you, didn't we?"

"That's an understatement. I had no idea, no idea at all. How long has this been going on?"

"You wouldn't believe me if I told you."

"Wouldn't believe what?" Rosalind asked, as she walked into the room.

Walter walked from behind his solid oak desk to greet Rosalind with a kiss on the cheek. He placed his arm around her. "Christina wants to know how long our relationship has been going on."

Rosalind stepped out of Walter's embrace. "He's right. You wouldn't believe it if we told you." She looked at her watch. "We'd better get started if we're going to finish by noon."

Christina nodded. She wanted to hear more about this relationship, but she could see that Rosalind wasn't going to discuss it now. Ah, well, Christina thought, maybe some other time. She turned her attention to the work.

"Let's go out for lunch," Rosalind said to Christina, when the meeting ended. Walter had another meeting, so he couldn't go with them.

Rosalind and Christina took the elevator to the lobby. "Walter and I have done a good job keeping our relationship out of the office," Rosalind explained. "I want to keep it that way."

"Do you think you're going to be able to keep it that way after you're married?"

Christina asked.

Rosalind gave a small laugh. "You saw Walter this morning. I don't think so."

"Walter surprised me when he held you like that. I had no idea he was so affectionate."

"He's really surprising me these days, too. I like it, but it makes me wonder how different our lives would have been if he had always been this way."

"Sounds like you two have a long history," Christina said.

"We do. I hope you and Jackson handle yourselves better than we did."

Christina pretended ignorance. "Jackson and me?"

"No need to deny it. Walter suspected something after your first trip here. And he saw something at the wedding that convinced him."

Christina didn't say anything until they were off the elevator. "We're that obvious?"

"Maybe to us because we're in the same situation."

Rosalind led her out of the building to Toffee, an intimate café nearby.

"So just how long have you and Walter been seeing each other?" Christina asked, after lunch had been served.

"Since his wife died ten years ago," Rosalind answered.

"How did it happen?" Christina asked. When Rosalind didn't answer immediately, she added, "It's really none of my business. You don't have to answer that. I'm sorry."

"I don't mind. Maybe it'll help you and Jackson not to make the same mistakes."

"What mistakes?" Christina asked.

"Choosing a career over a relationship," Rosalind answered. After a sigh, she began, "When I started at CL, women didn't have the options they have today. You were a wife and mother, or you had a career. Maybe you could teach and still be considered a good wife, but that was about it. I always thought I would get married. I went to college thinking it would happen, then on to graduate school, but it never did. I intimidated most of my male classmates. Dating was difficult. I wouldn't suppress the real me to be the fluff they seemed to want."

As Rosalind spoke, Christina realized it could have been her life that Rosalind talked about. She, too, thought she would end up married with children. The only difference was that Christina thought she would have the family, the children, and the career.

"You came to CL right out of college?" Christina asked.

Rosalind nodded. "I was so excited to get

the job. I was one of the first women engineers hired. I worked hard to show them they had made the right decision in hiring me."

"That's when you met Walter?"

"Yes. He started about six months before I did. He thought he'd show me the ropes. Actually, he wanted to boss me around." She smiled then as if she was reliving those days. "We had a few rows early on. I determined that he wasn't going to roll over me."

"Were you attracted to him even then?"

Again Rosalind smiled. "Was I ever! Walter's still an attractive man. Then, he was what you'd call 'fine.' "

"Was he attracted to you?"

Rosalind's smile faded. "Yes."

Christina sensed her sadness, and to cheer her up, she said, "You're fortunate. Now you have each other."

The comment must have helped, because Rosalind smiled again. "We did, but it wasn't an easy road. Walter didn't want a wife who worked, especially a wife who worked where he worked. CL didn't hire married people at the time. If we were to be together, one of us had to quit."

"You put your career first?"

"Walter never gave me that option. He married somebody else." Rosalind shrugged as if past pain was pain forgotten, but the hurt in her voice spoke the truth. "I honestly don't know if I could have done it if he had asked me. In those days I was so determined."

"How could Walter have done that to you? He should have talked to you about it first. He owed you that much."

"You're right, he did. And for years I hated him. After he married her, I considered leaving CL. I didn't know if I could handle being around him. But I didn't leave. I threw myself into the job instead. It worked."

Christina saw herself in the picture painted by Rosalind's words. "How did you two get back together?"

"I hated him, but I never stopped loving him. After his wife died, we came back together. He never stopped loving me, either."

Christina couldn't imagine pining for a man for all those years. "Why have you kept it a secret for so long?"

"When Walter and I started at CL, dating between employees wasn't allowed. Though the rules had changed when we got back together, Walter and I were still the same. At first it was too personal, too new, too private, to bring into the open. Later, it was just too complicated. We wondered what everybody would think. What effect it would have on the people working with us. We focused on all the negative consequences of our relationship. Maybe we should have looked for the positive."

"I know what you mean." Christina was thinking about herself and Jackson now.

"I have you and Jackson to thank for my upcoming marriage."

"How's that?"

"Walter wanted me to talk to you about the problems of office affairs."

Christina's face burned with embarrassment. It was as if she and Jackson had worn neon signs. Everybody knew about them. "You and Walter have talked about us?"

"Walter talked about you. I talked about Walter and me. His response to your relationship made me angry about ours."

"Why hadn't you told him before?"

"I didn't realize how much I resented the secrecy until then. Don't get me wrong — I never doubted Walter's love for me. When he began to talk about you and Jackson, I realized how much I was missing because of the restrictions on our relationship."

Christina gave a sad smile. "I'm glad we could help."

"How are things between you and Jackson?"

"There was nothing between us until this weekend," Christina answered honestly. She wanted to share this with Rosalind.

"How do you feel about him?"

Christina placed her napkin on the table. "I don't know. Right now my emotions are everywhere."

"Are you two going to see each other when you get back to Atlanta?"

Christina nodded. "We're going to see where this relationship takes us. I admit I'm a little scared about seeing him tonight and going into the office in the morning."

"What about that scares you?"

Everything. "I don't know."

"Are you in love with him?"

Christina pondered that question. Was she in love with Jackson? She wanted to be with him. She missed him even now. She believed she could trust him. But did she love him? "I don't even know what love is." She repeated Jackson's own words.

"Do you want some advice from someone who's been there?"

"Yes," Christina answered.

"Hiding your feelings won't make them go away. If you love him, say it and get used to saying it. You aren't going to hurt any less by not saying it, and you'll find more joy in your love if you do say it."

That made sense to Christina.

"Has he told you how he feels?" Rosalind asked.

"He says it's magic and he wants to see where the magic takes us. I think he's afraid, too."

"I'm glad that you see that. Jackson's a good man. I've known him a long time. Be good to him."

She's telling me to be good to Jackson? Christina thought to herself. This I don't believe. "If anybody's in over their head in this, Rosalind, believe me, it's not Jackson."

"Just be careful, Christina, and be good to each other."

Christina sat by the window on the flight back to Atlanta. She looked out and thought about Jackson. She had called him from the airport and he was meeting her flight. She couldn't wait to see him. He said he had a surprise for her.

She saw him as soon as she entered the gate area. He greeted her with a kiss. "Welcome back, stranger," he said. "I've missed you."

She kissed him back. "You saw me this morning, Jackson. How could you have missed me that quickly?"

"I missed you all right. Did you miss me?"

"I just saw you this morning," she said.

He pulled her into his arms and looked into her eyes. "Did you miss me?"

Her first instinct was to tease him, but she saw he was serious. "I missed you. A lot."

He grinned then. "Good. Now we can get going."

"Where are we going?"

"It's a surprise," he said.

When he opened the car door for her, she said, "I'm impressed. A red Porsche. Somehow, I should have known."

Jackson grinned again. "Even grown-ups have toys. If you're good, I may let you play with it. Now, buckle up."

Jackson got on I-85 and drove downtown. When he got off at Fourteenth Street exit, Christina asked, "You're taking me to the office, aren't you?"

Jackson shook his head. "Work is the farthest thing from my mind right now."

"Then where are we going?"

"You'll see," was all he said.

He pulled into the private garage at the Midtown Terrace Apartments. "Do you live here?" She remembered that he lived near work. This apartment complex was compatible with his Porsche.

244

"We're almost there," he said, getting out of the car. He opened her door and said, "You sure do ask a lot of questions."

She stepped out of the car. "You do live here, don't you?"

He used his key to open the elevator and they stepped on. "Yes, I live here," he answered finally.

"Looks pretty expensive," she said.

"Maybe you could tell my boss that I need a raise," he said, with a teasing smile.

"Close your eyes," he said, when they reached his door.

"Close my eyes? Why?"

"Will you just cooperate?"

She did. He led her through the door and across the room. She felt a light breeze and Jackson said, "You can open them now."

She couldn't believe what she saw. A table had been placed on the balcony. There were candles, red roses, and what seemed to be chilled wine or champagne. Plates and flatware were on the table as well. "Did you do this?"

He lit the candles and pulled out a chair for her. "A special night for a special woman." When she sat, he bent to kiss her on the lips.

He sat across from her and poured for them both, then lifted his glass to her. "A toast." When she lifted hers, he said, "To beginnings."

Christina couldn't believe this was happening. She took a swallow of the drink. It was champagne. She had to say something, and looking out into the Atlanta skyline, she said, "You have a beautiful view from here."

"It *is* a beautiful view," he said thickly.

She looked at him. He was not looking at the skyline. He was looking at her. No, he was devouring her with his eyes. She looked away again.

"Don't turn away," he whispered. "I like looking at you. You're a beautiful woman, Christina."

Christina knew she wasn't beautiful. She was average looking. Maybe pretty, but not beautiful. There was something in the way he said it, though, that made her feel beautiful. She turned back to look at him.

"If you continue to look at me like that, we may not get around to dinner," he warned.

She continued to look at him. He cleared his throat and got up from his chair. "I'm going to check on dinner."

Jackson walked into the kitchen. The evening was turning on him. He had intended to seduce Christina to christen their first night back in Atlanta, but the looks she was giving him threatened his control. They had been together this morning, but he wanted her again. He wanted her badly.

He looked in the oven. Not ready yet. He stayed in the kitchen longer than necessary to calm down. He had to get control if this was going to be the special night he had planned. He turned on the stereo on his way back out to Christina.

The notes of a soft ballad floated onto the patio. Jackson held out his hand to Christina. "Dance?" he asked, repeating the question he had asked at the reception.

She got up and walked into his arms. As soon as he felt her against him, he knew he'd made a mistake. Now he had to get through this dance and then through dinner. He could do it, he told himself. He knew he could do it.

Christina leaned her head against his chest and tightened her hold on him. He groaned aloud. She looked up at him. "I think it's going to be a while before I'm ready for dinner. How about you?"

"I'm sorry about your dinner, Jackson."

He leaned over and kissed her. "I'm not complaining. We just had dessert before the main course." They sat on his bed, eating his home-cooked meal. He was in his under-shorts; Christina wore one of his shirts.

"When are you going to take me home?" she asked.

"Do you have to go? You could stay. Waking up with you is something I could get used to."

"I like waking up with you, too, but I have to go home. There's work tomorrow," she said.

He slapped his hand against his forehead. "Oh, work. I forgot about that."

"Now, I know you're lying. You'd never forget work."

"You make me forget everything, woman. Why don't we take the day off and spend it right here? We could use a vacation."

"You can't be serious," she said.

"Why not? When's the last time you took a day off?"

She tilted her head and looked at him. "It's been a while, but we can't take a day off. They'll know we're together."

"Who'll know?" He reached over and pulled her into his arms. It was manipulative, but he felt he had a greater chance of getting her to agree if she were in his arms.

"Everybody in the office," she said. "Penny and Doris have probably already figured out that we spent the weekend together in

Boston. There would be nothing but gossip if we both took the day off."

"They're going to find out about us sooner or later. Why not sooner?"

"I'm not ready for that yet, Jackson. Let's keep a low profile for now. Just us."

He squeezed her to him. "I want to spend a lot of time with you. Is that what you want?"

"Yes," she answered, a bit too hesitantly for his taste, "but I need to take it slowly. I can't handle us and the world right now. Let's stick to us for a while."

He didn't like it, but he sensed that was all he was going to get. "Just us. You've got to remember that."

"Are you going to take me home now?" she asked.

He pushed her back on the bed. "Not yet. We need a little more time together."

CHAPTER 14

Christina saw the pink roses first. Reggie, she thought. What am I going to do about Reggie? She walked over to her desk and picked up the card. "Sorry I missed the wedding," the card said. Christina sat at her desk. She wondered what would have happened if Reggie had gone to the wedding with her. She certainly wouldn't have spent the weekend with Jackson. Maybe Jackson was right. Maybe they *were* destined to be together.

"When are you going to tell him," Jackson asked. She hadn't heard him walk into her office. She looked up to see him standing next to her.

She considered playing dumb. "Soon." It was too early in their relationship to play games.

"What are you going to tell him?"

"I don't know yet. What should I tell him?"

"I can't help you there."

"Did you want anything special?"

"Yes. I wanted to say good morning. Maybe get a kiss. What do you think?"

After closing her office door, Christina walked to him. She reached up and kissed him softly on the mouth. "Good morning."

When she moved to pull away from him, he pulled her back. He kissed her again then set her away from him. "Now it's a good morning. See you later," he said, and left the office, leaving the door open.

Christina looked after him. *I want this to work*, she thought. *I really want this to work.*

Penny stuck her head in the door then. "You have a call, Christina. Do you want to take it now or should I take a message?"

Christina hadn't heard the phone. "Who is it?"

"Reggie Stevens."

Not now. "I'll take it," she said, and picked up the receiver.

"Reggie, thanks for the roses. How are you?" she asked. She dreaded what she had to tell him.

"I'm great, now that I'm talking to you. How was the wedding?"

"Enlightening would be a good word." *Invigorating would be another. Intoxicating would be another.*

251

"What did you do in Boston?"

"I spent some time with friends." Well, more time with one friend than another, she elaborated in her mind. "Actually, I spent a lot of time with Jackson."

"I didn't know Jackson was going." She detected a slight change in his tone.

"I didn't, either. Robert must have invited him. They're fraternity brothers, you know."

"No, I didn't know. So, what did you two do?"

She didn't answer immediately.

"Is there something you need to tell me, Christina?" Reggie prodded.

She knew that he knew. "Jackson and I started seeing each other this weekend, Reggie."

"Started seeing each other? What does that mean?"

She gave a heavy sigh. "It means we're seeing each other exclusively."

Reggie didn't say anything.

"Reggie?"

"How long have you been seeing each other?"

Christina heard his pain and she regretted she had caused it. "I didn't want to tell you like this, Reggie. It wasn't planned. It just happened."

"I don't know why I'm surprised. I could

see there was something between you when I was in Atlanta. Why couldn't you tell me then?"

She had no idea he had noticed. "It's not like that. There was nothing going on between us then. We weren't even friends. Not really."

"Well, you sure moved fast."

She tried not to take offense at Reggie's words. She knew she'd hurt him, but she also knew that she hadn't made any promises to him. "I'm sorry."

"It doesn't help, Christina."

"What else can I say? What can I do?"

"You could love me instead," he said.

She heard him take a deep breath and she knew he wished he could take those words back. "I care about you, Reggie, but I'm not in love with you. We've talked about this before."

"I know. And I thought I'd handle this better. Let's talk about this later, okay?"

"Okay." She held the phone in her hand after he had hung up. Was there a better way to handle this? What else could she have said? Why do things have to be so difficult?

Christina kept herself busy for the rest of the day. She didn't even eat lunch. It was after six when Jackson stopped by her office.

"Ready to go?" he asked.

"I think I'm going to stay a little later," she said, without looking up from the papers on her desk. "You don't have to wait for me."

He walked over to stand next to her. "How much later?"

"Maybe an hour or so. You don't have to wait." She still hadn't looked up.

"What time did you get in this morning?" he asked casually.

"I don't know. Probably around six."

"And you're going to work till . . . say, eight?"

"That's right."

"That's thirteen, fourteen hours. When do you sleep?"

"I'll have plenty of time for sleep. I don't need much anyway."

"What about time for me?"

She stopped working and looked up at him. "We'll have time together."

"When?"

She didn't know when. "Okay. We both have busy schedules. What do you suggest we do?"

"The way I see it we only have two choices — either we cut back to more reasonable-unreasonable hours or we move in together."

Live together? She was flabbergasted. It was impossible. "What's your idea of more reasonable-unreasonable hours?"

"Something less than fourteen hours a day, for sure."

"That going to be hard, Jackson. There's a lot of work to do around here."

"What about the other option?"

"It's too soon for us to move in together. We'd be rushing it. We need time."

"I agree that we need time, but where are we going to get it?"

"We'll find ways," she said.

"Be sensible. You don't want us to spend any personal time together during the day. You're working until late into the night and we live a half-hour apart. Where's the time?"

She considered the options. "What if we worked together?"

"I thought you didn't want people in the office to know."

"I don't. We can work together in your apartment. It's near here. We can leave work each day around five, have dinner out or at your place, finish up on any pressing work, and then I could drive myself home."

"I don't like the idea of your being out all hours of the night."

"You need to be sensible now, Jackson. If I was working late in the office, I'd be driving home alone. What's the difference?"

"Why don't we go to your house and I'll drive back each night?"

She smiled. She liked his consideration, but it wasn't necessary. "You're not a sexist, are you, Jackson? Why don't we split it — two days at your place, two days at my place, and one night apart? The weekends we play by ear."

"That's a good idea. I guess that's why you're the boss."

The words caught Christina off guard. His tone didn't sound malicious, but neither was the teasing spirit there. "Is there something wrong?" she asked.

"Not a thing," he answered. "Are you ready to go now?"

Maybe she had misheard him. "Give me a couple of minutes."

Christina began putting her papers in her briefcase. She would get some reading done tonight. When she finished packing the briefcase, she locked it. "I'm ready."

Jackson walked to the door and held it open for her. As she walked through it, he asked, "Your place or mine?"

Christina thought about her first night at Jackson's apartment. She wanted to plan something special for their first night at her house as well. "Yours."

Jackson rode with Christina. He never drove to work. He lived close enough to walk, and he enjoyed the exercise.

Jackson pulled Christina into his arms as soon as they were in his apartment. "You're like a drug. The more I have you, the more I need you."

Christina returned his embrace. She needed this, too. She hadn't realized how much.

She pulled back to look at him. "I think I'm falling in love with you." There, she said it. She hadn't planned to say it. She meant it, but she wondered if she had said it too soon. She had an uneasy feeling.

He spoke directly to her heart. "I know. I'm falling in love with you, too."

She laid her head against his chest. "Don't you think it's too soon for this?"

"Who sets the time schedules? When is the right time? It's not too soon. It's not too late. It's just how it is."

It's just how it is, she thought, as they stood holding each other. The ringing phone intruded on their time together.

She moved to pull back, but he kept her pressed close against him. "Stay here. The machine's on."

Christina heard Jackson's voice on the machine. She realized that she had never called his home, never heard his machine voice, never left a message. There was so much they didn't know about each other. She then heard a familiar voice.

"Jackson, this is your tour guide. How was your trip to Boston? I have some new plans for you. Call me." The machine clicked off.

"You haven't talked to her since you've been back." It wasn't a question.

"No, I haven't had time," he answered anyway.

"I talked to Reggie this morning."

"How did he take it?"

"Not well," she said. She stepped out of his arms and moved to sit on the couch. "Reggie's a good man. I didn't like hurting him."

Jackson stood looking at her. "I know you didn't, but he had to know. Maybe I should call him. His family was very good to me when I needed them."

"I suggest you give it a few days, Jackson. He needs to work through his feelings right now. What about Angela?"

"What about her?"

She inclined her head toward the answering machine. "You haven't told her about us."

Jackson sat down then. "Actually, she told me about us."

"What?"

"After the Sunday the four of us spent together, she guessed there were some unresolved feelings between us."

Christina was shaking her head. "Did everybody see something? Liza did. Rosalind and Walter did. Reggie did. Angela did. God, I wonder who else has?"

"What did Rosalind and Walter see?"

"They picked up something during our first visit to Boston and then later at Liza's wedding. I wonder if they're talking about us in the office."

"Probably, but it's mostly innocent speculation. I'd bet Penny and Doris are doing most of the talking."

Christina nodded. She knew that was true. She just wondered how long it had been going on. "I don't doubt it. It's kind of scary that people were seeing things that we weren't even acknowledging to ourselves. What's going to happen, now that we're lovers?"

"Lovers, Christina?" Jackson asked, a gleam in his eyes.

"Well, what do you call it?"

"I like the image that 'lovers' conjures up."

She held up her hand to stop him. "I'm not even going to ask what images. Now, what else did Angela say?"

He nuzzled her neck. "I don't want to talk about Angela."

She let him nuzzle. "I'm meeting with her next week."

Jackson stopped nuzzling to ask, "About what?"

His tone surprised her. "Oh, just girl talk."

Jackson sat up then. "This doesn't sound good. You and Angela. Girl talk. I hope I don't live to regret this."

Christina laughed. "What do you think we're going to do? Compare notes?"

Jackson grunted. "There are no notes to compare."

"You never slept with Angela?" His answer was important to her, she realized.

He shook his head.

Though she would have understood if he had, she was glad that he hadn't. "Why not?"

"My relationship with Angela isn't like that. We're friends."

Though Christina couldn't imagine that Jackson and Angela weren't physically attracted to each other, she decided not to pursue it. "What are you going to tell your friend Angela about us now?"

"Knowing Angela, I think she'll know by looking at me. If she doesn't I'll just tell her that I took her advice. Can we stop talking about Angela now?"

"Sure. What do you want to talk about?"

"Who said I wanted to talk?" Jackson leaned over and started a conversation that Christina found all consuming.

He liked watching her sleep. She snores, he thought. Not a loud, obnoxious snore, but still a snore. He'd be sure to tell her about that when she woke up. He wondered what time it was and looked over at the clock. Nine-thirty. Nine-thirty and neither of them had done any work. He hated to do it, but she'd be upset if he didn't. "Wake up, sweetheart." He shook her lightly. "Christina."

She awoke slowly. She had a grin on her face. She reached up for him. "A girl can get used to this."

He wanted to oblige her, but she had to know the facts. "It's nine-thirty."

She blinked as if she didn't understand. "Nine-thirty? I just got here."

He stroked her breasts. "That's not quite true, sweetheart. You've been here quite a while, and you've been quite busy."

She stopped his hands. "I'm hungry." She lifted a brow at him. "We've got to start eating first."

"I do eat first," Jackson said. The gleam in

his eye told her not to pursue that one.

She got out of the bed. "What do you have in the kitchen?"

Jackson consumed her naked body with his eyes. He was glad she didn't reach for something to cover herself. He would never tire of looking at this woman.

"Stop looking at me like that."

His eyes moved to her face. "How was I looking at you?" he asked innocently.

Like I'm the most beautiful woman you've ever see, she answered in her head. Like you could devour me. Like you love me. "You know how. Now, are you going to feed me, or what?"

They microwaved last night's leftovers. "I should get ready to go now, Jackson."

"You're right, but I don't like it."

Christina gathered her belongings. "I haven't even opened this briefcase. You're a bad influence on me."

He was right. She didn't mean it. There was nothing in that briefcase that couldn't wait until tomorrow. "You think you know me so well?"

He nodded. "Better than you think."

"I'd better watch that. A predictable woman quickly becomes boring."

He kissed her goodnight. "I never said you were predictable. And there's no way I'd call you boring. You're exciting enough for me. Any more excitement and I just might have a heart attack and die."

Angela called Wednesday of the following week. "Can we get together tonight to work on our fundraising idea?"

Christina wondered if Jackson had spoken with her yet. He hadn't mentioned it. "Tonight looks good for me. What time were you thinking?"

"How about six? We can do dinner, like we did before."

"Good idea," Christina said. "If you like, we can meet at my house. That way we can work and eat and probably get more done than if we were sitting in a restaurant."

Christina gave directions to her home. When she and Angela hung up, she called Jackson.

"Are you missing me, or is this a work call?" Jackson teased.

"Angela's coming over tonight," she said.

"Girl talk, I imagine. Do I still get to come over, or what?"

"Sure you can come over. What have you told Angela about us?"

"I told her that love wasn't turning out to be such a bad thing," Jackson answered.

"You told Angela you were in love with me?"

"Don't sound so surprised. It's not exactly a secret."

"Jackson, you've never told me that you love me."

"Yes, I have. I've told you lots of times. I told you the first night we were together. I knew it then."

Christina couldn't believe Jackson was saying this. "You did not say you loved me. You said making love with me was special. You said you were falling in love with me, but you never said you were in love with me. Believe me, if you'd said it, I'd remember."

"How can you not know how I feel, Christina?"

She did have an inkling about his feelings for her. "I made some assumptions, but it's good to hear."

"I love you, Christina Marshall," Jackson said.

"You do?" Christina was grinning now. "Well you'd better, because I love you, too."

"Music to my ears, sweetheart. Are you sure you have to meet with Angela tonight? I feel the need to celebrate."

She understood the celebration he had in mind. "She won't stay all night. We'll have plenty of time to celebrate. You know what they say about anticipation."

"You'd better be ready for a long night, Miss Marshall. I hope you got a lot of rest last night."

He knew she hadn't gotten a lot of rest last night because he'd kept her up half the night. "I haven't been getting a lot of rest lately, but if you have the stamina, I'm sure I do."

"We'll just have to see, won't we?" was Jackson's response.

The doorbell rang just as Christina finished tossing the salad. Exactly six o'clock. Angela was punctual.

The doorbell rang again when Christina and Angela were about halfway through dinner and their agenda. Christina knew who was at the door. She looked at Angela.

"Something wrong, Christina? Were you expecting company tonight?"

Christina got up to get the door. "I guess you could say that. It's Jackson." She paused, then added honestly, "This feels awkward."

"It shouldn't," Angela said. "Jackson and I were never more than friends. There might have been something there, but I always figured he had a thing for you." The doorbell rang again. Angela smiled. "You'd better get that before he kicks the door in."

The doorbell rang again and Christina laughed. "I think you're right. I'll be right back."

Jackson kissed her in greeting. "Are you about done?" he whispered. "I've been anticipating all day."

"Behave yourself," she said. "You're going to have to wait a little while longer. Come on back, we're in the family room."

Christina deliberately let Jackson walk ahead of her. She was still unsure of this platonic relationship he and Angela shared. "Hi, Angela," was Jackson's greeting. No hidden message in that, Christina thought.

"Hi, yourself," Angela said. "If I had known you two had plans tonight, Christina and I could have gotten together another time."

"It's not a problem. We just decided today." He looked at Christina. "Sometimes things come up."

That wasn't just a look he gave Christina. It was a promise, a threat, and a dare, all rolled into one gaze. Christina cleared her throat. "We're almost finished," she said to Jackson. "You want something to eat? We have some left."

"Don't let me rush you. I'll get a bite and

watch some television. Never let it be said that I came between a woman and her work. Or in this case, two women and their work."

Christina looked at Angela to see if she had picked up on the double entendre. She didn't look as if she had. Christina looked back at Jackson, which was a mistake. He was slowly seductively licking mayonnaise off his knife. Christina felt a shiver go down her spine.

CHAPTER 15

Christina leaned against the armoire in her bedroom with her arms crossed. "You were bad tonight, Jackson," she scolded. Angela had just left.

"Actually, I was pretty tame. I could have been a lot worse," Jackson reasoned from his seat on her bed. The bed tray in front of him held a newspaper and his discarded dishes. "How did your meeting go?"

"Good." She dropped her arms and walked over to the bed. Jackson put the bed tray on the floor to make room for her. "We came up with a pretty detailed proposal for what we want to do. Angela has some other people she wants to involve. We did enough tonight to take the proposal to those people."

"It's a pretty big project, but a great way to raise money. You two will probably be a big hit."

"I don't know about all that. We're going

to need a lot of support. Are you sure you don't want to help?"

"No way. That's yours," he said quickly.

"Just thought I'd check again," she said. She hadn't really expected him to help. They had talked about the project and agreed that Jackson wouldn't get involved. Their lives were too intertwined as it was with work and this romance. There had to be room for separate interests.

Jackson touched his hand to the back of her neck. "Has the celebration started yet?" Jackson asked.

"I was thinking that we'd go out tonight. Maybe dancing." Her eyes twinkled. "What do you think?"

"I think we have different ideas of what a celebration is. Mine don't include leaving this room."

"I think we're becoming limited in our activities, Jackson. All this time in one room isn't good."

"Speak for yourself. It's very good for me."

She rolled her eyes. "That's not what I'm talking about and you know it."

Jackson's nimble fingers began a gentle massage of her neck. "Do you really want to go out?"

"Well . . ." she teased. "Not really."

Jackson shook his head. "Then why are

we having this conversation?"

"Because we need to look at how much time we spend in bed. Maybe we're having sex too often?"

Jackson laughed. "Sweetheart, there is no such thing as too much sex."

"Don't laugh. I'm serious, Jackson. What if all we have is sex? What if we don't have a real relationship?"

"That's not the case and you know it," he said in a serious tone. "What's brought this on?"

She moved so that his hand fell away from her. "I think about it all the time."

"Sex?" he asked.

"Making love with you," she clarified.

"What's so bad about that? I spend a great deal of my time thinking about making love with you. It's natural. We're in love."

Christina wasn't too sure about it being natural. "I wonder if Liza and Robert have sex this often."

"From what I saw in Boston and from what I remember from their wedding, I'd say they have sex at least as often as we do. Probably more."

Christina couldn't imagine more. "Why do you say more?"

"Their relationship is more established. They've found a rhythm for their lives together. I'm not just talking sex, I'm talking their lives. Look at Robert's ease with relocating to Atlanta."

"Are you saying we're going to have sex more often than we do now? That I can't imagine." Christina made a mental note to talk to Liza about this.

"What about the celebration?" Jackson asked again. "When does it start?"

Christina stood up. "I do have a surprise for you. Don't move." She went into her walk-in closet and closed the door.

When she walked out she was wearing a purple teddy trimmed with black lace. The gleam in Jackson's eyes told her that he liked it.

He gulped. "Did you buy that especially for me?"

She walked around the bed. "I bought it for myself, but I knew you'd like it." She bent over from the waist to pick up something from the floor. She knew she gave Jackson a good view of her derriere and her thighs. She stood up when she heard him moan.

"Everything all right, Jackson?" she asked innocently.

"I want to touch you," he said quickly.

"Not so fast," she admonished. "Tonight

I'm going to make love to you."

Liza began work the following Tuesday, two months after her wedding.

"When did you guys get into town?" Christina asked, over coffee in her office that morning. She and Liza were seated in adjacent chairs.

"Saturday night. We're still in a hotel. We looked at a couple of apartments yesterday. I think we're going to end up at the Midtown Terrace Apartments."

"That's where Jackson lives. You're going to love that building. It's close to work."

"Robert will like living close to Jackson. How is he, anyway?"

"He's great. The two of us want to take you and Robert out when you get settled."

Liza lifted a brow. "The two of you? Is anything going on here?"

Christina couldn't stop the grin that spread across her face. "As a matter of fact, there is."

"Details," Liza said, leaning closer. "I want details."

"Jackson and I are seeing each other."

"Seeing each other? What does that mean? Are you sleeping with him?"

Christina found Liza's eagerness amusing. "Yes, I'm sleeping with him."

"So, you finally did it. How was it? That was a stupid question. It must have been good, or you wouldn't still be seeing him. So, how was your first time? Was it as difficult as you imagined it would be?"

Christina felt as giddy as a schoolgirl. "That's the thing, Liza. I didn't have any reservations at all. I didn't think about my body or possible pregnancy or AIDS or anything. I just wanted to be with him." Christina paused, then added, "There were a couple of moments when I was apprehensive, but Jackson helped me through them. He's a considerate lover."

Liza reached over and hugged her. "Oh, Christina, I'm so glad it was good for you." Liza pulled back. "I have one question. Did you use protection?"

Christina nodded. "Jackson came prepared. Since then I've seen the gynecologist, so we're okay."

"Are you in love with him?"

"Yes, I love him. There are times, though, that I wonder if it's him I love or the sex. Liza, I never even considered how much I would like it. It scares me sometimes."

"Don't look for trouble where there is none," Liza advised. "Be thankful that you and Jackson are sexually compatible. There are thousands of women out there who'd love to be in your shoes, or maybe I should say, in your bed."

"So you think this is normal?"

"What's normal? As long as it makes you happy, it's normal and right for you."

"Are you and Robert very active?" Christina asked. It seemed that she was always asking Liza about her sex life.

"Very, and you don't hear me complaining. Making love binds you. It doesn't make the commitment, but it cements it. Making love also helps you keep your perspective. It's hard to fight when you're making love. And it's hard to remember what the fight was about in the afterglow."

Christina stored those comments in her memory bank. "I always thought that communication was the cement that held a relationship together, not sex."

"Making love is a form of communication. It's the most intimate conversation two people can have. It comforts, it relaxes, it reassures, it soothes, it excites, it stimulates. It can do all those things depending on the needs and wants of those involved. It can't be the only form of communication in the relationship, but it's a vital form."

"So you think I'm worrying needlessly?"

Liza nodded. "How does he feel about you?"

"He says that he loves me, too."

"Sounds like there's a but in there somewhere. What's the problem?"

"It all happened so fast. We've only been together since your reception."

"Who cares about time? There's no timetable for your emotions. You have to take love when it comes. Cherish it, don't question it away. Be happy. Isn't this what you wanted?"

"It is," Christina answered. "Sometimes I wonder why all these good things are happening to me."

Liza put her cup down and took Christina's hand. "Good things are happening to you because you deserve good things."

"I'm glad you're here, Liza. Jackson's a good listener, but I need to talk to another woman sometimes."

"I'm glad I'm here, too. I've missed your friendship. And I'm glad Jackson and Robert like each other. We can do some foursomes. That makes it all the better."

"Don't forget Jackson and I want to take you two out. Just give us a date. Let us know, too, if you need help with anything." Christina took a slip of paper from her desk and wrote her and Jackson's phone numbers. She handed the paper to Liza. "Call us anytime."

"Did you see Liza today?" Christina asked from her desk in Jackson's apartment. They were now spending weekdays at his place, since it was closest to work and weekends at her place. They had fallen into the comfortable routine of bringing work home and working until all hours of the night.

"In passing. We didn't get to talk, but she mentioned they were thinking about moving in here. That would be great, wouldn't it?"

Christina nodded. "We should plan something special to welcome them to Atlanta. I just have no idea what."

"We can have a party for them. Introduce them to some people. Not a lot of people, just a small dinner party."

"We'd host a party?" It made them seem like an official couple. Not that they weren't, but giving a party for his fraternity friends made a statement.

"Sure. Don't you like the idea?"

"It's not that. This'll be the first time we've hosted a party."

"I say it's about time. It would be a good time for you to meet Betty, Ellis's wife. I hate that you two haven't met each other yet. Let's pick a date that she and Ellis can definitely make it."

The plans began forming in Christina's mind. "Do you want to have it here, or at my place?"

"It doesn't matter. You decide."

Christina weighed the pros and cons. "We can have a larger group at my place. How many people were you thinking about?"

"No more than ten, including us. Ellis and Betty, Michael and Jewel, Robert and Liza, you and me, and one other couple. Who do you suggest?"

"Why don't we invite Angela? She's seeing somebody, isn't she?"

"I don't know, you spend more time with Angela than I do."

Christina detected his hesitation. "Does that bother you — my friendship with Angela?"

"Not at all. I just wonder if she'll feel awkward when we're with Ellis and Betty, Mike and Jewel. Jewel and Betty are the ones who wanted to pair me up with Angela originally. I don't want her to be hurt."

Christina remembered the first time she and Jackson had gone out with Mike and Jewel. She had sensed a need to win Jewel over. She had done it, and she now had a new friend. "She may be more hurt if we don't invite her. Jewel and Betty are her friends, too."

Jackson picked up his newspaper. "If you think that's best, let's do it. I'll talk with Ellis tomorrow and get some dates and we'll work it from there. Okay?"

"Okay," she said. She hoped Jackson hadn't acquiesced just to appease her. "Are you about ready for bed?"

"I have more reading to do. You go on ahead." He looked up from the paper. "Just don't go to sleep before I get there."

When Christina awoke Sunday morning, Jackson wasn't in bed with her. Maybe he's in the bathroom, she thought. Or the kitchen. She waited awhile, then, sensing something was wrong, got up to look for him. She found him in the family room. She stood in the doorway and watched him hang up the phone, then lean forward and place his head in his hands.

"Bad news?" she asked, as she walked toward him. He lifted his head from his hands and turned in her direction after she spoke.

"Just another call to my dad. Every call affects me this way."

She took a seat on the couch next to him and pulled him back so his head rested against her breasts. She began rubbing her hands across his chest. There was nothing sexual in her touch this morning, she only wanted to comfort him. "What did he say?" she asked.

"Why can't he get over her?" Jackson demanded to know. "She left fourteen years ago."

She heard the pain in his voice and she wished she had answers for him, but she didn't. "Neither of you have heard from her in all this time?" Christina found it hard to believe that his mother had just disappeared.

Jackson shook his head. "I haven't heard a word, and I don't think Dad has, either."

"How do you know nothing happened to her? Maybe she didn't leave willingly."

"She left a letter. I never read it. My dad sat me down and told me she was gone. He said she left a letter saying she needed her own space. Wanted to find herself," he said. "Can you believe that? The old man didn't even care enough to lie to me. How can you tell your fifteen-year-old kid that his mom just up and left. That she doesn't love him?"

Christina held him tighter. "It was cruel of your mother to leave, and your father handled it badly," she agreed. "Didn't you want to find out for yourself? Didn't you want to talk to her yourself?"

"Yes, and that talk led to the deterioration of my relationship with my dad. I called him a liar. I told him my mom did love me. I told him she left him, not me. I told him I was going to find her."

Christina wished she could absorb some of his pain. She hoped talking about it helped him. "What did you do?"

"I set my sights on getting out of that house and looking for my mom. I told myself that she didn't leave me. She was out there waiting for me somewhere. My dad was the bad guy."

"You never found her?"

"I didn't say that. During my second year in college, I hired a private detective. Can you believe that?" He didn't wait for an answer. "She was living in Los Angeles, married with two kids — twins."

Christina knew the ache he'd felt when he'd learned the truth was still there. Time had dulled it, but it was still there.

"She was pregnant when she left my dad," he continued. "She'd been having an affair. I didn't even want to know how long it had been going on. That day my mom died for me."

"Oh, Jackson, that's so sad."

"Not really. I learned how strong I was. I didn't need a mother."

Christina didn't believe Jackson didn't need his mother. The pain in his voice told the real story. "What happened between you and your dad?"

"Nothing. I wanted to forget her, all my dad wanted to do was remember her. That's the way it is now. He can't get over her."

"He must have loved her a great deal," Christina offered.

"If love did this to my dad, who needs love?"

The bitterness in his tone made Christina cringe. "What does it mean when you say you love me, Jackson? You don't have a real high opinion of love."

He sat up then and looked at her. His feelings for her were real. "I know that everything that's called love isn't love. I've seen the effects of false love in my mom and dad."

"Why did you pursue me, then? What were you looking for? A good time?" Christina wasn't sure she'd like the answers to those questions, but she wanted them.

Jackson must have sensed her uneasiness, because he turned and pulled her into his arms before he answered. "I was first attracted to you when I saw you walk in the building that morning before the interview. I liked the way you moved. Your legs and your breasts." He squeezed her left breast with his hand. "They bounced as you walked across the street."

Christina remembered that morning. She had known he was watching her.

"I was surprised to find that my mystery lady was also my boss. That information should have stopped me, but I couldn't help myself," he stated simply.

"Be for real, Jackson."

"I'm serious. You were on my mind constantly. When I started going out with Angela, I hoped she would help me not think about you so much. It didn't happen. The more I tried not to think about you, the more I thought about you. You got under my skin real quick, lady."

Christina liked hearing that. She turned and gave him a quick kiss.

"To answer your last question, I wouldn't have pursued you if all I wanted was a good time. I pursued you because I sensed there was something special between us."

"Magic," she whispered. She remembered he had called it magic.

"At the time, I didn't want to put a label on it. Somewhere in the back of my mind, I thought that we had a chance to have something as solid as Reggie's parents have. I'd never felt that before."

Warmth spread over her at his words. "Do you ever think that we'll end up like your parents?"

He didn't answer immediately. She gave him time. "Sometimes, when I'm thinking about how well we fit, I begin to wonder if it's all in my mind and I get scared. It's possible we'll end up like them, but I don't think we will."

"What makes you so sure?"

"A lot of little things. We share the same work ethic. We talk about everything. We're sexually compatible. I love being with you. We don't have to talk. We don't have to do anything. I just like being with you, being in the same room with you. Being in the same house and knowing that you're in the house, even if you're not in the same room. I like going to bed with you and I like waking up with you. You're good for me, Christina."

Christina pressed closer to him. "I feel the same way. I can't imagine coming home without you. It's as though you're a part of me. It's scary, but it's good." She peeked up at him. "You make me feel beautiful."

"You *are* beautiful," he said.

"You make me believe that," she said.

"You know that we're sounding like an old married couple, don't you?"

"I can't imagine feeling more committed

to you than I do now."

"I feel the same way," he said.

She listened to the regular thump of his heart and felt content to be in his arms, glad they had shared what was in their hearts. He surprised her when he spoke again.

"Do you want to get married?" he asked.

CHAPTER 16

"Married?" Christina's first thought was that this was a proposal.

"Yes, do you want to get married?"

"Now? Someday?"

"This wasn't meant to be a difficult question, Christina," Jackson said dryly. "Let's try 'someday.' "

"Sure, I want to get married," she said offhandedly. "There are a lot of benefits to having a man around."

"You don't have to be married to have a man around. You have me now and we aren't married. Do you want to get married?"

Christina thought again that Jackson was a lot like her mother. He always brought her back to the real issue. "Yes, Jackson, I want to get married. I've always wanted to get married."

He heard the wistfulness in her voice. "You didn't have any role models for marriages as a child, either, did you?"

"Not really. My mom was a great mom, but I missed having a dad. I've developed a lot of theories about the role a father plays in his daughter's life."

"That's only natural. You look at what you missed and you think he may have filled that. The reality is that even if he were there, he might not have filled those roles."

"You're probably right," Christina said. She often fantasized about life with a father. She wasn't ready yet to give up those dreams.

"Tell me your theories," Jackson said.

Christina pulled away from him to look into his eyes. "Are you sure you want to hear this? I've had a lot of years to develop these theories. It may get a little long."

Jackson kissed her softly on the lips. "We've got all day and all night."

Christina rested her head back against his chest. "My first theory is that girls learn to relate to boys by watching their mothers relate and interact with their fathers. Growing up in a house with no males make boys more foreign and, in some ways, more frightening. They're really an unknown quantity."

"That makes sense. All kids learn about the interaction of the sexes from their parents' model. You and I are proof of that. What's your next theory?"

"Well, I think that a little girl's confidence in her sexual self is given to her in her father's eyes."

"That I don't understand," Jackson said.

"It's difficult for me to express. The father is the first man in a girl's life. She wants to please him in all ways. His acceptance or rejection of her is what she expects to find in other men. If Daddy thinks she's smart and pretty, there's no reason for her to expect other men will think any differently. If Daddy thinks she's dumb or ugly, there's no reason for her to expect that other men will be any different in their view, either."

"What if Daddy isn't there?"

Christina had first-hand knowledge of that case. "If Daddy isn't there, the girl's first experience with a male is one of rejection."

"Not all fathers are absent because they want to be," Jackson reminded her. "What about cases where the father dies?"

She shook her head. "Children don't understand the difference. It's still rejection. The result — the little girl's expectation — is that every man will reject her."

"Is that how you felt?"

Christina expected the question. "I think so. I've never had to depend on a man, so I never had the experience of him being there when I needed him. You know, I remember a girlfriend in college saying that I had a lot of male friends. When she said that, I thought about it. She was right. I was friends with a lot of guys — none of them romantic, though. I was a friend who listened, but I didn't trust them and I didn't respect them."

"No trust and no respect. That's pretty cold, Christina."

"I know, but you have to remember my theory," Christina explained. "My expectation is that men will either reject me in the beginning or they'll reject me in the end. That kind of thinking doesn't allow for much trust or respect."

"Well, I hope your opinions have changed now."

"Of course they have. I know there are good men out there. I have professional relationships with men that I trust and respect."

He squeezed her to him. "What about personal relationships? What about me?"

She turned to face him. "You're a whole new experience for me." She turned back around.

"How's that?"

She heard the smile in his voice and

turned to face him again. "You make me feel things that I've never felt before. You make me think all my dreams will come true."

Jackson kissed her then. "I want to make them come true, Christina, if you'll let me."

Christina searched for the words to express to Jackson how much he had given her already. He had taken her dreams for love, marriage, and family and brought them so close that she could touch them. "I wish I could tell you how much I love you."

"I know, Christina. I love you, too."

She smiled. "And how are you so sure that I love you?"

He gave her a smug masculine smile. He touched her eyes. "I can see it here. They light up when you see me." He touched the corners of her mouth. "I can see it here. You have a smile that's reserved just for me." He ran his forefinger up and down her cheek. "You've taught me what love is."

She felt his intensity. At that moment, she was overwhelmed with love for him. She couldn't say anything so he put all her emotions, all her love, into a long, wet kiss. When it was over, she turned around and burrowed into his chest. "There's no place I'd rather be than in your arms."

He squeezed her. "Sometimes I want to

take you away so I can have you all to myself. Someplace where I wouldn't have to share you. You'd be all mine. All the time."

How beautiful that sounded. Beautiful and unrealistic. "You'd get tired of me."

"Never."

The forcefulness of that one word shook her. She knew he meant it. She realized he wasn't going to allow her to minimize his feelings for her. "Your love for me is hard for me to get a handle on."

"What do you mean by that?" he asked.

"I know you love me, but sometimes it's hard for me to understand and to believe that you have as much invested in this relationship as I do. I always think of the woman as having the greater emotional investment."

"I don't know who has the greater investment, but I'm as committed to this relationship as you are. I can be hurt as easily as you."

Christina waited before saying, "Rosalind told me not to hurt you. I thought it odd for her to say that. I thought she should have been more concerned with your hurting me. She also said that we should be good to each other."

"We're doing that."

Christina nodded. She picked up one of

Jackson's hands that rested on her stomach. As she began counting his fingers, she asked, "Do you want children?"

"A couple."

"Boys or girls?"

"I prefer boys, but as long as they're healthy I won't complain."

"What do you have against girls?" she asked.

"I'd rather spend the next twenty years telling my boys to stay away from other people's girls than spend them telling other people's boys to stay away from my girls."

She pinched him. "I want children, too. One boy and one girl." Christina thought for a while. She turned to look at Jackson. "Can you picture me pregnant?"

Jackson turned her so she faced him and her body was fully flush his. "I can't picture how you'd look pregnant, but I can definitely picture you getting pregnant."

"I checked with Betty, and next weekend is good for us," Ellis said.

"Good. It's about time she and Christina met."

"Betty's eager to meet her. Once she accepted that you and Angela weren't getting married, she was pretty receptive to hearing good things about Christina."

Jackson laughed, then signaled the waiter for a fresh drink. "Has Mrs. Matchmaker found another mate for Angela yet?"

"No, and between you and me, I think Angela's told her to butt out for a while."

"Good for Angela."

"Is she coming to this get-together?" Ellis asked.

"Yes. She and Christina are working together on a fundraiser. They like each other."

"You and Christina must be pretty serious if you're giving parties together," Ellis said, popping a pretzel in his mouth.

"We're pretty serious. I asked her to marry me the other night."

Ellis slapped Jackson on the back. "I don't believe it! What did she say?"

"She didn't understand the question, or maybe she chose not to understand the question. I'm still not sure which it was."

"What do you mean, she didn't understand the question?"

Jackson shrugged as if it didn't matter, but it did. "I asked her if she wanted to get married, and she said yes. Somehow, it was never clear that she wanted to marry me."

"I don't understand. Did you ask her to marry you or did you ask if she wanted to get married?"

"I asked if she wanted to get married. Who would I be talking about, if not myself?"

Ellis shook his head. "You have a lot to learn, man. Christina probably didn't understand your question. Imagine yourself in her position. What if she had said she would marry you and you had said, 'Well I wasn't talking about marrying me, I was talking about marriage in general?' When she answered in general terms, you should have told her the question was about the two of you. Why didn't you do that?"

He didn't do that because he'd been unsure what her answer would be, especially after their conversation about rejection. "I got scared, man. I hadn't planned to ask her."

"Join the club. I felt that way with Betty. I wanted her, but I never would've married her if I thought I could keep her without marrying her."

"That's the difference with me and Christina. I've never wanted to get married, but I want to spend the rest of my life with her."

Ellis slapped him on the back again. "Well, you'd better practice proposing if you want to get married, because what you did last time was a bust."

"Calm down, Christina," Jackson said.

"Everything's going to be perfect."

"Maybe we should have had it at your apartment, after all. We spend most of our time there anyway."

Jackson walked over to her and took both of her arms. "Why are you so nervous? It's only a party. They're people we already know."

She pulled away from him and leaned against the kitchen sink. "You don't understand, Jackson. This is more than a party."

He looked at her. "I'm not usually dense, but you'll have to explain that one to me."

"This is the first event we've held as a couple. We're inviting people to the home that we share together. It's not just a party." She wiped at her tears.

"There's no need to cry," Jackson said, and then he laughed softly.

"Don't laugh at me," she said between her tears.

"I'm not laughing at you, sweetheart," he said. "I love you too much for that. I'm laughing because you're so unpredictable. Sometimes I think you're two different women."

Christina sniffled and asked, "What do you mean by that?"

He pulled her to him. God, he loved this woman. The love had come quickly, but it was in no way shallow. She was a part of him now and he was determined to keep her. "Don't take it wrong. You're different at work than you are here at home. At work, you're all strong and in control. At home, you're just as strong, but nowhere near as in control." He wiped her tears and smiled. "I'm laughing because I'm so glad that I have you."

"You really think this is going to go okay?" she asked.

The doorbell rang then. "I do. Now I'm going to greet the first guest. Take care of your eyes, we don't want the guests to think that I beat you."

Jackson went to the door. He opened it to see Liza and Robert. "Glad you guys got here first." He looked at Liza. "Christina's in the kitchen. She could probably use a friend right now."

"Okay, I'm off for the kitchen," Liza said. "Don't you two get into any trouble."

Jackson led Robert to the living room. Before they could sit, the doorbell rang again. This time it was Jewel, Michael, Ellis, and Betty. "We drove together," Ellis explained.

"Come on in, Robert and Liza are already here," Jackson said.

Christina and Liza came out of the kitchen

and Jackson made the introductions. When they had all been introduced, the women went back to the kitchen.

"Jackson told us that you were a frat. We'll look to see you at the meeting next week," Ellis said to Robert.

"I'll be there," Robert said. "Where's it going to be?"

"Paschal's on MLK," Ellis answered. "Where do you live?"

"We were fortunate. We found a place in Jackson's building downtown."

"You and Jackson can come together, then."

Jackson spoke up. "I planned to do that, though we're usually out here on weekends."

Mike clapped Jackson on the back. "Yeah, he and Christina live in their downtown quarters during the week and they come to their country place on the weekend."

The men all laughed.

"You joke, but it's working well," Jackson explained. "Christina likes not having the long commute everyday, and I love being out here on the weekends."

"So, when's the big day?" Robert asked. He was looking at Jackson.

"Big day for what?" Jackson asked.

"The wedding, of course. You're acting married, you're talking married, you're living married. When are you going to get married?"

Jackson glanced at Ellis. He wasn't ready to talk to the other guys about his feelings. "We haven't talked about dates yet. We're enjoying being together."

The three married men all shook their heads. "He's a dead man and he doesn't even know it," Mike said.

"He thinks they're just enjoying being together, and I'll bet you Christina's already picked out the wedding dress," Robert added.

Jackson hoped they were right. "You guys don't know Christina. If she was ready to get married, I'd know. There wouldn't be any games."

Again the three married men all shook their heads. "Has she started naming the kids yet?" Mike asked.

Jackson shook his head. "No, we've only talked about how many we'd like to have."

"That's it, man, when you start talking about babies, it's all over but the ceremony," Robert explained. They all laughed. "We're kidding you, man. I, for one, wouldn't trade marriage for anything. You and Christina have a good thing going. We wish you all the best."

"Thanks, man," Jackson said. He knew he

and Christina had something special. And more and more each day he wanted to make it permanent.

"I didn't think I'd like you, Christina, since you busted up what was probably my best matchmaking effort, but I like you a lot," Betty said.

Christina didn't know to respond to that, but found she didn't have to.

"You'll get used to Betty, Christina," Jewel explained. "She has a tendency to say what she thinks without thinking about what she says."

"She's right," Betty agreed. "I didn't mean anything bad. Angela told me that I'd like you, but I wasn't too sure."

"Well, I'm glad we all get along, since our men are such good friends," Christina said. "Have you heard from Angela today? I expected her to be here by now."

"She didn't call you?" Betty asked.

Christina shook her head.

"She must have gotten tied up," Betty explained. "She's meeting with the producers for her talk show tonight. It came up suddenly and she couldn't get out of it."

"That's great — the show, I mean," Christina said. "I hope this means it's really going to happen."

"I think that's what it means," Betty said.

"I'm happy for her," Jewel added, "but I wanted to meet her new guy."

"Yes," Betty said. "So did I. This is the first guy Angela's dated who works at her station."

"This guy works with Angela?" Christina asked. "I didn't know that."

"She probably decided to give it a shot since it's working so well for you and Jackson," Betty said. "What's it like working with him and living with him?"

"It's good. You know, we've only been doing it for four months, but it seems like we've been doing it forever. He understands my day, I understand his. We support each other. I had my apprehensions, but now I recommend it highly."

"Ellis says you're his boss," Betty continued. "What's that like?"

"We don't think of it that way," Christina responded. Betty did ask a lot of questions, she thought. "Because of the nature of our work, we don't really have to deal with the boss-employee roles." Christina knew she wasn't being completely honest, but it wasn't Betty's business.

"That's right," Liza interjected. "I work for Christina, too, but we're also friends. It can work if you want it to." Christina gave

Liza a thank-you smile, then Liza added, "I'm a newlywed and I'm missing my man real bad right now. Can we go and see what they're up to?"

They all laughed. "Newlyweds," Betty repeated. "I'm surprised you two were willing to get out of bed to come here."

Liza winked at Christina. "It was tough, but we couldn't let Christina down."

"You were a hit tonight," Jackson said to Christina. She was in the bathroom, so he couldn't see her.

"It did go well, didn't it?" He heard the water come on.

"More than well," he replied. "What's taking you so long in there?"

She walked out of the bathroom then, turning off the light as she did.

"What are you so impatient about?" she asked. She sat on the side of the bed and began to lotion her legs.

"Let me do that," Jackson said. "Lie back."

Christina lay back on the bed and Jackson began applying the lotion to her legs. "You didn't warn me about Betty," she said.

"I didn't know I needed to. What did she do?"

"It's not so much what she did as what she said."

"I know she's a talker, but I thought she was basically harmless."

"She is. There's not a malicious bone in her body. She's just a bit more outspoken than I expected."

"Turn over," Jackson said. He began applying the lotion to her hips and the backs of her legs. "What did she say?"

"She said she liked me even though I did bust up her perfect couple, you and Angela."

Jackson laughed. "Betty said that? And what did you say?"

"I was at a loss for words. What could I say? I told her I was glad we got along since our men were such good friends."

"Did you like her?"

"I don't know if I'd use the word 'like.' She's a nice person. I don't know if I could be around her for an extended time, though."

"Well, I'll make sure you don't have to. We'll only see them at fraternity events and get-togethers like tonight's. How did she and Jewel get along with Liza?"

"They got along well. Liza enjoyed keeping Betty in line. And you know Jewel, she gets along with everybody."

Jackson slapped Christina softly on the

buttocks. "Finished." She turned over. He smiled at her and added, "Too bad Angela couldn't make it. She would have helped Liza keep Betty in line."

"I wish she could have come, too. Jewel and Betty said Angela was dating a new guy, somebody she worked with. Did you know that?"

Jackson shook his head. "I hadn't heard. It doesn't sound like Angela, though. She had strong convictions about dating co-workers. If it's true, this guy must be something special."

Christina reached up and touched his face. "Betty said she was following our example."

Jackson covered her hand with his own. "We set a pretty good one, don't you think?"

She raised up and kissed him on the lips. "I sure do." When she moved to lie back down, Jackson followed her. He was about to kiss her again when she asked, "How did Robert get along with the guys?"

"I think they got along well. He's a frat, and that makes it easier." He kissed her above each eye. "They had something else in common, too."

Christina closed her eyes and let herself enjoy him. "And what was that?"

He continued with kisses all over her face.

"They're all very much in love with their wives. It's obvious."

Christina tilted her head to give him better access. "Same with the women. Three solid marriages right before our eyes."

"They seem to think that we should be next," Jackson said casually. His kisses continued.

"What did they say?" she asked.

"They said we're obviously in love and we're acting married, so we may as well get married."

She opened her eyes then. "What do you think?"

Jackson stopped kissing her and looked into her eyes. "I think they're right."

She didn't say anything. All she could think was that it was too soon. They had known each other six months and they'd only been together for four months. Marriage now would be a disaster. It just wasn't done. They needed more time to get to know each other.

Jackson asked, "What do you think?"

"I love you, Jackson, but it's too soon to think about getting married." At his pained look, she added, "You haven't even met my mother. I haven't met your father."

"I don't want to marry your mother. I want to marry you."

Christina couldn't think of anything to say. She had dreamed of hearing those words from this man. But it was too soon, wasn't it? Didn't they need more time to be sure? What if he decided later that he'd made a mistake? It was better to be sure than to make a mistake and end up in divorce court. That she couldn't handle. "I couldn't marry you before you've met my mom or I've met your dad. It wouldn't be right."

Jackson sat up. His back was to her. He admitted his surprise, his disappointment, at Christina's hesitation. Was she looking for an excuse not to marry him? Maybe she didn't want to marry him. "I don't understand. We're living like we're married already. What would change?"

"I don't know," she said softly. "I do love you and I'm committed to you. I want to marry you and have your babies. I want to grow old with you, but I need time to get used to this." When he didn't respond, Christina added, "I don't want to lose you. Tell me I'm not going to lose you because of this."

Jackson turned to face her. He saw the fear in her eyes and knew that a part of her expected that she would lose him. That was the past. He was the present. He couldn't erase the past. All he could do was hope that she would believe in his love for her.. "You're not going to lose me, Christina."

Christina sat in her office preparing for the Friday status meeting with Liza and Jackson. Today they had to select the first application site for OPTIMA. Christina studied the papers. She hoped they could agree.

"Let's start with site selection," Christina said, when Liza and Jackson were seated in her office. "Who wants to go first?"

"I will," Jackson said. He spread out four charts that he had pulled together. "We should start with E-Manufacturing. They're aggressive and they're prepared to do a full conversion within six months."

"That's what concerns me about E-Manufacturing," Liza said, "They're too aggressive for a new product like OPTIMA. We need to start on a smaller scale. Maybe Kenner Limited. They have one line that they want to bring up, then see what happens. We could use that time to work out the kinks."

"The kinks ought to be worked out before we deliver to the field," Jackson explained. "Kenner Limited won't be a showcase site for this product. E-Manufacturing will give us the cover page of every major manufacturing journal in the country."

"You're right, Jackson," Liza said, "but it's too risky. We shouldn't go that big until we're sure."

Jackson knew it was no use talking to Liza. She was much too conservative. He turned to Christina. "What do you think?"

"There's merit to Liza's concerns. We need the extra time that Kenner would give ₁us. We go with Kenner."

"Surprise" didn't adequately capture Jackson's response. Had Christina gone conservative on him, too? He definitely did not like the way the scales had been tilting around here lately.

Jackson walked out on the balcony of his apartment to talk with Christina. "That's the second time this week that you've sided with Liza against me."

Christina turned from the railing to look at him. "What did you say?"

"At the status meeting today . . . you sided with Liza. It's the second time that you've done it."

"I didn't side with Liza. I made the best decision for CL. Nothing more, nothing less."

"So you think Liza's judgment is better than mine?" He vowed not to get angry, but he felt his temper rising.

"Not really. I think she's more cautious than you some of the time."

In his opinion, Liza was cautious to a fault. "You think I don't use caution."

"You're deliberately misunderstanding me, Jackson. That's not what I'm saying at all. You're good at your job. Liza's good at her job. Most of the time we're able to come to a consensus. When we can't, it's my job to decide. Sometimes it'll be in your favor, sometimes it'll be in Liza's favor. I'm not being disloyal to you, if that's what you're implying. This is business, plain and simple."

"Whatever you say, Christina," Jackson said smugly. "You're the boss." He turned and walked back into the apartment.

CHAPTER 17

"It's not the end of the world, Christina," Liza said. "All relationships have problems. You've got to find out what your problem is and fix it."

Christina looked across the conference table at her friend. "Easier said that done."

"How's the sex?"

"It's been better. We go through the motions, but I can tell something's wrong and I know he can, too."

"Have you talked about it?"

"We've talked around it. I think it's a lot of different things."

Liza nodded. "I thought something was up."

"You did?" Christina didn't know why she was surprised. From the beginning, outsiders knew what was going on with her and Jackson before they did.

"I've noticed lately that you two aren't as relaxed with each other as you were before.

The staff has noticed, too. I overheard Penny and Doris talking about it."

"Penny and Doris? What were they saying? Do they know we're living together?"

"There's speculation, but no one really knows. They know there's tension between you that wasn't there before."

Christina stood up and walked to the windows. Looking out, she said, "I knew this would happen."

"Knew what would happen?"

"I knew we couldn't keep this relationship out of the office. That's part of the problem."

"What are you talking about, Christina?"

She turned around and looked at Liza. "I think Jackson resents my being his boss."

"That's a pretty serious charge. You need to talk to him about this."

"I know. That's why I can't bring it up."

"Keeping it bottled up inside isn't going to work. You've got to talk to him about it."

Christina began to pace. "Our relationship was going so well. It was almost too good to be true. Maybe it was."

"Don't blow this out of proportion now. Remember that you love this man and he loves you. Whatever's wrong can be fixed."

Christina stopped pacing and looked back at her friend, wanting very much to believe her words. "I wish I were as sure as you, Liza. I wish I were as sure as you."

"What do you want to do this weekend?" Jackson asked. He and Christina were in his apartment.

"I don't care. What do you want to do?" She wondered if she had imagined the friction between them.

"I was thinking about taking in a ball game with Ellis, Mike, and Robert this weekend. Mike has tickets for Saturday and Sunday."

Then again, maybe she wasn't imagining it. "Don't worry about me. I understand you want to spend some time with your friends."

"Are you sure you don't want to do something else?" he asked.

"I'm sure. You go and have fun. Maybe Liza and I'll do something."

He walked into the kitchen. "And since the games are downtown, I thought I'd spend the weekend in town."

"Oh," was all she said. Our first weekend apart, she thought. We've only been together five months and he wants a weekend alone. This is the beginning of the end.

"Don't say it like that."

"Like what?"

He walked back into the living room. "Like I've said I don't love you anymore."

She didn't say anything. *Is that what you're saying, Jackson?*

"What are you thinking?" he finally asked.

I'm thinking that maybe you don't love me anymore. "This will be the first weekend we've been apart since we've been together."

"I'm only going downtown, not across the country," he said. The irritation in his voice made her angry.

She got up. "That's not the point."

"Since you know so much, you tell me. What is the point?"

"You know as well as I do that things between us have been strained for the past couple of weeks. I wonder if this is your way of dealing with it."

Jackson took a deep breath. "I'm beginning to feel crowded. We could use some space, Christina."

First he wants to get married and now he's crowded. Bull . . . "Crowded?"

"Maybe 'crowded' isn't the right word. We're together all the time. We need some space."

Doesn't sound like a man serious about marriage. She was right not to consider his proposal. "We? So now you're speaking for me?"

"All right. I need some space." He turned her to face him. "I love you, Christina, but I need some space and some time to figure out where this relationship is going."

"A few weeks ago you were ready to get married. What's going on here, Jackson?" Christina feared asking the next question, but she had to. "Have you stopped loving me?"

"I love you, Christina, but I wonder if that's enough. Maybe you've been right all along. Maybe this is moving too fast."

Christina felt each of his words like a dagger in her heart. Jackson wasn't supposed to leave her. They were supposed to be together forever. "You've felt this way and you've never mentioned it to me?"

"I didn't know where to start. I couldn't talk about it."

"Can you talk about it now?"

"No more than what I've said. It's not you, it's me. I'm not feeling good about myself lately. I've got to work through it."

"You have to work through it alone? Without me?" Tears were in her eyes, but she was determined not to let them fall.

Jackson nodded.

"If that's the way it has to be, there's nothing I can do." Christina began putting her papers in her briefcase.

"What are you doing?" Jackson asked.

"What does it look like I'm doing? I'm going home."

"You don't have to leave."

"What good will my staying do? Maybe you're right. Maybe we both need some space. My staying here tonight wouldn't be right."

She wanted him to take it all back. She wanted him to say that it was all a joke. He didn't. He looked at her with a sad expression on his face.

She gathered her belongings and went to the door. She opened it and walked out without saying anything more.

When she closed the door behind her, her knees buckled. She held on to the wall for support. It was over! She and Jackson were finished. The tears she held back fell freely now.

When she got into her car, she rested her head on the steering wheel and cried. She cried for herself, for what she had, and for what she had lost. After about fifteen minutes, she started the car and began the drive home. As she drove, she played and replayed the past couple of weeks in her mind. What if she had done this differently? What if she had done that differently? What if? What if?

Her tears were all gone when she reached

her house. All she had now was a heart that felt as if it weighed two tons. She walked into the house. She missed him already. She saw him in every room. She dreaded going into the bedroom, but she finally decided to get it over with. She walked in and flipped on the light. Jackson's jacket was lying at the foot of the bed. She smiled. He could never decide which jacket to wear. If they'd spent weekdays here, her bed would probably be full of jackets. She picked up the jacket and held it close. It smelled of him. Chastising herself, she took the jacket and hung it up in the closet, their closet. His clothes were now mingled in with hers. It was amazing how quickly and completely their two lives had become intertwined.

She lay down on the bed. It, too, smelled of him. She remembered the nights they'd slept together in this bed. She remembered the night she had worn the purple teddy for him. God, it had been so good then. She lay there thinking of him until the tears came again. She was asleep before they stopped.

Jackson lay alone in his bed and missed her. Though their relationship hadn't been too good the last few weeks, he preferred being with her to being without her. He replayed tonight's conversation. He could think of any other way he could have handled it.

He loved her. There was no doubt about it. He just couldn't handle the new emotions he was feeling. He didn't like the way he felt when Christina chose Liza's judgment over his. It felt like a slap in the face. They had disagreed before Liza had come on board. But it was one thing for your woman to disagree with you when it was just the two of you. It was a whole other thing for her to do it in front of a friend. Liza probably went home and told Robert about it, too.

Jackson turned over onto his stomach. He missed her softness pressed against him. He knew he had no one to blame but himself, but he couldn't talk to her about it. How could he tell her that it made him feel less a man when she overruled him on a matter? How could he tell her that he needed her to respect his opinion?

He had told her that he could handle her being the boss. He had even joked about it. It was no joking matter. How did a man resolve his need to protect and care for his woman with the reality that his woman didn't need or want his protection? He rolled over onto his back.

He had changed a lot since he'd met

Christina. He thought he wanted an independent woman. Maybe he did, but he also wanted a woman who looked up to him, a woman who knew she could look to him for help. Christina didn't need him. She might not know it now, but she would come to that conclusion sooner or later, and then she would leave. Just as his mother had left, she would leave.

When Christina awoke she didn't know where she was. Then she remembered. She was home. Alone. She lay there looking at the ceiling for a while. She knew thoughts of Jackson would come. She couldn't stop them and she wouldn't try. She turned, opened the top drawer of her nightstand, and pulled out her small black notebook. She rubbed her hands up and down the cover, then opened it and turned to the page labeled, "Personal Goals." She read numbers 4, 5, and 6: fall in love, get married, and have three children. She had certainly fallen in love. She closed the notebook and put it back in the drawer.

She closed her eyes and let the tears come. She opened them when the phone rang. She considered not answering, but she did.

"Hello," she said.

"I called to see how you're doing." It was Jackson.

Maybe he's calling to say it's all a big mistake. "I'm doing fine. How about you?"

I've been better, he thought. "I'm fine. Are you sure you're okay?"

Strangers. They were talking like strangers. She was pissed at herself for getting her hopes up. "I'm a big girl, Jackson. You don't have to worry about me."

"That what I thought," he said sadly, and then hung up.

Christina held the phone in her hand. The nerve of that man. Was that sadness she heard in his voice? What did he have to be sad about? I'm the one who's been wronged here. Men.

Christina didn't feel like going to work today. She dreaded the staff meeting with Jackson and Liza, but she'd be damned if she'd let him think she was home crying over him. She got up and dressed for work.

She arrived in her office later than usual. Penny was not at her desk. When she walked into the office, she saw a bouquet of red roses on her desk. Her heartbeat sped up. Maybe he wants to make up. She rushed to the desk to read the card. She held it to her heart and wished. Then, she opened it and dropped down in her chair. "Not again," she said aloud. "Not again."

Christina couldn't bear to see Jackson today. She told Penny to tell him and Liza that the status meeting was canceled and left the office.

When she arrived at her house, she went straight to the kitchen. She needed something cold to drink. She placed her briefcase on the counter, took a glass from the cabinet, and went to the refrigerator. She stood with her back to the counter as she drank. From her position, she could see her front porch. And something on the porch caught her eye. She went to the front door. "Oh, my God," she said.

She was still seated at the kitchen counter when Jackson let himself into the house a few hours later. "I was worried when you canceled the meeting this afternoon," he said. "I called. When nobody answered I came to check on you. Is everything all right?"

She looked at him and wondered who this man was. "Thanks for the roses," she said dryly. "There was no need to send two bouquets."

"What are you talking about?" Jackson asked.

She pointed toward the dining room. "See

for yourself."

Jackson saw the roses through the open dining room door. "When did you get these?"

"They were here to greet me when I got in from work."

"Where's the card?"

It was on the counter. She pushed it in his direction. He read it, then asked, "Have you called the police?"

She shook her head. "I got more roses today at work. I called security."

"What did they say?"

"They came to a dead end in the last investigation, but they did come up with one bit of information that you might find interesting."

"And what's that?" he asked.

"The last bouquet came from Wall's Flower Shop in the Midtown Terrace apartment building." That bit of news had sent her home early. Security should have given her this news as soon as they found out.

"My building? The roses came from my building?"

"You sound as surprised as I was to get that piece of information."

Jackson looked at her then. The look in her eyes was one he had never seen before. "Christina, you can't think . . ." he began.

"I don't know what to think. Maybe you can help me." Christina knew her voice was calm. She was falling apart inside, but her voice was calm.

"You can't think I sent them," he said.

There was something in his tone that made her want to go to him and wrap him in her arms. She didn't give in to the feeling. "Who do you think sent them?"

"I don't know. What would I gain by sending them?"

"I've been asking myself that same question."

"And what answer do you come up with?"

"I don't have an answer. I just have a lot of pieces that make a real ugly picture."

"What pieces? What are you talking about?"

"When I thought about it, I began to see a pattern. The roses started after our fiasco in Boston the first time. I stopped getting them after our weekend together at Liza's wedding. They started coming again after our first real fight. What do you conclude from that, Jackson?"

"There's no need for me to say anything. You've figured it all out yourself."

"You don't have anything to say?" she asked. She wanted him to deny it, to explain it.

"You're a smart woman. You've figured it all out. What more could I possibly add?"

She didn't answer.

"I didn't think so," he said, and turned to leave. He stopped when she spoke, but he didn't turn to face her.

"Leave my key on the table on your way out," she said.

He turned then to look at her. She saw the plea in his eyes, but she chose to ignore it. He turned, put the key on the table, and left the house.

Christina remained seated at the counter after he had gone. She waited for the tears to come, but they didn't. She waited for the overwhelming sense of hurt and pain to come, but it didn't. She finally realized that she was numb. She felt nothing. She didn't know if she would ever feel anything again.

Jackson made it to his car. He drove out of the driveway and down the street. He made it about one mile before he had to pull over in a Denny's parking lot.

He shook with anger. How could she think that I would do something like that? he asked himself. What kind of man does she think I am?

Jackson leaned his head back against the headrest. Memories of times he and Christina had shared passed in his thoughts. He saw her face the first time she'd had an orgasm. He heard her voice when he'd told her he loved her the first time. He remembered her anxiety the day of their first party. He felt the same emotions he had felt when the events had occurred. He patted his face because it felt funny. When he looked at his hands, they were wet.

Christina needed to talk to someone. She considered calling Liza, but Liza was too close to Jackson. She picked up the phone and dialed. "It's me," she said. "Are you going to be home this weekend?"

"Yes," her mother said.

"I should be there in four hours," Christina said.

"Is something wrong? Did you and Jackson have a fight?"

"I don't want to talk about it now, Mom," Christina said. "I'll tell you everything when I get there."

It was dark when Jackson opened his eyes. He looked at his watch. He'd been sitting there for more than three hours. He felt his face. It was dry. He looked in the rearview mirror and couldn't believe what he saw. Though his heart was crushed, he looked the same. Shaking his head, he started the car.

He considered stopping by Ellis's house, but decided against it. He and Betty were too close to him and Christina, and Robert was out of the question. Then Jackson had an idea. Instead of taking the Interstate downtown to his apartment, he made a detour.

CHAPTER 18

Jackson arrived at the Oklahoma City Airport at 2 A.M. He rented a car and took a room at a nearby hotel. He admitted that he may have been a bit rash in taking the flight out, but now that he was here, he was going to make the best of it. He had no clean clothes and no sleepwear. "What the hell." He pulled off his clothes and went to bed nude.

The light streaming through the hotel room window greeted him when he awoke. He sat up in bed and wondered again that he had decided to fly out to Oklahoma without any clothes and without telling anyone that he was coming. He looked at the clock. It wasn't too early, he decided. He walked over to where his pants hung on the chair and pulled his wallet out of the pocket. He sat back on the bed, shuffled through the wallet, and found the number. Jackson weighed the decision. What were the chances he'd be there? It didn't matter. He needed to talk and the Stevens were the closest thing to a real family that he had. He picked up the phone and dialed.

"Stevens' residence," a young male voice answered.

"Hello, this is Jackson Duncan. Is Mr. or Mrs. Stevens around?"

He heard the phone drop and the young voice yell, "Grandma, telephone."

"Hello," a familiar voice said.

Hearing her voice made him feel better. "Hello, Mrs. Stevens. This is Jackson."

"Jackson?" she asked.

"You've forgotten me that quickly? I'm crushed. It's Jackie Duncan."

"Jackie? Is that you, Jackie? How are you doing boy? Where are you calling from?"

She was the only person who called him Jackie. Hearing the enthusiasm in her voice, Jackson was transported back to his college days. "I see you still ask a lot of questions," he said. "I'm doing fine and I'm here in Oklahoma City."

"You're here in Oklahoma City," she repeated. "What are you doing here? Where are you staying? You're welcome to stay with us, you know."

Jackson was relieved she hadn't changed. Her home was still open to him. "I'm at a hotel now, but I'd like to come visit."

"What are you doing in a hotel? You should have stayed with us."

"My flight got in late last night. I didn't want to disturb you."

"You wouldn't have been a bother. George stays up all hours of the night, anyway."

"How is Mr. Stevens, by the way?"

"George is fine. He retired last year. He's been around here worrying me to death, but he's doing fine."

"I can't wait to see you both again. Do you still live in the same place?"

She laughed a rich, full laugh. "You know better than to ask that. Where would we go? All our kids grew up here, and now the grandkids. This is home for the rest of our days. Now, when are you going to get over here?"

"I should be there in the next couple of hours. I have a few errands to run first."

"Take your time. We're not going anywhere."

The shopping took longer than he'd expected, and he arrived at the Stevenses' an hour later than planned.

"We were beginning to wonder if you'd gotten lost," Mr. Stevens said, after he and Mrs. Stevens had given Jackson big hugs.

"I had no problem at all getting here. It

was like being on automatic pilot. I got in the car and it brought me here."

"It sure is good to see you again, son," Mr. Stevens said. "Reggie told us that he saw you when he was in Atlanta. How long have you been there?"

"Almost eight months," Jackson answered. *But it felt like a lifetime.* "My job transferred me there."

"How do you like it?" Mrs. Stevens asked. "I've never been to Atlanta. Always wanted to go, but I never got around to it."

A month ago he would have given an enthusiastic, "I love it," but now . . . "It's a good city. It grows on you."

"Reggie liked it, too. He was dropping hints about moving there for a while," Mr. Stevens said.

Jackson knew the reason for that. "Is Reggie around this weekend?" he asked cautiously.

Mrs. Stevens shook her head. "He's out of town today, but he'll be back tomorrow. I hope you get to see him."

"Me, too," Jackson lied. Reggie was the last person he wanted to see. "How's William? Reggie told me married life was treating him well."

"He and the wife and kids are fine," Mrs. Stevens said. "They're out of town this weekend, though, and won't be back until Wednesday."

"I hate that I won't get to see them."

"Their oldest answered the phone when you called. He left about a half-hour ago to spend the weekend with one of his friends," Mrs. Stevens said.

"You missed out all the way 'round," Mr. Stevens added.

Jackson looked from Mr. Stevens to Mrs. Stevens. He was glad they were still the same happy family. "I didn't miss out at all. I have the two of you to myself this weekend."

Mr. and Mrs. Stevens laughed, and then Mrs. Stevens stood up. "Do you still have a good appetite, Jackie?"

Jackson smiled and patted his stomach.

"Good. Let me go see what I can rustle up for you."

Jackson stood in the garage of the Stevenses' home with Mr. Stevens. He watched from a seat on the workbench as Mr. Stevens tinkered with his lawn mower.

"What really brings you out here, Jackson?" Mr. Stevens asked casually.

Jackson stood up at that question and walked the length of the garage. He didn't know how to get started. "You don't buy that I'm just in the area?"

Mr. Stevens looked up and Jackson saw the concern in his eyes. "I have three boys of my own. I know when a man needs to talk."

Jackson sat back down and clasped his hands in front of him. "I don't even know where to start, Mr. Stevens."

Mr. Stevens stopped working on the lawnmower and sat next to Jackson. "It helps to start at the beginning."

When Jackson didn't say anything, Mr. Stevens added, "You can start with her name."

Jackson looked up at him. "How did you know it was a woman?"

Mr. Stevens's eyes gleamed. "I might be old, Jackson, but I'm not dead."

Jackson gave a half smile at that, then looked back at his hands. "Christina." From Mr. Stevens's response, or lack thereof, Jackson assumed that Reggie hadn't mentioned Christina before.

Giving him more help, Mr. Stevens asked, "Do you love her?"

"Very much." There was no doubt in Jackson's mind about his feelings for her.

"Does she love you?"

Jackson raised his head and looked straight ahead. He shrugged. "I really don't know.

She did. Now, I'm not so sure."

"Did something happen?"

Jackson stood up again. "A lot happened."

"Just start at the beginning," Mr. Stevens coaxed.

"She's my boss," Jackson explained. "I work for her. We both knew it was risky to start something, but we were attracted to each other. We fought it as long as we could." Jackson thought about his early advances and Christina's rejections. He wondered now if it would have been better for both of them if he'd left her alone. He had thought that he couldn't live without her. Now he wondered if he could live after losing her.

"That's understandable, Jackson. Emotions don't know positions."

Jackson was so lost in his thoughts, he'd almost forgotten Mr. Stevens. "She's the first woman I've ever loved. I thought we could get past any problems our professional relationship might cause. We did, at first." I couldn't handle it though, he added silently.

"What happened to change that?"

Jackson knew that question was coming. "Me. I changed. I thought I could handle her being the boss. At first I could, I really could. If we disagreed and she overruled me, it wasn't a problem. We were colleagues working together. I could handle it."

"What happened?"

"Liza happened," Jackson said. He couldn't handle Christina choosing Liza's opinion over his.

"Who's Liza?"

Jackson looked back at Mr. Stevens. The concern and love in his eyes were comforting. "Liza works with us. She and I report directly to Christina. Initially, Christina and I decided everything together. Now, there are three of us who have to work together." Jackson began to pace. "I thought I could handle it. I had no idea I would feel this way."

"Hold on there, Jackson. I think you're leaving something out. What couldn't you handle?"

Jackson stopped pacing. "I couldn't handle Christina choosing Liza's opinion over mine." Jackson shook his head. "If anyone had told me this would happen to me, I would have laughed. I thought I was a bigger man than this."

"Doesn't have anything to do with how big a man you are," Mr. Stevens said. "It's about feelings. Did you talk to Christina about it?"

Jackson shook his head again. "I couldn't.

I knew that what I was feeling was irrational. How could I explain it to her?" Jackson didn't wait for a response. He knew the answer; he couldn't explain it to her. "Christina is a smart woman. She has her life together. She really doesn't need me. I knew that from the beginning, but I also knew she loved me and respected me. That was enough for us. When her decisions started falling with Liza's opinions instead of mine, I began to wonder if she still respected me. And if she didn't respect me, I began to wonder if she would soon stop loving me. The more she agreed with Liza, the greater my insecurities became."

"Is that why you don't think she loves you now?" Mr. Stevens asked.

"That's part of it, probably the smaller part," Jackson answered. "I mentioned my feelings to her once and she said, as I knew she would, that it wasn't personal. She was making what she thought were the best decisions for the company."

"And that made you feel worse," Mr. Stevens finished for him.

"That's right," Jackson said, glad somebody understood what he'd been feeling. "Finally, I told her I needed space. Our relationship was strained, but we were going on as if nothing was wrong. I had to do something."

"You decided to leave her before she could leave you," Mr. Stevens concluded wisely.

Jackson jerked his gaze to Mr. Stevens. "That wasn't my intention. At least, not my conscious intention. But that's exactly what Christina thought. I tried to tell her that I still loved her, but she didn't buy it."

"Can you blame her?"

Jackson lowered his eyelids. "What do you mean by that?"

"Think about it. She knows something's wrong. You won't talk about it and then you want to leave. What did you expect her to think? It probably didn't look like a man in love to her."

He looked up again. "I do love her. I even asked her to marry me."

Mr. Stevens held up both hands. "Hold on a minute here. You asked her to marry you?"

Jackson nodded.

"What did she say?"

Jackson gave a hollow laugh. "She said it was too soon. She said she loved me and wanted to marry me, but she needed more time."

"How did you feel about that?"

"I was disappointed, of course. And hurt."

And he still hurt. "But I understood her reasons."

"Are you sure you understood her, or did you just let it go?"

Jackson didn't answer immediately. He had tried to understand Christina's reasons. He wanted to understand them. He told himself that he did. A part of him knew her childhood scars were the cause of her fears and cautiousness. Yet another part of him wanted her love for him to be stronger than all that. "Maybe I just left it alone."

"Why do you think you did that?"

Jackson knew why. "Because I was hurt. And I was afraid. What if she really didn't love me? That's why I'm here, Mr. Stevens. I have to figure out how to handle my feelings, my fears."

"That's where you're wrong, Jackson," Mr. Stevens said. "Your feelings aren't your problem, your refusal to share those feelings with Christina is the problem. I've been married for forty-two years, and I'll tell you this, talking about it might cause a problem, but not talking about it causes even greater problems."

Jackson didn't respond immediately. "It did lead to bigger problems."

"Always does, my boy, always does."

Jackson thought Mr. Stevens was getting

carried away. "Now she thinks I've been sending her red roses with offending cards."

"Why would she think that?"

Jackson told Mr. Stevens the story of the roses and how Christina thought that he sent them.

"Whew, you do have yourself in a pickle," Mr. Steven said. "That's what happens when you don't talk about things. One person starts wondering what the other is thinking and drawing conclusions from everything. Things that aren't even related."

Jackson nodded. "You're right about that. How could she even think I sent those roses? I'm in love with her."

"That's what you say, Jackson, but that's not what you've been showing her lately. All she's seen lately is your discontentment, your silence, and then your decision to leave. I'm not saying that she's making rational decisions, but she's using what you give her."

"I wish I knew who was sending those damn roses," Jackson said. He started to pace again.

"I wish you did, too," Mr. Stevens said.

Christina was exhausted when she reached her mother's house. She pulled into the driveway and sat there a few minutes trying to get herself together. She couldn't understand how or why Jackson had betrayed her as he had. When the front porch lights flicked on, Christina gathered her belongings and headed for the house.

"How long had you been sitting out there?" her mother asked, after Christina had put her bags down and sat on the bed in the guest bedroom.

"Only a few minutes, Mom," Christina answered. "I'm so tired."

"It's late. Do you want to go to bed now, or do you want to talk?"

Christina thought about that. "The truth, Mom? Right now, I could use a hug."

Louise sat next to her daughter and opened her arms. Christina leaned into them and her tears began again. She let them flow freely as she rested in the protectiveness of her mother's embrace.

When the tears finally stopped, Christina remained in her mother's arms. "It's over, Mom," she said slowly. "Jackson and I are finished."

Louise brushed her daughter's hair with her hands. "What makes you say that?"

"He said that he needed space."

"That doesn't mean it's over. It means he needs space."

Christina tightened her embrace on her

mother. "That's not all, Mom. Do you remember the roses I was getting a while back?"

"Yes, I remember. I thought those had stopped."

"So did I." Christina paused to get her breath. She was choking up again. "Well, I got two dozen today. One at work with a card that said *'Bitch,'* and another at home with a card that read *'Whore.'* "

Louise's hold on Christina tightened. "Oh, no, darling. Have you reported this to the police?"

"I don't need to report it to the police. I know who sent them."

"Christina, you can't possibly think . . ."

"Jackson sent them, Mom," Christina interrupted. "That's the only explanation."

"Could you be jumping to conclusions? What makes you think it was him?"

She explained the incidents to her mother as she had explained them to Jackson.

"Those could be coincidences," Louise said. "There's no real evidence implicating Jackson."

"Looks like evidence to me," Christina corrected. "Anyway, he didn't deny it."

"You accused him of sending the roses?" Louise asked. Her tone expressed her surprise.

At that tone, Christina became wary. Maybe she had gone too far with Jackson. "I didn't exactly accuse him. I merely laid the information out to him and asked him to explain it."

"And what did he say?"

She'd never forget the scene or the look in his eyes. "He didn't say much. He actually had the nerve to look affronted, like I was in the wrong. That man is a good actor."

"Either that, or he's innocent."

Christina pulled back to look at her mother. "You can't seriously believe that he's innocent, Mother. Have you heard a word I've said?"

"I heard you, Christina. I heard you loud and clear."

"Then how can you say he could be innocent?"

"I'm not saying whether he's innocent or not. That's your call to make, but do you think you've given him enough room to explain himself?"

"Why should I do that? So he can tell me more lies? What do I owe him?"

"You don't owe him anything. This isn't about Jackson. This is about you and what you owe yourself. A few days ago you were in love with this man. You were thinking marriage. Now you're ready to believe him guilty of the vilest of acts without even really discussing it with him. You owe yourself more than that."

Christina was beginning to get uncomfortable with this conversation. Why was her mother saying that she had been hasty? "I did discuss it with him, Mother. I told you, he didn't deny it."

"It's your decision, Christina."

Christina was silent for a while. She pulled away to sit next to her mother. "I hate it when you do that."

"Do what?" Louise asked.

"Back down like that. You know you're not really backing down and I know you're not really backing down. Why don't you just say what you mean?"

"I have said what I meant. You don't like it and now you want me to change it. I can't. You haven't said anything here tonight that makes me believe Jackson sent you those roses."

Christina stood up then. "So you think I'm overreacting?"

"No, not overreacting. Maybe reacting to the wrong thing."

"And what do you mean by that?"

"I wonder how you'd be feeling now if Jackson hadn't said he needed space."

Christina didn't say anything immediately.

"That wouldn't have changed the facts."

"No," Louise agreed, "it wouldn't have, but it might have changed your interpretation of those facts."

When Christina didn't respond, Louise said, "We've had enough talk for tonight. You need to get some rest. A good night's sleep will do you good. We can talk about this tomorrow, if you like." Louise kissed her daughter on the forehead and left the room.

Christina watched as Louise walked away. She didn't understand her mother's reaction. Why was she taking sides with Jackson? Well, it doesn't matter, Christina thought. I'm not going to give Jackson another chance to hurt me. He did send the roses. I'm sure of it.

Christina was up early the next morning. She hadn't slept well. Her mother's questions had caused her considerable unrest. Had she been too hasty in her decision? Did Jackson deserve a chance to explain? No, she thought, she had given him a chance. Jackson wanted space; well, he'd gotten space.

"Up early, aren't you, Christina," Louise asked, still dressed in her gown and housecoat.

"I didn't sleep very well," Christina said.

"Thinking a lot, huh? Did you come to any conclusions?"

Christina shook her head. "No conclusions, really. Even if Jackson didn't send the roses, it's still over. He doesn't want to be with me anymore. He said so."

"That's not what he said," Louise corrected.

"He needs space. I think that's a euphemism for 'I need to get out of this relationship.' "

"I think you're reading more into it than necessary. Why didn't you ask him what he meant?"

Christina got up and poured herself another cup of tea. "We had practically stopped talking, Mother. He wasn't sharing his thoughts."

"When did this start?"

Christina shrugged. Maybe it was there from the beginning. Maybe it was never as good between her and Jackson as she'd wanted to believe. "I don't know exactly when it started. It's been the last month or so. It all happened so suddenly. Our relationship was going great, then it hit bottom. I don't understand it."

"That sounds strange. You have no idea what happened?"

Christina shook her head. "He went from asking me to marry him to accusing me of siding with Liza at work. That was ridiculous. I told him I wasn't siding with anybody."

"What did he say to that?"

Christina searched her memory. "I don't remember him saying anything."

"Maybe that's where your problem is, Christina," Louise reasoned.

Christina was not ready for her mother to analyze her problems. "Jackson and I are articulate adults, Mom. He's had more than enough time and opportunity to speak with me if he had a problem. Why should I go looking for a needle in a haystack? If he can't talk to me, it wasn't much of a relationship in the first place."

CHAPTER 19

Jackson was sitting on the top step of the Stevenses' front porch when Reggie came up the walk.

Reggie stopped in front of him, his legs apart, his arms crossed. "I'm surprised to see you here."

"Not as surprised as I am to be here," Jackson said. His apprehensions about this meeting with Reggie were proving well founded.

"We may as well get this out of the way," Reggie began. "How's Christina?"

Jackson didn't want to talk to Reggie about Christina. It was obvious Reggie still had feelings for her. "Christina's fine."

"That's not a very enthusiastic answer. Is something wrong?"

Jackson raised a brow in his direction. "Nothing's wrong."

Reggie dropped his arms. "So how is she? Why didn't she come out here with you?"

"You're overly concerned with Christina, aren't you?"

"You know that I had a thing for her, Jackson. That's no secret."

Jackson leaned back on his elbows and stretched out his legs. "And you know that now she has a thing for me."

"That what you say, but you're here and she's still in Atlanta. Maybe things have changed."

"And if they have?"

"Well, if she's not seeing you anymore, maybe she'll see me again."

"So you'd move in on my woman like that?" Jackson asked. He knew Reggie would do just that, given the chance. There were no rules when it came to women.

"I don't remember your holding back when I was in the picture," Reggie minded him. "As I see it, what goes around comes around."

Jackson knew Reggie was right. He pursued Christina even after he'd realized Reggie was in her life. From Jackson's viewpoint, though, Christina was his before she was Reggie's anyway. "I'm not going to argue about this, Reggie," he said. "Just know that I'm in love with Christina and she's in love with me."

"If you say so, man," Reggie replied, but

Jackson saw the challenge in his eyes.

The ringing telephone greeted Christina when she entered her house Sunday night. "Reggie," she said. "I'm glad to hear from you." She sat and cradled the phone in her arm. She had been tempted to call him, but she didn't want to hurt him any more than she already had.

"I've been thinking about you a lot," he said. "I wanted to apologize for our last conversation. I didn't handle what you had to say very well."

"There's no need for apologies. I'm glad to hear from you again. I'd hate to think we couldn't be friends."

"Oh, no, the dreaded friends," he said. "I guess Jackson was right. You're still in love with him."

Christina sat up straighter in her chair. "Jackson? When did you talk to Jackson?"

"I saw him this weekend."

Christina didn't understand. "You were in Atlanta?"

"No," Reggie said. "Jackson was here in Oklahoma City."

Christina slumped back in the chair. "Jackson was in Oklahoma City? What was he doing out there?"

"Your guess is as good as mine. I walked

into my parents' house this afternoon and there he was."

She wondered what Jackson was doing out there. "He thinks highly of your parents."

"Well, he had them all to himself for two whole days. My mom can't stop talking about him. Dad, either. They had a good time with him."

"I'm glad he got to see them," was all Christina could say.

"It's none of my business, Christina, but are things between you and Jackson okay?"

"Things aren't as good as I'd like them to be," Christina said, hedging. She didn't know what Jackson had told them.

"Do you want to talk about it?"

Christina considered that offer. "I don't think it would be such a good idea."

"Maybe you're right," Reggie admitted. "I wouldn't be an unbiased listener. I still care a lot about you."

Christina wished she loved Reggie, but she didn't. She was still in love with Jackson. There was no future for them, but she loved him. "I know you do, Reggie, and I don't want to hurt you again."

"I'm a big boy," Reggie reminded her.

Christina didn't want to argue, so she changed the subject. "What's going on with you?" When Reggie didn't answer immediately, she thought he might not make this easy for her. When he said, "Nothing much," she breathed a relieved sigh, glad they could have friendly conversation.

Christina arrived at the office at her regular time Monday. A part of her hoped to get roses. If she got them today, she could be sure that Jackson hadn't sent them. He wouldn't be stupid enough to send more. She didn't see any roses on Penny's desk. Maybe they're on my desk, she thought. She opened the door to her office cautiously and looked around the room. No roses anywhere. She walked to her desk and sat down. Who's sending those damn roses? she asked herself. If not Jackson, then who?

She looked up when there was a knock on the door. Jackson stood in the open doorway. "It's open," she said. "You didn't have to knock."

He walked in. "I didn't know if I was welcome."

"You know I have an open-door policy. Every CL employee is welcome."

"That the way it is, then?" he asked.

"This is a place of work, Jackson. We should confine our conversation to work-related topics. Don't you agree?"

"If not here, then where?"

"Where what?"

"Where and when are we going to talk?"

"I did all my talking Friday. You haven't talked in a while. Are you sure we have something more to say to each other?"

"We need to talk, Christina." He walked closer to the desk. "I have something —"

"Excuse me, Christina," Penny interrupted. "Walter's on line 1. He says it's urgent."

Christina stared at Penny. She hadn't heard her come in. "All right, Penny, I'll take it." To Jackson, she said, "We'll have to continue this later."

"You can bet on it," Jackson said. He walked out of the office, closing the door behind him.

Christina picked up the phone. "Walter," she said. "What's so urgent this morning?"

"There's good news and bad news," Walter said. "Which do you want to hear first?"

"Let's try the good news first."

"Rosalind and I are getting married three weeks from Saturday and you're invited to the wedding," Walter said gleefully.

"Congratulations," Christina said. "I'm so happy for you and Rosalind. Give her a big kiss for me." Christina deliberately did not say she'd attend the wedding. It was too soon after her and Jackson.

348

"I'll do that," Walter said. "This is going to be some wedding."

"I bet it will be," was her reply. That was noncommittal enough, she thought.

"Now the bad news. Jackson's promotion has come through and he has to be back in Boston by the end of the week."

"The end of the week? That's too soon," she said. Too soon for me to let him go.

"I'm sorry, but there's no other way. You knew this was coming. Have you looked over any of the résumés we've sent you? You're going to have to pick a replacement."

"I haven't even started looking at résumés. I thought Jackson would be around until the demo was done. You can't do this now."

"It's done, Christina," Walter said. "You'd better get started on that replacement because if Jackson wants this job, he has to be in Boston by Friday. Now, who's going to tell him, me or you?"

It was all happening too fast. "You tell him."

"Who knows, Christina, maybe he'll turn down the job and stay in Atlanta."

"Be serious. You know as well as I do that Jackson is going to take the assignment."

"Yes, I do think he's going to take it, but I'm sure he'll talk with you about it. Anything else we need to discuss while I have

349

you on the phone?"

"No, I can't think of anything."

"Okay, I'll talk with you later in the week. And don't forget the replacement."

Christina hung up the phone. Everything was falling in place for them to be apart. He wanted space. Well, there was definitely a lot of space between Boston and Atlanta. One week. Less than a week and he would be gone.

She stood and looked out the window. She could see his apartment building from her office. She remembered the first time she'd been in his apartment. Everything. The dinner he'd prepared and the dessert they'd shared. It was only one of the memories that bombarded her thoughts this morning. She wanted to hold on to every one of those memories because she knew there would be no others for her and Jackson. And that made her sad, very sad.

Jackson stood in the door of Christina's office later that day. He was glad Penny wasn't at her desk. This gave him time to study the woman he loved. He never figured he'd fall in love so deeply and so quickly. He smiled as he remembered the first morning he'd seen her. That seemed ages ago, but it was only eight months, less than a year. She'd gotten to him when no other woman could. She found a place in his heart that he hadn't even known existed. As he looked at her now, he knew he'd always love her.

Then why, he asked himself, are you leaving her? Jackson had been surprised at his own reaction to Walter's news. He'd wanted this promotion for a long time. His joy at hearing the news was dampened by the knowledge that it would mean leaving Christina. If their relationship was going well, it would have been hard to leave her, but they could have worked at a long distance relationship. Since it wasn't going well, he knew this would be the end for them. He had asked for space and he'd gotten space. Be careful what you wish for, he reminded himself.

Christina looked up when he cleared his throat. Her face didn't hold the smile it usually held for him, and that made him sad. "I just talked to Walter."

She stood. "Congratulations. I know how much this means to you, and I wish you the best."

"Thanks," he said. "I'm sorry I have to leave so quickly. I know you'll be short-handed." *I feel like I'll be leaving a part of myself.*

"I knew this day was coming. I just didn't

think it would be this soon. We're really going to miss you around here."

"I'm going to miss you, too." He saw by the way her eyes widened that she understood he meant it personally.

"Do you think we should announce it at the staff meeting today?" she asked.

"We need to tell Liza before then. You and she are going to have your hands full until you get a replacement, but I'm sure you'll handle it."

"I know we'll do it, but we'll miss you. You added a lot to this project. Where we are with OPTIMA now is largely due to the work that you did when you first came on board. Even before Liza got here."

He knew that, but it was good to hear her say it. He wondered how often she'd have to say it before he believed she meant it. "Thanks. That means a lot to me."

"It's true, and I know Liza feels the same way. When do you think you'll be leaving?"

"Walter wants me to report Friday, so I need to leave Thursday night." He paused. They were talking about work, not daring to discuss the personal issues between them. What cowards they were. "You, Liza, and I will need to plan some type of transition."

"This is going to be near impossible. You know that, don't you?"

And not just the work. It was going to be impossible to leave her. "I'll do what I can to make it easy. I'll make myself available after I'm back in Boston. Do you have anybody in mind to replace me?"

"I haven't thought about that, Jackson. To be honest, I haven't wanted to think about it."

He was glad for that. "I'm going to clean out the apartment soon, too. What do you want me to do about your belongings?"

She didn't even blink. They could have been discussing the weather. "I can pick them up over the weekend while you're away, if that's okay. I'll leave your key on the counter."

He was disappointed they were discussing this so unemotionally. Didn't their love deserve more? "That's fine. When can I pick up my stuff from your place? I no longer have a key."

Christina took the hit. She remembered asking him to return the key. "I'll be in every night this week, so you can come over anytime."

"I'd like to take you to dinner before I leave," he said. He needed her to agree to dinner, at least.

"I don't know if that's such a good idea, Jackson."

He couldn't let it end like this. "Christina, we've shared too much, been too close for me to just leave. There's still a lot we need to talk about. I'm still in love with you."

"Don't say that, Jackson," Christina pleaded. She was determined to make it through this with her dignity intact. It was all she had. "You wanted space and you're getting it."

"I know, but I don't want us to be over. Not yet. Not like this."

She wanted to believe him, but too much had happened. "So, you don't need space?"

"Yes, but I need to know that you'll be there for me. I don't want this to be the end."

"That's not fair, Jackson. You want your space to think, but you want me to wait for you. What am I supposed to be doing while I'm waiting?"

He wanted her to continue doing what she was doing, but he didn't want her to see other people. This made no sense, even to him, but it was how he felt. And he couldn't tell her. She'd really think he'd lost his mind.

"I don't know, Christina. I just don't want to lose you."

"You didn't lose me, Jackson," she said,

close to tears. "You threw me back."

Jackson came over Wednesday night. He had called, so Christina expected him. She had most of his stuff packed.

"Thanks," he said. "You didn't have to do that."

She knew it was easier than watching him do it. "It was nothing."

"I . . ." Jackson began.

"Let's not make this any harder than it has to be. We have some problems that we can't work out long distance. Let's just call it quits and leave it at that."

"Is it that easy for you, Christina?" Jackson asked.

"It's not easy, Jackson, but it's easier than you want it to be."

"We need to talk," he said.

She shook her head. "We needed to talk last week. So much has changed since then. Talking is not going to change anything."

"Don't you want to give it another chance?"

More than anything she wanted to try again, but she didn't have the courage to say it. "What's the use, Jackson? You're leaving, I'm staying."

"That's the way you want it?"

No. "That's the way I want it."

He looked at her for a long while. Then he moved as if to come closer, but changed his mind. "Goodbye, Christina," he said and left.

"Goodbye, Jackson," Christina said. When she heard the door close behind him, she added, "I still love you, too."

"We're glad to have you back, Jackson," Rosalind said, directing him to a chair in front of his desk.

"It's good to be back, I think," Jackson said. It was his second week in Boston.

She sat down after he was seated. "Are you having any problems getting settled?"

"No, the work is fine."

"What's the problem, then? I expected you to be happy in your new job."

"I am happy, but not as happy as I thought I'd be. This is all I've wanted for the last three years. I've got it and I'm on my way, but it feels hollow." He shrugged. "Maybe my expectations were too high."

"Or maybe you've found that work is not enough."

He studied her. "You know about me and Christina, don't you?"

She nodded. "Christina and I talked the weekend of Liza's wedding. Are you two not adjusting well to the separation?"

"Not exactly. We decided to end the relationship."

"Why would you do that? You wouldn't be the first couple in a long distance relationship."

"There were other reasons and she . . . we thought it was best to end it."

"What do you think now?"

"I miss her. I miss her a lot. I miss working with her. I miss being with her."

"Have you told her this?"

He couldn't count the number of times he'd picked up the phone to do just that. "No, I haven't told her, and I can't tell her. She wants something I can't give her right now."

"Well, Jackson, you've got some decisions to make. I'd advise you to make them quickly. Christina is not going to wait forever."

"What makes you think she's waiting now?"

Rosalind smiled like she had a secret. "Remind me one day to tell you the story of a woman who waited twenty-five years for a man."

Jackson saw Robert and Liza first. "Hey, you two, how's it going?"

"No complaints, man, no complaints,"

Robert answered.

Jackson let his gaze roam the ballroom. "This wedding was almost as nice as yours."

"Almost," Liza said, and smiled at Robert.

"It's one thing to watch and another thing to be in it. That was the most special day of my life," Robert said. He put an arm around Liza's waist and pulled her to him. "We're an old married couple now."

Liza pushed against him. "Hardly. We're still on our honeymoon."

Jackson watched them. They were as in love today as they'd been the first time he'd met them, as they were on their wedding day. He used to wonder if he and Christina would be as good a couple as they were. Thinking about her, he asked, "Did Christina come?"

Liza looked at Robert before answering. "No, she decided not to come."

Jackson voice registered his concern. "Is she sick or something?"

Liza placed her hand on his. "She's fine, Jackson. She just didn't feel up to a wedding right now. She sent her love to Rosalind and Walter, though."

Jackson understood. Christina didn't attend because she didn't want to see him. She was really trying to get him out of her system. "She's okay?" he asked again to be sure.

"She's fine," Liza reassured him.

CHAPTER 20

Christina sat on the examination table in Dr. Johnson's office. "I feel tired all the time and it's getting worse each day," she said. She'd dismissed her fatigue as depression at first, but when it had gotten progressively worse, she'd become concerned.

"Any other problems?" Doctor Johnson asked.

"None that I can think of. Maybe I need vitamins or iron tablets."

He flipped open her chart, and scanned it, then closed it. "Before I prescribe anything, I'm going to take some blood and do a physical. It's about time for one anyway. How does that sound?"

"Right, now Doctor, I'd go for anything that was going to make me feel better."

"Give us a little time, Christina, and we'll figure out what's wrong."

Three days later, Christina got a call from Dr. Johnson. "I may have found the reason for your fatigue, Christina. Are you sitting down?"

My God, Christina thought, I must be dying. "Is it serious, Doctor?"

"Not exactly. You're pregnant, Christina."

Christina thought she had misheard him. "What did you say?"

"You're pregnant. I don't know how far along you are, you'll need to see your gynecologist."

"Pregnant? You must be joking, Doctor. How can I be pregnant?"

Dr. Johnson laughed. "You don't really need me to answer that, do you?"

She was pregnant. It must be a joke, a cruel joke. She and Jackson had been so careful. "Oh, no. I know how other people get pregnant, but how could it happen to me?"

"The same way, I'd say."

"That's not what I mean, Dr. Johnson. I wasn't planning to have a baby. Not yet, anyway."

"I thought you'd be happy about this, Christina."

Christina wondered if he was crazy. "Doctor, I'm a single woman with no marriage prospects. What makes you think I'd be happy about this pregnancy?"

"Every day single women are making

choices to have babies. You're financially and emotionally capable of raising a child. It's conceivable that you'd be happy about it. Surprised, maybe, but happy."

"A word of advice, Doctor. The next time you tell a single woman that she's pregnant, try to tone it down a little." She hung up. The doctor was right about one thing. She was definitely surprised.

Pregnant. Christina couldn't believe it. She was pregnant. She touched her hand to her abdomen. A baby is growing in there, she thought. Jackson's baby. She took her hand away. What am I going to do?

"How about a movie?" Liza asked. "Robert is out doing some male-bonding so I'm free to do some male-bashing. Are you game?"

Christina gave a wry laugh. Male-bashing. She could really get into that now. "I'm not up for it tonight, Liza."

"Tired?"

"More tired than I've ever been," Christina said morosely. She was seated on the bed with the phone propped between her shoulder and her ear.

"What's wrong, Christina?"

I need to talk about this. "I'm pregnant, Liza."

"What? You're kidding."

"I wish I were. I found out today. I'm pregnant."

"Do you want some company?"

Very much. "Thanks, Liza, I could use a friend right now."

Forty-five minutes later, Liza sat in Christina's kitchen.

"How do you feel about it?" Liza asked.

"I don't know. I certainly don't feel pregnant."

Liza didn't comment.

"I feel stupid. How could I let myself get pregnant? I'm a grown woman, Liza, an intelligent woman. I swore I'd never end up in this situation. How could I let this happen?"

"What did happen, Christina? Did you and Jackson get careless?"

Christina shook her head. "I was faithful with the birth control pills. Before that, Jackson faithfully used condoms."

"That may be it."

"What?"

"Did Jackson always use a condom even after you started taking birth control pills?"

Christina shook her head. "Most of the time, but not all of the time." She paused, then added, "But I faithfully took the birth control pills."

"Unfortunately, they aren't one hundred

363

percent effective."

Christina lifted a brow. "I remember telling you that once before."

"I remember, too. Too bad we didn't know Betty then."

"What does Betty have to do with this?"

"She was taking birth control pills when she got pregnant with her youngest, Anne. Now she jokes that even though she's still on the pill, Ellis can't come near her without a condom."

Christina knew Liza and Betty got along, but she didn't know they were as close as this conversation indicated. "You and Betty have been talking about birth control?"

Liza nodded. "You know Betty. She has an opinion on everything. When I told her that Robert and I didn't plan to have children anytime soon, she shared the Anne story with me. Needless to say, the condom is now Robert's constant companion."

Christina smirked. "One of you could have clued me in."

Liza lifted her shoulders and let them drop slowly. "It happens less than point-three-percent of the time. I just figured it would be my luck to be one of the point-three."

"Well, it seems I made it into that lucky group." Christina smiled. "I have an idea for one of Angela's shows. Women who got pregnant while taking the pill."

Liza laughed. "Probably put a scare into the whole female population."

Christina laughed, too. "I'm glad you came over, Liza. I was getting depressed about this. You're helping me feel better."

"Have you decided what you're going to do?" Liza asked.

"Not really. I'm only beginning to believe I'm really pregnant. I've been thinking that maybe the blood tests got mixed up, maybe it's a tumor." She laughed again. "Maybe this is *Dallas* and it's all a dream."

Liza didn't laugh. "I know the feeling."

Christina looked around, surprised. "You've been pregnant before?"

Liza turned away. "Once."

"I didn't know. What did you do, Liza?" There were only three options — adoption, abortion, or miscarriage.

"Abortion," Liza said quickly.

"I never knew," Christina said.

"No one knew. Not my parents. Not the guy. Nobody."

Christina could see the memory was painful for her friend. She was sorry to have caused her to think about it. "You went through it by yourself?"

"I had to. There was nobody to go through

it with me."

"Why didn't you tell the guy?"

"He didn't love me and I didn't love him. It happened at a bad time in my life."

At the sadness in Liza's voice, Christina walked over and put her arms around her. "I'm sorry, Liza."

Liza's eyes filled with tears. "Don't be. I knew what I was doing. It was a painful time in my life."

Neither woman said anything for a few long minutes.

"Abortion actually crossed my mind," Christina said softly.

Liza looked at her then, "You can't be serious."

Christina nodded. "It seemed the easiest way. You know how I felt about becoming an unwed mother."

"But you decided against it?"

"Yes. It was only a passing thought. I really want children, Liza. I just wanted a husband to go with them."

"I want them, too," Liza said. "I just didn't want one then, and I don't want one now. That's why Robert and I use birth control. Now, about the husband. When are you going to tell Jackson?"

Christina looked away.

"You *are* going to tell him, aren't you,

Christina?"

"I haven't decided yet."

"What do you mean, you haven't decided? You *have* to tell him. It's his baby."

Christina shrugged.

"It is his baby, isn't it, Christina?" Liza asked.

Christina let out a deep breath. "Of course it's his baby."

"Then you have to tell him."

Christina had been debating this with herself. Jackson deserved to know, but she didn't want him back just because of the baby. There had to be more than that. "Why should I. You didn't."

"That was different. You and Jackson are in love. He deserves to know, regardless of the problems you're having now."

Christina wrapped her arms around herself. She wasn't sure of Jackson's feelings for her. "I'm not sure Jackson would think this is good news. If he felt crowded when it was just me, how's he going to feel about a baby?"

"I can't answer that, Christina, but you have to tell him. What if he wants to be a father? Don't you want your baby to know its father?"

Christina flinched. That hit a nerve. More than anything she wanted her baby to have a mother and a father. She hadn't planned this pregnancy, but she was going to handle it the best way she could. "Liza, I want my baby to grow up in a happy home, but I can't use this baby to force Jackson back to me. He wouldn't be happy with that, and neither would I."

"So you're planning to raise this baby alone? Without a father?"

Unwed motherhood would not have been her choice, but this was the hand she was dealt and she was going to play it. "My mom didn't do too bad a job with me, did she?"

"You can answer that better than I can, Christina. Do you want your baby to have the kind of childhood you did? Can you keep your baby away from its father? Your mother didn't have an option, your father was dead. Jackson is very much alive."

Christina knew she couldn't risk Jackson rejecting her or the baby. It would hurt too badly. "What if he doesn't want this baby, Liza? What if he doesn't want me?"

"I believe he'll want you and the baby."

"I'm not so sure about that. I'm not sure I want him."

"Come on, Christina," Liza pleaded. "You're still in love with Jackson. Even if you aren't, you can't keep your pregnancy a secret. He's bound to find out."

A plan began to form in Christina's mind. "Don't be so sure about that, Liza."

"What are you thinking, Christina?"

"I can't tell you now, Liza, but you have to promise not to tell anybody about my pregnancy." She paused, "Not even Robert."

"That's not fair. I don't like keeping secrets from Robert. Especially something like this."

"It's really not his business, Liza. Besides, he might feel obliged to tell Jackson."

When Liza didn't respond, Christina added, "I need your help on this, Liza. Promise me you'll help."

Walter slammed his fist on her desk. He had come down to Atlanta. "It's out of the question."

Christina forced herself to remain calm. A calm head would get her what she wanted. "It can work, Walter. I know it can."

Walter began to pace the room. "You want to take a year's leave of absence and you say it can work." Walter stopped, looked at her and shook his head. "Have you lost your mind?"

She thought Walter was going too far, but she was not going to lose her temper. "It will work. Tom Haydn has fully assumed

Jackson's duties and he's doing a great job. Liza can take over my responsibilities. She's due for a promotion, anyway. We both knew we'd have to replace her."

"Not this soon, Christina."

"Now's a good time. The major OPTIMA milestones have been met. The demo was a success and the first office application site selection is complete. Now's the perfect time for a change."

Walter sat in the chair across from her desk and began tapping his pencil on the desktop. Christina knew he was trying to think of more reasons for her not to leave. She also knew he was having a difficult time.

"What about your career?" he asked. "What will taking a leave of absence do to your career?"

She wasn't surprised. She knew Walter would end up here when nothing else worked. "You tell me, Walter. What will happen?"

He started slowly. "All you've done here will be forgotten. You'll have to build everything again. People will wonder if you're dedicated. They'll wonder how important CL's work is to you. It will be hard to get back to where you are now."

Christina knew Walter had spoken honestly. "Do you think I could do it, Walter?

Do you think I could get back to where I am now?"

Walter looked away from her and she knew she had won. "It'll take time, but you could do it," he answered. He paused. "What do you want, Christina? Sometimes I get the feeling Rosalind and I want the vice presidency for you more than you want it for yourself."

"I've been asking myself that same question. I can't give you any answers now. I love my work, but beyond that I don't know. Maybe the time off will help me focus and decide what I want to do."

"There's nothing that I can do to get you to change your mind, is there?"

Christina shook her head. "No, Walter, I've decided." At his look, she added, "And neither can Rosalind."

"Does your leaving have anything to do with you and Jackson?" Rosalind asked. She and Christina were having lunch.

"Jackson and I are no longer together," Christina answered. She wasn't telling Rosalind any more than she's told Walter.

"I know you think Walter sent me here to convince you to stay, but that's not the reason I'm here."

Christina was skeptical. "Walter didn't

send you here?"

"Walter told me about your conversation," Rosalind explained. "But it was my idea and my choice to come and see you." She reached over to touch Christina's hand. "I'm here as a friend today, not as a colleague."

Christina looked at the hand that covered hers. She wanted to believe Rosalind. "I'm listening," was the best she could do.

"Leaving CL is not going to help you get over him. I know; I've been there."

"I'm not running away from Jackson, Rosalind. Jackson's already gone."

"Can you honestly say that you don't feel anything for him?" Rosalind challenged.

Christina enfolded Rosalind's hand in her own. She knew her friend was trying to keep her from repeating her and Walter's mistakes. "Jackson will always have a place in my heart. He's the first man I've ever loved. A part of me will always love him." And I'll have his baby, she added to herself.

Rosalind was slow to speak, and Christina knew she had given in. "What are you going to do during this leave?"

Christina gave Rosalind's hand a quick squeeze, then pulled away. "I'm going home to spend time with my mother. She'll probably work me to death. She's opening another nursery."

Rosalind smiled. "So you're going from the boardroom to the greenhouse."

Christina laughed lightly. "I guess you could say that. It'll be good for me."

"Do you think you'll come back to CL?"

Christina didn't expect that question. "It's my plan to come back, but I don't know what will happen. Maybe I'll find that I prefer greenhouses to boardrooms."

"So what do you think, Liza?" Christina asked.

"I don't know what to say," Liza said. She stood and looked out of Christina's office window. "I'll have to talk it over with Robert."

"You say that like you think he might object. Do you?"

Liza turned around to face her. "Just the opposite. He'll go crazy with the idea. He's been pressuring me lately to cut back on work."

"The house won't exactly help with that, will it? You can still work long hours."

Liza nodded. "I could, but not living so close to work will help some."

"So what's the problem?"

"I just can't believe you're taking a leave of absence. What about your job?"

Christina lifted her hands. "What about it? It'll be here when I get back. Besides, look how my leave benefits you. You get my job. Haven't you wanted it?"

Liza smiled. "You know I've wanted it. Not your job, but I wanted a promotion. I'm glad about that."

"Then what's the problem?"

Liza shook her head. "I can't believe you're doing this. Not at this point in your career."

"Well, I am. There's more to life than a career. I hope you haven't forgotten that."

"Now you're beginning to sound like Robert. Of course, I haven't forgotten. It's just that I want it all — the career and the family. And right now the career needs most of my energy."

Christina didn't want Liza to sacrifice her relationship with Robert for her job, but she knew she was in no position to give advice. "So when do you want to move in?"

"I like being downtown. It's so convenient to work. I don't know."

"The commute from Christina's house wouldn't be that bad," Robert said. "You need to put some space between you and your work anyway. You overdo it sometimes."

Liza got up from her seat on the balcony and stood next to Robert at the railing. She ran her fingers through his hair. He needed a haircut. "I know I've been working long hours. I appreciate your being a good sport about it."

He caressed her face with his hand. "That doesn't mean I like it, Liza. Will this promotion mean more hours for you?"

Liza thought before answering. She was ambitious and she was willing to work hard for what she wanted. And she wanted Robert, her job, and someday, children. "It doesn't have to."

"What does that mean?"

"It means it's my choice. I can set the pace and the schedule that I want to work."

He dropped his hand from her face. "What are you going to do?"

She thought again. If she was going to have it all, she was going to have to do one hell of a balancing act. But she was determined. "I'm excited about this promotion, Robert, and I want to do a good job. I want to be a vice president at CL one day, the sooner the better. That's going to mean a certain amount of commitment from both of us."

Robert turned away from her. "What

about us? Do we rate as highly as your work?"

She moved so he faced her. "How can you ask that, Robert? Our marriage is much more important to me than the work, but I don't want to have to choose between them. I want both."

"I don't have a problem with that. I just don't want to lose you to your work."

She hugged him to her. "You won't. I'm going to need you to keep me honest, though. We need to have talks like this when you feel that I'm getting out of balance. I love you and I want us to be happy together for the rest of our lives."

She felt the tension ease out of him. "I love you, too, Liza."

They stood holding each other for a long while. Robert broke the silence. "What are we going to do about Christina's offer?"

"We should move out there. You're right. Some distance between me and work would be good."

She felt Robert's arms tighten around her and she relaxed. It was hell being Superwoman.

CHAPTER 21

"Hi, Mom," Christina said into the telephone. "How'd you like to have a houseguest for a few months?"

"Depends on who the guest is," Louise responded. "Are you thinking about taking a vacation?"

"A very long vacation."

"Well, that's hard to believe. I've never known you to take more than a couple of days at a time. What bring this on?"

"I've got some news for you."

"By the tone of your voice, I'd guess it's happy news."

"It is."

"Are you going to tell me now or are you going to make me wait?"

"I'll tell you now. Are you sitting down?"

"No, I'm not sitting down," Louise answered. "Are you sure this is good news?"

Christina laughed. After all her initial misgivings, she was finally feeling good.

Good about the baby. Good about her decision to take a leave of absence. Good about life. "I'm positive it's good news, but you'd better take a seat."

Christina held on while her mother found a chair. "I'm seated now, Christina. Tell me your good news."

"I'm pregnant, Mom. Can you believe it? I'm going to have a baby."

Christina enjoyed being back in Selma. She spent most of her days in the new nursery with her mother. She liked not having to dress for work every day, not having to prepare for meetings, not having to direct employees. She worked in the nursery and she thought about her baby. It was the good life — with one exception: Louise was upset. She was happy about the baby, but she disagreed with Christina's decision not to tell Jackson. For once, Louise wouldn't leave it alone.

"How long are we going to continue like this, Mom?" Christina asked one night after dinner.

Louise didn't pretend not to understand. "Until you come to your sense and tell Jackson about this baby."

"This is *my* decision, Mom," Christina said gently. "I'm doing what I think is best.

Can't you support me in this?"

Louise shook her head. "Not this time. I don't want you to make the same mistakes I did."

Thinking Louise was talking about her pregnancy, Christina explained, "I don't think of it as a mistake anymore, Mom. It's an unplanned but welcome surprise. I wanted a baby and I wanted a husband. At least I'm getting one of them."

"It'll be all my fault," Louise said.

"It's not anyone's fault. I loved Jackson and I got pregnant. Unfortunately, our love ended before we found out about the pregnancy."

"It's a cycle," Louise said. "I have to break this cycle."

Christina didn't know what her mother was talking about. Again, she assumed it was her pregnancy. "You were a great mother to me and I'll be a great mother to this baby. I hope I can be half the mother that you are."

Louise stood up. Christina had no idea what she was mumbling about. "I should have told you the truth. I never should have lied."

As Christina watched her mother, a nervous feeling settled in the pit of her stomach. "What are you talking about, Mother? What should you have told me? What did you lie about?"

"I'm so sorry, Christina," Louise said. She was crying softly now. "I thought I was doing the right thing."

Christina rubbed her hands across her head. "What are you talking about?"

"I hope you don't hate me, Christina. I thought it was the right thing to do."

Christina went to her mother. "Tell me what you're talking about." *Please don't let it be bad. God, please don't let it be bad news.*

"It's your father." Louise looked directly at her daughter. "Your father is alive, Christina."

Christina couldn't believe her ears. Surely she had heard wrong. "Alive?"

Louise didn't look away. "Yes, Christina."

Christina heard a ringing sound in her ears. "Alive? He can't be alive. All these years you told me he was dead."

"It was a lie. All these years I lied."

Christina couldn't stand any longer. She sat down and stared at her mother. "You lied?" she asked softly. "Why did you lie?"

"I had to."

"Alive," Christina repeated. "All these years and my father has been alive. All these years that I've needed him and you told me he was dead. Why did you do that to me,

Mother? Why? Did he not want me? Is that the reason?"

Louise shook her head. "He never knew I was pregnant, Christina. I never told him."

"You never told him," Christina repeated, dazed.

"You can't make the same mistake I did, Christina. You must tell Jackson about this baby."

Christina just stared at her mother. "All these years you were lying. How could you do that to me, Mother? How could you do it? What about all the stories you told about the two of you? Were they lies, too?"

Louise had dreaded this anger, but she understood it and she had known she would see if it Christina ever learned the truth. "No, Christina, they weren't all lies. I loved Christian and he loved me."

"Then why didn't you tell him about me?" Christina demanded.

Louise hoped Christina would understand. "It was the best thing that I could think to do. There was no way Christian and I could be together."

"Then what kept you apart?"

"My parents didn't approve of him. And his parents wouldn't have approved of me."

"Why didn't Big Momma and Big Daddy like him? What did he do?"

Louise saw the confusion on her daughter's face. "It's not what he did, Christina. It's what he was. They liked him, they just didn't approve of our relationship."

"What was he, Mother? An ex-convict?"

"No, he wasn't an ex-convict. He was a law student, like I told you."

"Why don't you just tell me, Mother?"

Louise took her daughter's hand. "Your grandparents didn't approve because Christian was white."

"White? White?"

"Yes, dear. He was, is, white."

"My father is a white man?" Christina's mind felt numb.

Louise nodded. Please God, don't let my daughter hate me, she prayed.

"I don't believe you, Mother. How can that be? I don't look white."

"That's an ignorant thing to say, Christina. There's no doubt about it, Christian is your father, and he's white."

Louise watched Christina absorb this news. She saw pain, disbelief, begrudging acceptance, and then anger cross her daughter's beautiful face. Anger was the emotion that remained.

"If you knew there was no hope for the relationship, Mother, why did you sleep with him?"

"I loved him, Christina. You don't choose the person you fall in love with. You should know that. It just happens."

When Christina didn't speak, Louise continued. "If he'd known I was pregnant, he'd have defied his parents and married me. That's the kind of man he was. I wanted so much for you to know him."

"You had a strange way of showing it," Christina said. "What makes you so sure he would have married you? Maybe he didn't love you. Maybe it was curiosity. You saw *Jungle Fever*."

That stung. That question had haunted Louise over the years. She knew Christian loved her and she believed that he wanted to marry her, but there was still a niggling doubt. "It wasn't like that; he asked me to marry him. He asked me. He asked, and he didn't know about you."

"If you loved him so much, you should have married him."

She's so young, Louise thought. "It wasn't as easy as that. We would have had to give up so much and face so much. It may have killed our love. I couldn't risk that."

"For the sake of love, you decided to have an illegitimate child?" Christina asked, her pain evident. "Did you lie to me all these years because you loved him? Did you think

I'd want to see my daddy and that might cause him some discomfort? Is that what you thought, Mother?"

"I can see you're distraught, Christina. Maybe we should talk about this later."

Christina shook her head vigorously. "No, I want to talk about it now. Why did you lie to me?"

Louise knew she had to make Christina understand. "I didn't even tell him. What was I going to tell you? How could I tell you he was alive when he didn't even know about you? You would have wanted to see him."

"Of course, Mother. He's my father. I'm a part of him." Christina broke down then and tears streamed from her eyes. "All these years I've dreamed about my father, he's been alive. He's alive, and he doesn't even know that I exist."

Louise got back to the reason she had told Christina this news. "Don't make the same mistake I made, Christina. You have to tell Jackson about this baby."

My father is alive, Christina thought. He's out there somewhere. My father. My father. She placed her hands on her abdomen. She knew she had to tell Jackson. Her mother was right, she couldn't deprive her baby of its father.

Christina was still angry with her mother. Louise should have told her before now. A knock on the door interrupted her thoughts.

"Come in, Mother," Christina said.

Louise poked her head through the door first. "Are you sure it's safe for me in here?"

Christina smiled, almost. "Come on in. I don't have any lethal weapons."

Louise walked all the way into the room, closing the door behind her. She sat on the bed, facing Christina. "What have you been doing up here? I've been worried."

Christina saw a pattern here. Jackson breaks my heart, and then he wonders how I'm doing. My mother breaks my heart, then she wonders how I'm doing. Why do I have to love crazy people? she wondered. "I'm not going to do anything stupid, Mother." She aimed for humor. "I told you there were no lethal weapons in here."

"That's not what I meant, Christina. How long are you going to be angry with me?"

"I really don't know. Let's see, you lied to me for thirty years. Don't I at least deserve to be angry for thirty days?"

"You do have a right to be angry, Christina, but I'm not used to this tension between us. It's been a week."

Christina picked up a pillow from the bed and pulled it to her. "Me either, Mom. You were always the person I could count on. It's hard for me to come to grips with your lying to me. I can understand your not telling me when I was a child, but I'm thirty years old. I deserved to know."

"You're right. I should have told you sooner, but I was afraid. What was I supposed to say, 'Christina, by the way, your father's not dead, pass the salt?' I didn't know how and I was afraid I would lose you." She paused, then added, "I love you, Christina. Whatever wrong I've done or whatever else I've lied about, I do love you."

Christina heard the sincerity in her mother's voice. And the pain. She just wasn't ready yet to give Louise the forgiveness that she wanted. "Will you tell me about him now? The truth, this time?"

Louise took her daughter's hand. "Everything I told you about Christian was true, except that we didn't meet in Selman, we met in Huntsville. We were attracted to each other from the start. We couldn't really date in the open, so we attended rallies together and worked on a lot of the same work teams. Our feelings grew as we came to know each other. Though it was difficult, we found ways to be together. He told me he loved me early on, and even proposed, but I couldn't even think about that. As the summer went on, I realized he was serious and so was I. We made love once, the night before he left to go back home. It was beautiful." She squeezed Christina's hand. "I have never regretted what we shared or the result of it."

"You mean you got pregnant that first time?"

Louise nodded. "I've always considered myself fortunate."

Christina couldn't ignore the similarities in their situations. Her mother and Christian. Her and Jackson. History was repeating itself. "You considered being an unwed mother fortunate?"

"No," Louise said. "I consider having the child of the man I loved fortunate. I knew society, his parents and mine, would never allow us to be together. Having you allowed me to have him. It was worth all I suffered."

Christina wanted to know more. She could understand her mother's feelings because they were much like the feelings she had about Jackson and their baby. "What was it like, Mom?"

Louise breathed deeply. "It was hard, Christina. For me and your grandparents. When they found out about Christian and me, they told me to end it. They said some awful things. That Christian was using me. That a white man only wanted one thing from a colored woman. It was awful."

"But you didn't end it?"

"I couldn't. I was young and in love. I was reckless."

"How did they find out?"

"Your grandparents?" Louise asked. At Christina's nod, she answered, "Gossip. I never knew who, but people were talking about us."

"So what happened after he left?"

"He promised to write, and he did. While he was away, I came to my sense. Or maybe your grandparents' influence just affected me more. When I found out I was pregnant, I was scared. Your grandmother knew before I did. She and your grandfather sat me down and told me they would disown me if I told Christian about the baby, but they would help me if I didn't tell him. They said there was no way those white folks would want a black baby in the family, even if it was part white. Soon, I was believing them."

"What did you do?"

"The hardest thing I've ever done. I wrote Christian and told him that I was mistaken, I didn't love him. That it was wrong. That it was a sin for us to be together. White folks and colored folks don't mix, I told him. I never heard from him after that."

That didn't make sense to Christina. If Christian had really loved her mother, he wouldn't have given up so easily. "Why didn't he write you back or try to get in touch with you?"

"Because of what I said. It was the thing about it being a sin for us to be together. The whole basis of our relationship was that somehow God had ordained the two of us to be together. To say it was sin denied the entire relationship. What could he say? I never expected an answer."

"What did you do then?"

"Your grandparents sent me away to have the baby. We never told anyone about the father. After you were born, I came back home. People talked for a while, but it soon died down. So much was going on then that people really didn't care."

"That's it?"

"That it. The rest, as they say, is history." Louise smiled, then asked, "Do you think you can ever forgive me?"

"He's not in the office today, Miss Marshall," Jackson's secretary said. "He took the day off."

Christina felt relieved. She had decided to

tell Jackson about the baby, but she wasn't looking forward to doing it. This was a welcome reprieve. "Thanks," she said, and walked toward the elevator.

The elevator doors opened and she saw Rosalind standing there.

"What are you doing here, Christina?" Rosalind asked. "Tired of greenhouses already?"

Christina laughed. It was good to see Rosalind. "Not yet. I think I'm growing a green thumb."

"Good for you," Rosalind said. "I'm glad all is well. What brings you here?"

Christina considered her answer. "I'm here to see Jackson, but he's out today."

"You can find him at home. Do you have his new address?"

Christina didn't, so Rosalind gave it to her.

"I wish I had more time to talk," Rosalind said, "but I'm on my way to a meeting. Are you going to be in town long? Maybe you can have dinner with Walter and me."

"Maybe another time. I'm leaving tonight." I'm here just long enough to tell Jackson about the baby, she added silently.

"I'm sorry we can't get together this time. Let me know the next time you're going to be in town and we can plan to get together.

Good luck with Jackson," Rosalind said, and walked away.

Christina looked at Jackson's phone number and address as she pressed the button for the elevator. She debated calling first. She decided to just show up. She didn't have enough nerve to call first. By the time she got on the elevator she had changed her mind, she was going to call first. When she reached the lobby, she had changed her mind again, she would just show up. She hailed a taxi.

CHAPTER 22

"Christina?" Jackson asked. He couldn't believe it. What was she doing here?

"Hi, Jackson." She met his gaze and he saw the flicker of uncertainty in her eyes.

He stood looking at her for a few long moments. She was as beautiful as ever. Looking at her reminded him how much he missed her.

"Are you going to invite me in?" she asked. She was smiling now and he felt like an idiot.

He stood back so she could walk in. "I'm sorry, yes, come on in." When she was in, he pointed towards the sofa. "Have a seat. Would you like something to drink?"

Christina sat on the sofa. "No, I'm fine right now."

Jackson couldn't get his fill of looking at her. It was so good to see her again. He thought he'd gotten over her, but now he knew that wasn't true. And, God knows, he had tried to get over her.

What brings you to my apartment? Jackson wondered. "What brings you to Boston?"

She didn't answer immediately. While he waited, a noise from behind got his attention. God, he'd forgotten that quickly.

"Jackson," the sexy voice called, "where do you keep the shampoo?"

Jackson didn't answer. He looked at Christina and let his gaze follow hers to the hallway. Angela walked into the doorway. She stopped when she saw Christina.

Angela pulled the towel tighter around her. "Hi, Christina."

Jackson looked at Angela. He couldn't look at Christina. He could guess what she was thinking. Angela wore a towel and nothing else.

"Hi, Angela," Christina said. She stood up. "Congratulations on your TV show. I've seen it a couple of times and I've liked it."

"Thanks. I'm sorry I had to cut back on my help with the fundraiser. I know you guys have been working hard."

Jackson looked from one woman to the other. He couldn't believe they were carrying on this conversation as if they had met in a restaurant or something.

"You got us off to a good start," Christina

was saying. "I was supposed to contact you about doing a spot on the variety show."

"I hope I can. Call me next week and I'll let you know."

"I'll do that," Christina said. She turned to Jackson. "I guess I'll be going now. It was good seeing you." She included Angela in her goodbye. "You, too, Angela."

Jackson followed Christina as she walked toward the door. "Don't rush off."

Christina looked up into that face that she knew so well. "I think I'd better go. I didn't know you had company. I should have called."

Jackson was shaking his head. He knew she couldn't stay, shouldn't stay, but he didn't want her to leave yet. "Wasn't there something you wanted to talk to me about?"

Christina looked at him. There was no way she could tell him about the baby today. "It can wait."

Jackson saw something in her eyes that could have been pain. He wanted to comfort her, to tell her that what she saw was not what she saw. He couldn't, so he let go.

"It was good to see you, Christina. Take care of yourself." I still love you, he added silently.

Jackson stared at the door after she had gone. He turned quickly when a hand touched his shoulder. Angela was standing next to him. He'd forgotten she was in the room. His mind and his heart were with Christina.

"It was harder than you thought it would be, wasn't it?" she asked.

He nodded. "I thought I'd gotten over her."

Softly, Angela said, "So did I."

Jackson looked down at her then. "I'm sorry, Angela. I didn't . . ."

Angela raised her hands. "Don't apologize, Jackson. That'll only make it worse."

"I do care about you."

"I know you do." They were both silent for a while. "I should leave tonight," she added.

Jackson thought it might be best. He needed some time alone, but he didn't want to hurt her feelings. "You don't have to go."

He could tell from the look in her eyes that she knew what he was thinking. "We've always been honest with each other, Jackson. Let's not start lying now."

What could he say to her? Beautiful Angela. He could love her if he didn't love Christina. He wished he did love her. It would be easier. "You're a special woman, Angela, a very special woman," was all he could say. He knew it wasn't enough, but there were no words to express what he felt. Angela had been there when he'd needed her. She'd listened to his pain and she'd comforted him. And when she'd believed him ready, she'd made love with him. As he looked in her eyes now, he knew she regretted that. He regretted it, too.

It was a long drive home from the Montgomery Airport to Selma. Tears fell freely from Christina's eyes as she drove. She hadn't thought it would hurt this badly. Or this long. But it did. She wondered if the pain would ever stop. It had to. She knew she couldn't continue these emotional highs and lows. They weren't good for her and they weren't good for her baby.

Louise walked out the door as Christina pulled into the driveway. Great, Christina thought. I don't need this right now. "Hi, Mom," she said with mock cheerfulness when she walked up to the porch.

"How did it go?" Louise asked, the anxiety evident in her voice.

"It didn't," Christina answered.

"What? Didn't you see him? Didn't you tell him?"

Christina walked past her mother and into the house. "Yes, I saw him, and no, I didn't tell him."

Louise followed her into the house. "What do you mean, you didn't tell him? You went all the way to Boston and you didn't tell him? Why not?"

Christina sat down before answering. "It wasn't the right time or place, Mother."

"What's that supposed to mean?"

"It means he had guests. Rather, he had one guest."

"A woman?"

"How'd you ever guess?" Christina asked, with a tinge of sarcasm.

"I'm sorry, Christina."

"Don't be sorry. I should have known he'd be seeing someone else by now. It's been almost three months." *I just didn't know it would hurt so much.*

"Just because he was with a woman doesn't mean he's sleeping with her."

"Oh, but in this case I know he is. She walked out dressed only in a towel. She looked pretty comfortable, too."

"That still doesn't mean anything. Men have needs," Louise reasoned. "It doesn't mean he cares for this woman. He's only known her a short time, anyway."

Christina shook her head. "Good try, Mom, but wrong. Jackson has known this woman for a while. It was Angela, from Atlanta. Jackson wasn't just having his needs met, he's starting a relationship, a life, with someone else."

"Angela? Your friend from the radio?"

Christina nodded. "She was Jackson's friend first. It was her." Christina could still see Angela standing there in that towel. She had wanted to double over. She felt like someone had punched her in the stomach.

"That really doesn't change anything, Christina," Louise said calmly. "You still have to tell him."

She stood up. "I know that, Mother. I couldn't tell him then. I just couldn't."

"When *are* you going to tell him?"

Christina placed her hands across her face. "I don't know." How could she tell him now?

"It's not going to get any easier. The longer you put it off, the harder it'll be."

Christina lashed out. "You're a fine one to talk, Mother. You never told Christian."

"I did."

Christina stood then. "When will the lies stop, Mother? You told me the other day that you didn't tell him. Which is it?"

Louise was not affected by Christina's outburst. "I hadn't told him then, but I have told him now."

"What?"

"I told Christian about you."

"How? When?"

"I called him right after you left for Boston."

Christina sat down. Things were moving too fast for her. "You knew his phone number."

Louise nodded.

"How?"

Louise looked away. "A while back I had a private detective do some work for me."

Christina was incredulous. "You tracked him down? Why?"

"I was thinking about him a lot. I always think about him around your birthday. In the year you graduated from high school, more than ever."

Christina stared at her mother. She was learning so much about her these days. "Where was he?"

"Chicago. He runs a law firm there."

"Was he married?"

"No," Louise said sadly, "he wasn't."

"Did you call him? Let him know you were thinking about him?"

"Not then."

"Why not? He was single."

"Because so many years had passed. So many things had changed. What would I say?"

Christina thought about that for a while.

"I guess you really couldn't just walk back into his life, could you?"

"No, but I wanted to."

"You loved him that much?" Christina was beginning to understand how long it took for love to fade.

"It surprises me, too. I haven't seen him in more than thirty years, but in my heart we've never been separated." She looked at Christina. "A lot of that has to do with you."

Christina walked over to her mom. "Do you still keep up with him?"

Louise nodded.

"Where is he? What's he doing?"

Louise didn't answer.

"Did something happen to him?"

"Nothing happened to him."

"Then where is he?" Christina asked again.

"He's at the St. James."

"The St. James Hotel?" Christina asked.

Louise nodded.

"Here in Selma? What's he doing here?"

"I called him and told him about you. He wanted to meet you, so he came here."

He's here. My father's here, she thought. "You what?" she asked.

"I called him."

"You should have talked to me about this first, Mother."

"No, this was my decision."

Christina spoke rapidly, her words matching the beat of her heart. "What's he doing here?"

"I told you he wants to meet you."

"Why?"

"You'll have to ask him that. He's coming for dinner tonight."

"Tonight?" It was too soon. She needed time to prepare. She wasn't ready for this yet. "How did you know I'd be back tonight?"

"I didn't. It was just going to be the two of us. He wants to know more about you. Now, he can go directly to the source."

Christina couldn't speak. She was going to have dinner with her father tonight. She was going to see him for the first time. She looked at the clock on the wall. It was five o'clock. "What time is he coming?"

"He'll be here around six."

That's not long, she thought. Then she commented, "You aren't excited or nervous about this. Why is that?"

"The telephone call was the hardest part. Seeing him yesterday was easy compared to that. I look forward to seeing him tonight. I want you two to know each other."

I want that, too, Christina thought. "Don't get your hopes up too high, Mom. It's a little late for us to become a family." Having said that, she turned and left the room.

Christina found herself watching for him. She passed the front window more times than necessary and stopped to peek out each time. She couldn't keep still. I hope he likes me, she thought, then chided herself for the thought. She didn't like how important this night was turning out to be. A car pulled into the driveway then. Christina stepped back from the window. If it was him, she didn't want him to see her looking. A tall, sandy-haired man stepped out of a blue four-door Chevy sedan.

She watched him stride up the walkway to the door and ring the doorbell. I should answer it, she thought, then decided against it. He rang the bell once more before Louise opened the door. Christina heard Louise lead him into the living room, but she couldn't hear what they were saying. While she was debating whether to go in now or to wait, Louise came to get her.

"He's here, Christina," Louise said, "and he's eager to meet you."

Christina took one step toward her mother, then stopped. She couldn't do it.

"What's the matter?" Louise asked.

"I'm scared, Mom. When I was small I

used to dream that he wasn't really dead. That he would come back for me. Now that he's here, I'm scared. What if we don't get along?"

Tears formed in Louise's eyes. "He already loves you, Christina. He loves you because you're his daughter. He just wants to get to know you."

"I've wanted a father for so long. What if he can't be what I want him to be?"

"You can't make up for the time you were apart, and I'll always blame myself for that, but you can start something new here today. Don't you want to try?"

Christina didn't say anything. Louise extended her hand and Christina took it. They walked into the living room together.

Christian stood as they walked in the room. He smiled. "Hello, Christina. I'm Christian."

Relief washed over her. One of her worries was what to call him. His introduction made it easy. "Hello, Christian."

Louise ushered Christina into the room so the two of them stood facing Christian. "I'll get tea." She looked at Christian. "You still drink tea, don't you?"

Christina could have sworn that her mother blushed when he nodded. She watched as Louise left the room.

"She's giving us some time alone," he stated.

Christina looked at him and knew where she got her height from. And the texture of her hair. "I know."

"Shall we sit then, and get to know each other a little bit?"

Christina sat, but she could think of nothing to say. Fortunately, Christian could. "Louise tells me that you're on a leave of absence from your job. Are you enjoying yourself?"

Christina wondered what else her mother had told him. "I needed the break. I'm something of a workaholic."

Christian smiled at that. "I can believe that. I'm known to be somewhat of a workaholic myself."

"Mom says you have a law practice in Chicago. What's that like?"

"I like it. I've been doing it for nearly thirty years now."

"What kind of law?"

"Family law."

"Divorce?" This was stupid. She really didn't care about his law practice.

"Some divorce. I also do estate planning, wills, adoptions. That kind of thing."

"Did you love my mother?" Christina surprised herself with the question.

"Very much," Christian answered. "I've never loved anyone else."

"What did you think when she called you?"

"Shocked. Angry. Scared. Expectant. All those emotions."

Christina relaxed then. "I felt the same when she told me about you. I used to dream about you when I was a little girl."

"I bet you never quite pictured me, though."

Christina smiled because he did. "You're right about that. I imagined you were tall, though. I always thought I got my height from my dad."

"I thought that when I first saw you myself. You've probably been taller than Louise for a long while."

Christina nodded and laughed softly. "I passed her around eighth grade."

"Have you forgiven her yet?"

"She told you?"

He nodded. "She loves you a lot. She made a mistake, but she had the best intensions. At the time, it was all she knew to do."

"I'm not the only one she lied to. Have you forgiven her?"

"In my case there was nothing to forgive. I was there. I understand the pressure she was under. I regret not spending my life with the two of you. I was angry and hurt that Louise didn't feel confident enough to tell me she was pregnant, but I understand. I blame myself, anyway."

"Why is that?" Christina asked. How could he blame himself if he didn't even know?

"In my day, a man showed his love for a woman by waiting until marriage. We didn't do that. If we had, none of this would have happened."

"And maybe I never would have been born."

Christian smiled again. "I like to think that you would have been born, but you'd have been born to a family, a mother and a father, who cherished you. I envy Louise the time she had with you."

"She was a great mother to me," Christina said. Her anger subsiding now.

"That doesn't surprise me. She's a great woman."

Christina detected that Christian's feelings for Louise were still strong. "What was she like when you met her?"

"She hasn't changed. She's as beautiful now as she was then, and unless I'm mistaken, she's as strong-willed now as she was then."

Christian smiled and Christina felt they were sharing a secret. It was a good feeling.

"She is," Christina agreed. "She's always done things her own way, been her own person. And she's managed to be happy."

"She tells me you're a lot like that yourself. You've built quite a career for yourself."

"I've done well in my profession, but there's more to life than work."

He nodded. "There should be. I've found that work can fill up a lot of places when other parts of your life aren't working right."

"Right about what?" Louise asked, when she walked back into the room with the tea.

"Christina and I were just comparing notes on work," Christian answered.

Louise set the tray on the cocktail table. "Things must be changing, since you both have taken leaves from your work."

Christina looked at Christian. This was the first she had heard about a leave. "How long are you planning to be away?" she asked.

Christian looked from Louise to Christina. "As long as it takes for me to get to know you. I've got nothing but time."

Christina was at a loss for words. She didn't know what to think.

"I think I'm the real winner in this," Louise said with a lilt in her voice. "I get to have time with both of you."

Christina looked at Louise. Her mother wore a shy smile. She looked at Christian. He wore a contented smile. What's going on here? she wondered.

CHAPTER 23

"How is she?" Jackson had been on the phone with Robert for almost fifteen minutes. He couldn't wait any longer.

"She?"

"You know I'm talking about Christina." Jackson hated putting Robert in the middle like this, but he needed to know.

"She's fine. Why do you ask?"

"She was in Boston last week and she came by my apartment." Jackson couldn't shake the feeling that Christina had wanted to discuss something important with him. When she saw Angela, she had closed up.

"What happened?"

"Nothing happened. I'm trying to figure out why she came by. Do you know anything?"

"Not really," Robert said slowly.

Jackson didn't believe him. "Come on, man. I need to know."

"Why do you need to know? I thought you

and Christina had broken up. Liza said you were seeing Angela again."

News travels fast, Jackson thought. "I was seeing Angela, but I'm not anymore. I'm still in love with Christina, Robert. I need to know if there's still a chance for us."

"Then shouldn't you be talking to her?"

"Yes, but she's not talking to me these days."

"What happened?"

If he asks one more question, I'm hanging up, Jackson thought. "Angela was here when she came to visit. I could tell she wanted to tell me something, but after she saw Angela in my apartment, she changed her mind."

"Oh, man, do you have bad timing!"

"Tell me something I *don't* know," Jackson said. "What's going on, Robert? Do you have any idea why she was here?"

"Did you know that she has taken a leave of absence from CL?"

Walter and Rosalind didn't talk to him about Christina anymore. They kept this news from him as well. "A month or so ago. Liza took her old job. She's pretty excited about it, too."

"Give her my congratulations," Jackson said absentmindedly.

"And we've moved into her house in Decatur," Robert added.

"You've moved into her house? Where is she? Why did she take a leave of absence?"

"You should be having this conversation with her, Jackson," Robert said.

"You do know something, don't you?"

"I may have heard something from Liza," Robert said. It was obvious he didn't want to give away any information.

"Come on, man," Jackson pleaded. "This is important."

"She's pregnant, Jackson."

Jackson jumped up from his chair. "Pregnant? Christina?"

"Yes."

"When? Who?" Jackson asked, but he already knew the answers.

"I'd think that you'd know that better than me."

"Are you sure? She's pregnant?"

"That's why she took the leave. She wanted to get away . . ."

Jackson sat down. *God, did I have bad timing. First I need space, and then those damn roses.* "She didn't want me to know, did she?"

"You really should be having this conversation with her, Jackson. I only know bits and pieces."

Christina came to tell me about the baby, Jackson concluded. In spite of all that had happened between us she wanted me to know about the baby. That meant there was still a chance for us. "That's all right, man. You've helped a lot."

"What are you going to do?"

I've got to move fast, Jackson thought. First, I've got to find out who sent those roses. "I don't know yet, but I'm not going to let her keep me away from my child. I'm going to be a father." Jackson thought back to Christina's visit. She hadn't been show-ing then. "Do you know how far along she is?"

"No, man. I've told you all I know."

"I appreciate it, Robert. Thanks a lot."

Jackson continued to hold the phone to his ear even after Robert hung up. I'm go-ing to be a father, he thought. Christina and I have made a baby. The recording signaled him to hang up.

He wondered what kind of father he'd be. He'd be better than his father, that's for sure. His father. Today was the first Sunday of the month and Jackson had yet to call his dad. Now is as good a time as any, he thought. He picked up the phone again.

"Good morning, Dad."

"Good morning yourself, Jackson. How you doing?"

His dad was sober. "I'm doing great, Dad.

I've got some news for you. I'm going to be a father."

"A father? I didn't even know you were married."

"I'm not yet, Dad, but I soon will be."

"Who is she?"

"Her name's Christina."

"I don't recall you mentioning her before. How long have you been seeing this woman?"

"For a while now. I just haven't talked much about her."

"Do you love her, son?"

"I do, Dad. I love her a lot." The words seemed inadequate to express the depth of the feelings he had for Christina.

"Be careful. I loved your mother, too."

That was the closest thing to criticism his father had said about his mother in a long while. Maybe he was getting over her, Jackson thought. He wasn't going to bet on it, though. "I know, Dad."

"A woman can hurt you real bad, Jackson. You be careful."

"You'll have to meet Christina. She's not like that. We're going to be together forever." Jackson prayed he was right.

"Just be careful, son."

"I will, Dad." Now that he was an expectant father, Jackson wanted a better relationship with his own dad. "What are you doing next weekend?"

"Nothing much."

"How about my coming for a visit?" Jackson hadn't seen his father in more than two years.

"I'd like that, son. I'd like that a lot."

Jackson heard the surprise in his dad's voice and he smiled.

"Your move," Jackson's father, Jim, said.

Jim and a friend had been playing checkers on the porch when Jackson drove up. After the friend had left, Jim coaxed Jackson into a game. Jackson wasn't playing very well. He was distracted because he still hadn't come up with a plan for finding out who had sent the roses. He moved one of the red men without much thought.

"How long are you gonna be staying?" Jim asked.

He had an appointment with a private investigator Monday morning. "I'll be leaving tomorrow afternoon."

"That's a short time to stay after such a long flight. You must have plenty of money." Jim jumped two of Jackson's men.

"I do all right, you know that." Jackson studied the board. He didn't have a free

move left. He could only prolong the inevitable.

Jim nodded. "Always knew you'd do good
for yourself."

Jackson was surprised at that comment.
Jim didn't hand out praise often. "Did you,
Dad?"

"Too stubborn not to do good." Jim
jumped all of Jackson's men with a single
man. The game was over. "But you didn't
do too well in this game."

"I was not stubborn," Jackson argued.

Jim began setting the board up for the
next game. "Yes, you were, too. When you
got something on your mind you were like a
dog with a bone. Wouldn't give up until you
had it whipped."

Jackson was surprised at the pride on his
father's face. He couldn't recall ever seeing
it before.

"Remember when you first joined the
track team?" Jim continued.

"Yeah, I remember. You told me I wasn't
going to be any good."

Jim laughed at that. "Proved me wrong,
though, didn't you? Came in first in every
race."

"I didn't even know you kept up with the
races." Jim had never come to any of his
meets.

Jim smiled as if remembering. "I knew about 'em, all right."

Jackson could only stare at his dad. He wondered at his dad's tone. He sounded as if Jackson should have known that he kept up with his activities. "You never mentioned them to me."

Jim picked up a checker and twirled it in his hand. "We argued about everything back then."

Not everything, Jackson thought, *some-one.* "You still love her, don't you?"

Jim didn't answer immediately. "Too much." He was quiet again. "And too long."

Jackson agreed. "Don't you think it's time you stopped?"

Jim pointed to his heart. "I loved your mama way down in here."

Jackson didn't think Jim had really tried to get over Sarah, but he didn't want to get Jim on his soapbox about her, so he changed the subject. "How about me taking you out to dinner? Catfish?"

"Your mama made the best catfish in town. Did I tell you that?"

Jackson groaned. It was going to a long visit.

"So she thinks you've been sending the roses?"

Jackson had been determined not to spend the entire dinner listening to Jim cry over Sarah, but he couldn't believe he'd told Jim the full story of him and Christina. "That's what she thinks all right."

"If you ask me, any woman who'd believe something like that about her man doesn't know what love is. I say, be glad to get rid of her."

That wasn't the response Jackson wanted. "I'm not exactly rid of her, Dad. She's pregnant, remember?"

"How do you know it's yours?"

There'd never be any doubt about that. "It's mine, all right."

"You'd best be careful, boy. Women, these days, you can't trust 'em. They'll do about anything to get a man."

Jackson put two hushpuppies in his mouth to give him time to prepare a suitable response to Jim's negative comments. "Christina doesn't need to trap a man, Dad. She doesn't need me." That's the problem, Jackson added to himself.

"Don't be too sure about that. She don't have no man, does she?"

Jackson knew this conversation was going nowhere. "How about apple pie for dessert? They used to have the best in town."

Jim nodded. "They have good apple pie,

right enough, but your mama made the best apple pie, in town."

"How did you know where to find me?" Christina asked. She had just come in from a day at the nursery.

"I ran into Angela in the Atlanta Airport last weekend," Reggie answered.

She sat down in the chair next to the telephone table. "Angela told you were I was?" She wondered if Angela had also told Jackson.

"She mentioned it in passing. She was on her way to Boston."

That figures, Christina thought. Angela must have found out from the Radio-thon Committee. "You were in Atlanta?"

"No," Reggie answered. "I was on my way to D.C. I'm spending a lot of time in airports these days. As a matter of fact, I'm in one now."

"Where are you?"

"Montgomery."

"Montgomery? What are you doing in Montgomery?"

"I'll give you three guesses."

Christina didn't need three guesses. "Reggie . . ."

"If you invite me to dinner, I can be there in less than ninety minutes."

Two hours later they were seated in Rob's Steakhouse. "I thought you were going to cook for me."

Christina laughed at that. "I don't cook anymore."

"How are you going to be a good mom if you don't cook?"

Christina had been pleased with Reggie's response to her pregnancy. He had looked at her and smiled. Her emotions had gotten the best of her and she had begun to cry. He had pulled her into his arms and let her do just that and he hadn't asked any questions . . . yet. "I didn't say I can't cook, I said I don't cook. Anyway, I can handle milk and formula. How many babies do you know that come here eating solid food?"

"You have a point there," Reggie conceded. "But they tell me babies move from milk to solid food pretty fast."

"I don't think that's a problem. Mom can cook and she's going to spoil this baby rotten."

"Aren't you going back to Atlanta and your job after the baby is born?"

Christina leaned back against the booth. She had thought a lot about that. She didn't know if she could go back to the memories and she didn't know if she wanted to go back to CL. "I don't know. It surprises me,

419

but I really don't miss work. I thought I would."

"What would you do?"

Christina pushed her plate away. "Oh, I don't know. There are a lot of things I could do. I could go into business with my mom. She's thinking about opening another nursery in Montgomery."

"You could go from being a top business executive to running a small nursery?"

"In a heartbeat. I've even thought about opening a preschool. That way I could be with my baby all day."

Reggie reached over and took her hand. "I knew it."

"Knew what?"

He squeezed her hand before letting go and settling back in his chair. "You're more like my mom than I thought."

She remembered him telling her something like that before. "Maybe a little."

"More than a little. Don't tell me you haven't thought about being a full-time mom."

"More like dreamed about it. That's not a choice for a single mom, though."

"You don't have to be single," Reggie said.

"I've decided. Jackson's not going to be a part of this baby's life." She had come to her decision and she didn't want to get into a discussion of Jackson and the baby. She'd had that conversation often enough with her mother.

"I'm not talking about Jackson."

Christina didn't know what to say. "Reggie, you can't be serious."

"Oh, but I am," he said.

She placed her hand on her extended belly. "Why would you want a wife who's pregnant with another man's child?"

"I don't want a woman who's pregnant with another man's child. I want you, and I'll love this baby like my own."

This was all happening too fast for Christina. "You only found out about the baby today. How can you make such an offer?"

"I've been in love with you for a while, Christina. You know that."

She did know it. "I know, but . . ."

"There are no buts. My hat's in the ring. I want to marry you. I want to have other babies with you. Now what do you want?"

She wanted marriage and she wanted a family. But she also wanted it with a man she loved, and she didn't love Reggie. "This isn't right, Reggie."

"It *is* right, Christina. You can turn me down, but you can't ignore my proposal. We can go shopping for a ring tomorrow."

"Reggie —" she began.

He interrupted her. "Don't turn me down out of hand. Think about it. We could have a good life together. I love you. You like me. You could grow to love me."

"It's too much," she said.

"All I ask is that you think about it. Will you do that?"

She saw the sincerity in his eyes and nodded. "I'll think about it."

"He's a nice man," Louise said later, after Reggie had brought Christina home. He had stayed awhile, talking with them.

"He asked me to marry him."

Louise put down the paper she was holding. "What?"

"He asked me to marry him."

"Doesn't he see that you're pregnant?"

Christina put her hand on her stomach. "The man isn't blind. He sees."

"The baby isn't his."

"He's not stupid, either. He knows the baby isn't his."

"You told him no, of course."

Christina put her feet up on the ottoman. They tended to swell by the end of the day. "I tried."

"What do you mean, you tried? Either you told him or you didn't. Which is it?"

"I didn't exactly tell him no," Christina

explained. The more she thought about Reggie's proposal, the more she convinced herself that it wasn't such a bad idea. A lot of marriages started with less than the friendship she and Reggie shared. Maybe they could make it . . . maybe . . .

"What did you tell him?"

"I agreed to think about it."

"I don't believe this, Christina. You can't seriously be thinking of marrying this man when you're carrying Jackson's baby."

"I don't know, Mother. Maybe I am."

"This isn't right, Christina. You need to tell Jackson about this baby."

"I'm not getting into that with you again. As for Reggie's proposal, I'm thinking about it."

"I don't believe you."

"I'm not thinking seriously about it, but I am thinking about it. Is that so wrong, Mom? He loves me."

"Do you love him?"

No, I don't love him. "I could love him if I tried."

"Sometimes you're so young, Christina. Love doesn't happen that way."

Reggie spent the next day at the nursery, helping Christina do the books. "Has your mother ever thought about expanding out

West? Oklahoma City could use more nurs-
eries."

Christina looked up from the ledger she
was working on. "Reggie . . ."

"Just trying to help you make a business
decision. Maybe I should talk to Louise
about this."

"Maybe you shouldn't."

He laughed. "Maybe you're right. Last
night I thought she liked me, but this morning she treated me like I have the plague.

"Let me guess. She doesn't think it's a
good idea?"

Christina smiled at him. "Let's just say
she thinks it's bad timing."

"The baby?"

She nodded. "And the baby's father."

Reggie got up from the desk where he was
working and walked over to the table where
Christina sat clipping stems. "We haven't
talked about that."

"I know, and I'm glad."

"Why haven't you told him?"

She remembered Angela in the towel.
There was no way she could share her baby
with Jackson and Angela or whoever he
chose as his wife. No, that would be too
painful for her. "Jackson has moved on with
his life. I'm his past. The baby was an accident. Why should it haunt him now?"

"Is that what the baby is to you, an accident?"

"No." This baby was her life now. She loved it already. She'd transferred all the love she had for Jackson to their baby. It didn't end the pain and hurt she still felt, but it did lessen it.

"Then why do you think he would look at it like that?"

Christina didn't like the way the conversation was progressing. She didn't want to think about Jackson and Angela. It was all she could do to take care of her own feelings. "Do you really want me to tell him?"

Reggie moved closer. "No."

Christina turned to look at him. She hadn't expected his honestly. "Then why are we having this discussion?"

Reggie scratched his chin. "Want to get married?"

She threw a plant stem at him.

Five weeks passed and Jackson was no closer to finding out who'd sent the roses than when he'd started. He hadn't talked to Christina, and he was getting restless. He needed to see her, but he was afraid to go to her without having some concrete information about those roses. He'd have a hard enough time explaining what had gone on with Angela. He picked up the phone and dialed. He was glad to hear Robert's voice. He got right to the important stuff. "What's the latest on Christina?"

"You haven't talked to her?"

"No. There are some loose ends that I need to tie up before I see her."

"You'd better hurry up and tie them. Christina's engaged. She might even be married by now."

Jackson jumped out of his chair. "Engaged? What the hell are you talking about?"

"Don't yell at me, man. I'm just telling you what I heard. She's getting married."

Jackson pinched his nose with his fingers. Things have gone from bad to worse. "To who?"

"I don't know. Liza doesn't tell me anything. She doesn't want us in the middle."

"How would you two get in the middle?"

"You know, her taking Christina's side and me taking your side."

"You're not taking sides. You're doing the right thing. I was supposed to know about the baby. It's also my right to know about this engagement. She can't be engaged when she's pregnant with my baby."

"I'm just telling you what I heard."

Jackson sat down again. He needed to be calm if he was going to get the information he wanted. "Who is he? She couldn't have met somebody new this quickly, could she?"

"Maybe it's somebody she already knew. I don't know, man."

"I can't believe she'd actually plan to marry somebody else and keep my child from me. That doesn't sound like Christina."

"Maybe I got it all wrong. Maybe she's not engaged."

Jackson didn't believe that. Christina was engaged. She was going to have the baby without telling him. And she was going to marry some man and give that man his child. "Thanks for the info, buddy. I owe you one," he said.

Jackson hung up the phone slowly. "So Christina is planning to get married. Over my dead body."

CHAPTER 24

Christian walked up behind Louise and placed his hands on her shoulders. "You can't live her life for her, Louise."

Louise leaned back against him. "I want her to be happy, Christian. I don't want her to make the same mistakes that I did."

Christian gently turned Louise around. "It's her decision."

"I know, but can you believe she's really thinking about marrying this Reggie character?"

Christian spoke calmly. "He's a good enough fellow. You can see that he loves her."

"She doesn't love him, though. She's still in love with Jackson."

"How can you be so sure? She and Reggie get along very well. And he's excited about the baby. He's been there for her. That has to count for something."

"He's a good friend. You can't build a

marriage on that. You need the passion."

"Are you talking about Christina or your-self?"

He was right . . . she was thinking about herself. She'd never married because she'd never felt the passion she felt with Christian with anyone else. "I'm talking about Christina."

Christian put his arms around her waist and pulled her to him. He placed his chin on her head. "You still feel it, too, don't you?"

Louise placed her hands on his. "It's almost like it was yesterday."

"I love you, Louise."

She knew it. She had known it from the first phone call. Theirs was a forever love. "I love you, too."

She knew he was going to kiss her. She leaned up on her toes as he leaned down to her. He tasted the same. She remembered it. She lifted her arms around his shoulders. He was bigger, wider, more muscular. He had been a boy then; he was a mature man now.

When he lifted his head, she saw tears in his eyes. She wiped them away with her fingers and smiled. "Now, what are we go-ing to do about our daughter?"

Christina placed her hand on her abdomen. "Reggie, it's moving. My baby's moving."

Reggie moved his hand next to hers. "Let me feel."

She looked at Reggie's hand resting next to hers. "It's a miracle."

Reggie moved his hand across her belly. "I don't feel anything."

"He's stopped," Christina said. "You missed it."

Reggie pulled his hand away. "What did it feel like?"

Christina smoothed down her top. It felt like she had a bad case of gas. "It felt like . . . I can't describe it. It felt like something moving inside me."

"Next time, tell me as soon as it starts."

She put her hands on Reggie's face. "You're disappointed, aren't you?"

He placed a hand atop hers, but didn't say anything.

"What are you thinking about?" she asked.

He looked at her. "Are you going to marry me, Christina?"

"That's not the right answer for either of us, Reggie."

"It is. I already love this baby and he's not

even born yet. And you know I love you. I'd be a great father and a great husband."

"But I don't love you," she whispered.

"I think you do," Reggie responded. "You can't tell me that you don't feel more for me now than you did a few months ago."

Christina knew her feeling for Reggie had intensified. He had been there when she'd needed him. That meant a lot. But. There was always a but. Jackson. He was never out of her thoughts. How could she marry someone else when she was carrying Jackson's child? Their child. "You're right. I do feel more for you now, but how do you know that it's love?"

"It's a start." He leaned in closer to her. "I can help you forget him, if you let me."

She wondered if he knew how often she thought about Jackson. She pulled her hands away and looked at her stomach. "How could you do that? The baby is his. I can never forget him."

"Maybe you don't want to forget him."

The accusation in his voice surprised her. "What does that mean?"

"You have to start living your life, Christina. If you want Jackson, you should go to him. If you don't want him, you've got to stop pining for him. It's not helping you. And it's not helping the baby."

Christina had said as much to herself. "I'm not going to tell him."

"Then you've got to start thinking about this baby and what you want. The baby needs a father."

"That's where you're wrong. I can provide everything this baby needs."

"I know you're more than able to provide financially for you and the baby. You even have enough love to give, but that's not enough for you."

She had to hand it to him, he knew her well. "I don't know. That sounds like all the bases have been covered. What more could I want?"

"You want the little white house with the picket fence. You want a traditional family."

"You know a lot about what I want. What do you want?"

"I want what you want. I want what my mom and dad have."

Christina massaged her stomach. "Sometimes I think I'm trying to make up for my childhood. I want to give my baby what I didn't have, and that's a father."

"I can be that father."

She stood then. "You don't understand, Reggie. I want it all. I want passion. I want fireworks."

Reggie stood next to her. "What about

commitment? What about being there? Don't they count?"

"Why do you want to marry a woman who keeps telling you she doesn't love you?"

"That's an easy one. As I said before, I think you do love me. We have different definitions of love. If you can stop fantasizing about Jackson long enough, you'll see that we have more than enough to build a life together. Can you do that? Can you stop the fantasies?"

The following week Christian came to visit Christina at the nursery.

"You've been away from your work a long time," Christina said to him. "If you're away any longer, you may lose all your clients."

Christian leaned against the counter and watched Christina sort the day's mail. "I doubt that. I haven't taken a real vacation in the last twenty-five years. This time has been good for me. It's been more than worth whatever it may cost me in clients."

Christina saw the sincerity in his eyes. "Do you still love her?"

"I've loved her forever," Christian said, the love evident in his eyes. "That's why I've never married. Louise was my first and only love."

"If you loved her, really loved her, you

could have come back for her."

Christian had wondered the same thing over the years. Had he been a coward? "The world was a lot different then. Louise and I knew our chances were slim. The only way it would work was with one hundred and fifty percent from both of us. When I got her letter, I knew it was over. I couldn't fight her, my parents, her parents, and God. It was best to leave it alone."

"So what's going to happen now?" Christina asked.

"I'm going to spend as much time as possible getting to know my two girls."

"Your two girls?"

"Yes, you and your mother. I know it's too late for me to be a father to you, Christina. Louise has raised you well. You're a beautiful woman and you don't need me. Not as a father. I would like to be your friend, though. Do you think that's possible?"

Christina wasn't so sure she didn't need a father. She looked up at him with hope in her eyes. "I don't know how to go about being your daughter, either, Christian. I think friends may be a pretty good place to start."

Jackson saw them through the front window. His first thought was that this was the man

Christina was going to marry. He couldn't hear them, but he recognized the look in the old man's eyes. It was love, pure and simple. Christina's eyes showed a deep caring. Jackson shook his head. An old white guy. Who would have thought it? What could she possibly see in this guy? he wondered. Well, he was going to put a stop to this right now.

The chimes sounded when he entered. They both turned to look at him. The man's eyes were clear. Christina's registered astonishment and something else he couldn't quite place. Probably guilt, he reasoned.

"Surprised to see me, Christina?" Jackson asked. "I really don't know why." He looked at Christian, then he allowed himself a long look at Christina's extended belly. It hit him that she was carrying his child. That belly carried the result of their love. He wanted to reach out and touch it. He looked back up into Christina's eyes. "You're carrying my baby." He looked again at Christian. "You did know it was mine, didn't you?' He extended his hand. "I'm Jackson Duncan. Who are you?"

Before Christian could answer, Christina asked, "What are you doing here, Jackson?"

"Where else would I be darling?" His

words dripped with sugar. "You're here, the baby's here. It's only natural that I'd want to be with my family."

"Your family? What are you talking about?"

He looked directly into her eyes, daring her to challenge him. "The three of us. You, the baby, and me. We're a family. I figure we'd better have the wedding pretty soon, though." He nudged Christian. "The preacher ought to beat the stork, if you know what I mean."

Christina stood staring at him. "Have you gone crazy? How dare you come walking in here, talking about a family? How dare you make any claim to me or my baby? You can leave now."

Jackson controlled his anger. He was going to play this scene his way. "I know you're upset it's taken me so long to get here, sweetheart, but I'm here now and we'll never be apart again."

"Uggg . . ." was all Christina could say. She looked at Jackson, then at Christian, then stormed out to the office in back of the nursery.

Jackson watched her waddle away. He had definitely ruffled her feathers. He glanced at the other man, who also watched her. Jackson took this opportunity to study the man. He didn't appear too upset by the things Jackson had said and he still had that dumb love look on his face. "I'll ask again," Jackson said. "Who are you and what are you doing here with Christina?"

Christian smiled as he answered. "I'm Christian Van Dorne, Christina's father."

Jackson couldn't believe his ears. "Christina's *father?*"

"Who else would I be?"

Jackson spoke before thinking. "I thought you were the man she planned to marry."

Christian shrugged, but kept smiling. "And I thought you said she was going to marry you."

"I know what I said. If you're not the man she's planning to marry, who is?"

"You'll have to ask her that."

Jackson wondered what the guy was smiling about. "You're her father?"

Christian nodded. "That I am."

"I thought her father was dead."

"As you can see, I'm very much alive."

"How can you be her father?" Jackson asked. The man was white, after all.

"Young man, if you don't know the answer to that, you're in much more trouble than I think you're in." Christian inclined his head toward the back room.

"She didn't look too happy to see me. Did

she?" Jackson asked.

Christian shook his head slowly. "Happy is not the word I'd use."

"Maybe I should go back there and talk to her?"

Grabbing Jackson's arm as he turned to go after Christina, Christian asked, "Want some advice?"

"Given the way this has started, I need all the help I can get. What's your advice?"

"Don't go in there now. She was shocked to see you. Give her some time to get her feelings together. She, her mother, and I are having dinner tonight. Why don't you join us? I know Louise would love to meet you."

Jackson wondered at the man's helpfulness. "Tonight? I have to wait until tonight?"

"That's best. You could probably use the time to do some adjusting of your own. You won't be able to browbeat her into doing what you want. You need to come up with another strategy."

Jackson didn't like having his style critiqued. "Why are you being so helpful?"

"She's my daughter. I want her to be happy, and she has to reconcile her feelings for you if she's going to be happy."

Jackson nodded. Maybe this guy would turn out to be an ally, he thought. "Are you going to tell me about this guy who wants

438

to marry her?"

Christian shook his head. "I can't do that, son. That's between you and her."

Jackson looked closely at Christian. "Are you sure you're her father?"

Christian laughed.

Christina heard the chimes again. She hoped Jackson was leaving. She tensed up when she heard the office door open.

"He's gone, Christina," Christian said. "You can come out now."

"You make it sound like I'm hiding. I'm working."

Christian walked all the way into the room. "What are you working on? That book in front of you is upside down."

Christina looked up at Christian. "Okay. I was hiding. What did he say before he left?"

Christian shrugged. "Nothing much."

"Oh . . ."

"I invited him to dinner with us tonight."

Christina tried to jump out of her seat, but her stomach was a hindrance. She eased herself up instead. "You *what?*"

"I invited him to dinner with us tonight."

"You had no right to do that!"

"I'm sure Louise wants to meet him."

"Then the three of you can go to dinner. I'll stay home."

"If that's what you want."

Christina had expected Christian to offer to withdraw Jackson's invitation. "You don't want me to come? I thought this was a family dinner."

"You can't keep running from the man, Christina."

"Why can't I?"

"Because it's his baby."

"It always comes back to that, doesn't it?"

Christian nodded. "As it should."

Christina wondered if Christian was talking from his experience with Louise. "It would have been so much easier if he'd stayed away."

"You really think so?"

Christina sighed. "Not really."

"Do you still love him?"

"I don't know how I feel. This morning I was seriously considering Reggie's proposal. Now Jackson's here. It complicates things."

"You were really thinking about marrying Reggie?"

Christina sat down again. "Not really. I don't love him that way."

"Does Reggie know how you feel?"

She nodded. "I've told him more than once."

"And he still wants to marry you? He must love you a lot."

"I've told him it's crazy, but he won't listen. He's turned into a great friend, but it'll never be more than that. I know that now for sure."

"Because of Jackson?"

Christina covered her face with her hands. "I still love him. I never stopped. I knew it from the moment he walked into the shop. I guess I always knew it."

"Then why are you fighting it so hard? Being in love should make you happy."

She dropped her hands from her face. "Only if the person you're in love with is in love with you."

"And you don't think Jackson is in love with you?"

How she wished it were true. "He took his own good time getting here, didn't he?"

"You can't very well hold that against him. You didn't tell him about the baby. How did he know you were here?"

Her first thought was Liza or Robert. Most likely Robert. Maybe Angela. But she didn't like to think of Angela and Jackson together. "I don't know. My guess would be that friends in Atlanta told him."

"From his display of ownership when he walked in here, my guess is he loves you, too."

Christina wished Christian was right, but

she couldn't bet on it. "There's a lot you don't know about Jackson and me. It's a lot more complicated than that."

"Do you want to talk about it? I'm a good listener. That's what friends are for."

Christina really didn't want to talk now, but there was something Christian could do for her. "Could you hold me for a while? I could use a good cry about now."

Christian walked over and for the first time in his life, he pulled his daughter into his arms. It felt good. It felt right.

Christina's tears started immediately. She cried for herself and Jackson, for her and her father, and for her mother and her father. She cried for all the times as a child when she had needed her daddy to hold her. She cried until she could cry no more.

CHAPTER 25

Jackson broke the silence. "It was good of your parents to give us this time alone."

They could have been a little less obvious about it, Christina thought. Louise practically fawned all over Jackson throughout dinner. Then Christian's bright idea was for him and Louise to go for a walk. "Maybe they didn't do it for us. Maybe they wanted to be alone."

"Do you think they'll get back together after all these years?" Jackson asked, his gaze on her stomach.

"It looks that way." Christina wished Jackson would stop staring at her stomach. He was beginning to make her nervous.

"Theirs must be a really strong love. If circumstances had been different, your parents would have been married for more than thirty years now."

"Thirty years is a long time." Not as long as Reggie's parents, she thought, but a long time. "I heard that you had been to Oklahoma City."

"I was out there. How did you find out?"

"Reggie told me."

Jackson lifted his gaze to her face. Reggie. He wondered why it hadn't occurred to him earlier. "You've seen Reggie?"

She nodded. "He's visited."

"He's been here, to Selma?"

Her nod was so slight he almost didn't see it.

Jackson moved from the chair across from her to sit on the couch next to her. "What was he doing here?"

"That should be obvious. He was here to see me. We're friends."

"Friends? Nothing more?"

"Friends." No need to mention Reggie's proposal. He knew the answer, but he asked anyway. "Is Reggie the guy you were thinking about marrying?"

Christina picked up on his controlled anger and moved closer to the end of the couch, away from him. "He has asked me."

"And you're considering his proposal?"

"I don't have many options, Jackson."

"The hell you don't. You have me. I'm the baby's father."

"You have a short memory. I did come to you. You were otherwise occupied at the time." Christina could still see Angela wrapped in that towel. The pain she had felt that day was still with her. "How is Angela, by the way?"

"I wouldn't know. I haven't seen her since that day in Boston."

Christina didn't respond. Why should she believe him?

"It's true, Christina. I haven't seen her since then."

"You slept with her, though, didn't you?"

Jackson knew he'd have to answer that question. "I did, and I'm sorry it happened."

"Well, I hope you didn't tell Angela that. It's cruel, Jackson. That's not your style at all."

"You know Angela and me. I didn't have to tell her. She knew."

It still hurt that Jackson had taken Angela to his bed so soon after their breakup. "Why did you sleep with her, Jackson? Didn't what we had mean anything to you?"

He heard the pain in her voice and for the hundredth time regretted what he'd done. "I thought it was over with us. I was trying to go on with my life."

She couldn't hold that against him, since she was trying to do the same thing herself. "When did you decide it was a mistake?"

"The day you came to the apartment. I still love you, Christina. I faced it that day. There was no place for Angela in my heart. It all belongs to you."

She wanted to believe him. These were the words she had waited so long to hear. "You sound pretty fickle to me, Jackson. First, you tell me you need space. Then you sleep with Angela. Then you tell Angela it was a mistake. Now you come back telling me you want us to be a family. How do I know you won't change your mind tomorrow?"

That hurt. He deserved it, but it still hurt. "I'm not fickle, as you put it, Christina. It was easier for me to give you the 'space' story rather than discuss the real problem with you. If I had done that, maybe none of this would have happened. We'd still be together."

"What was this real problem?" Christina asked.

Jackson moved closer to her and took her hand in his. He was relieved she didn't withdraw it. "It took me a while to figure it out myself. A part of it had to do with the way our work relationship was changing."

"But I told you that I wasn't siding with Liza against you. I was just making the best decisions for the company."

"I know you said that. And it hurt me that you did."

Christina was confused now. "I didn't say it to hurt you. I was trying to reassure you."

"It wasn't reassuring to know the woman in my life thought my judgment was unsound."

"I didn't think that. In some cases, I agreed with Liza's position."

"I know. I was there. Remember?"

"I'm not understanding, Jackson."

"I felt threatened, Christina." He wouldn't let her interrupt. "I found out some things about myself that I didn't like. I felt threatened. I felt I was going to lose you."

"Now I'm really confused. You left me because you thought you were going to lose me?"

"Don't try to make sense out of it. It doesn't really make sense. I thought I was losing you and I couldn't bear to wait around for the end to come. So I bailed out first."

"I loved you, Jackson. Leaving you never crossed my mind."

"You're a pretty intimidating woman, Christina. You don't really need anybody. You could have your pick of men and I feared one day you'd think you had made the wrong choice."

Christina was beginning to understand. She knew many of Jackson's insecurities stemmed from his mother's desertion. "You could have talked about this before now. Why didn't you?"

"I tried to a couple of times."

She remembered the conversations. "You could have tried harder."

"Maybe you could have listened a little better, too?"

She thought about that. "Maybe."

"Are you going to marry Reggie?" he asked.

"No, Jackson. I'm not going to marry Reggie."

His relief was obvious. "Are you going to marry me?"

She looked at him and she thought about her parents. Did she want her and Jackson to end up like them — trying to recapture a love that they lost for no good reason? "I haven't received a proposal from you."

Jackson remembered the pain from the first time he had asked her. "Yes, you have. I asked you before and you turned me down. That's the other part of what was bothering me. After you turned me down, I became convinced that you didn't really love me."

"Oh, Jackson," Christina cried. "How

could you have thought that I didn't love you? I didn't turn you down. I just said your timing was off."

Keeping her hand in his, he got down on his knees in front of her. "I love you, Christina. Will you marry me?"

"I like him. How about you?" Louise looked up at the starry sky as she and Christian walked along Main Street.

"Yes, I like him. I hope they can work out their differences."

"So do I. It's obvious he's in love with her and more than obvious that she's in love with him. One day they'll regret the time they wasted."

Christian took her hand and they continued to walk. "You're thinking about us, aren't you?"

"Their situation is like ours in many ways." She looked up at him. "There are differences as well."

"Do you think we have a chance, Louise?"

She'd been asking herself the same question. Thirty years was a long time. She was old and set in her ways, and so was he. "There are so many things to work out. Where would we live? Your business is in Chicago. Mine is here."

"People are relocating everyday. We could

work that out if we wanted to. The real question is whether you want to take a chance on me again." He stopped walking and tilted her face up to look at him. "I want to spend the rest of my days with you, Louise. We can't make up for our lost past, but we can have a future together. I love you. Will you marry me?"

"I love you, too, Christian. After all these years I still love you. Though some things have changed, a lot of things remain the same."

"You're talking race now?"

"Yes. The social environment will be more tolerant, but not any more accepting than it was thirty years ago. Are you sure you want to go through that? What about your business? Would it be affected?"

"I'd like to think my clients judge me by the work that I do. Honestly, I can imagine some effects, though. I may lose a few clients, but it doesn't matter. I've managed to build a sizable business and I seriously doubt that our marriage will cause it to crumble."

If it did, you'd hate me, she thought. "What if it did? What if you lost your business?"

"That's not going to happen. If it did, it wouldn't matter. I love what I do, but I stopped doing it for the money years ago. We'll have more than enough to last us the rest of our days." He smiled then. "There'll probably be some left over for our grandchildren. Now, what's your next problem?"

Louise turned and started walking again. He kept up with her. "You aren't taking this seriously, Christian."

"Yes, I am," he corrected. "You're worrying about the wrong thing. We made a mistake thirty years ago. Do you want to make the same one again?"

She had known that one day he'd blame her for the decision she'd made. "So, you think I was wrong not to tell you about the baby?"

"Not exactly. I think we didn't trust our love enough. I think it would have survived. It would have been difficult, but I believe we would have made it."

Tears filled Louise's eyes. "I'm so sorry, Christian," she said. "I did what I thought was best."

Christian stopped walking and pulled her into his arms. "I know you did, Louise. I'm not blaming you. You did what you had to do, and I accept that. I just don't want you to turn me away again. This is our last chance."

She knew he was right. It was a miracle

they'd found each other again, a miracle their love still lasted. More than anything, she wanted to be with him. She squeezed him to her. "I love you so much, Christian, and I want to be your wife, but I need time to get adjusted to the thought of marriage." She looked up at him. "Will you give me some time?"

He smiled and she knew it was going to be all right.

Jackson scooped dirt from the barrel. Helping in the nursery was not as easy as he expected. "We haven't talked about the roses."

Christina dreaded talking about them. "I know."

"Do you still believe I sent them?"

She answered honestly. "A part of me thinks it's possible." He visibly flinched at that and she added, "Another part of me doesn't believe you would ever hurt me."

"Which part is stronger?" he asked.

She reached into her heart to find the answer. "The part that trusts you."

He visibly relaxed. "That's good to know. Now, what will it take to get rid of the doubts?"

Christina moved to sit next to him. She was amazed at how quickly they had fallen back into their relationship. It was almost as though they'd never been apart. They were back to their preproblem days now. Only better. Now, they talked about things, especially things that hurt, instead of allowing them to fester. "Do you think we can find out who sent them?"

"I've been thinking a lot about it. Someone set me up. They wanted you to think I was sending the roses."

"Why would anyone want to do that?"

"I don't know. That's what I'm trying to figure out. Who would want to break us up?"

She spoke her first thoughts. "Reggie and Angela, but I won't believe either one of them did it."

"They crossed my mind, too, but I dismissed them immediately. Maybe the answer is professional, not personal?"

"I never considered that. So, you think someone thought that causing problems in our personal relationship would affect the work we were doing at CL?"

"Possibly. Frankly, I'd rather think that over the other. I've hired a private detective."

"When? What has he found out?"

"I hired him after I learned you were pregnant, but he hasn't come up with anything yet."

"How did you find out I was pregnant?"

"Robert."

She had guessed it was Robert. "I knew it. I knew Liza couldn't keep it from him."

"You shouldn't have kept it from me, Christina. Regardless of our problems, I deserved to know."

She knew he was right. She shuddered to think that she would have had this baby without telling him. "I know. I came to Boston to tell you, but when I found you and Angela together like that, I couldn't. If you could fall into bed with her so quickly, I began to wonder if you ever really cared for me. I couldn't risk finding out that you didn't."

"We've both made mistakes in this relationship. Let's make a pact now to keep doing what we've been doing since I've been here — talk, even when it hurts. That's the only way we're going to make it." He extended his hand to her. "Deal?"

"Deal," she said.

He pulled her into his arms and kissed her when she reached for his hand. "If you get any bigger, my arms won't go around you." he teased.

"Are you happy about the baby, Jackson? It wasn't something we planned."

He pulled back to look at her. "Very

happy. I think I'm going to be a great father. I've been practicing."

She chuckled. "Practicing?"

"Yes. I even went to see my dad."

"Your dad? When?"

"Right after I found out about the baby. I don't want any estrangements in our family."

"How did it go?" she asked. She was glad that he was building bridges.

"Dad hasn't changed, but he's not so bad. I learned a lot about him that weekend. With a little training, he'll do okay as a granddad."

"It's all working out, isn't it, Jackson? You and your father, my mother and father, you and me. Everything is falling into place."

He hugged her to him. "Almost everything. We still don't know who's been sending the roses, and unless I'm mistaken, Reggie still thinks you might marry him."

She lowered her eyelids. "I don't like the idea of hurting him. He's been a good friend to me and the baby."

Jackson knew, on some level, that he should be grateful for the way Reggie had supported Christina, but he just wanted the guy out of their lives. "I don't like to think about that. I appreciate that he was there for you when you needed somebody, but I don't like that he's always hanging around you."

"Jealous?" she teased.

"Maybe. The man planned to be a father to my child. I don't like it. Did he tell you that we almost came to blows on my visit to Oklahoma City? Mr. Stevens told me to talk to you, tell you how I felt."

"You could have done that."

"Not then. My feelings about our work relationship got mixed up with my feeling about my own manhood. I needed to work that out. And the situation had been complicated by the roses. I didn't know what to do. Then the Boston job came through and I took it."

Christina put her hand to her mouth. "Your work? I had almost forgotten about that. When do you have to get back?"

"I left it open. We have to decide what we're going to do. Are you going to marry me?"

Her mind went to the roses. Her heart went to his eyes. She wanted a life with him. It all boiled down to whether she would trust him to share his life with her.

"Yes," she answered.

His eyes lit up. "When?"

"Soon."

He reached down and touched her belly.

"I'd say the sooner the better."

She laughed. "I agree."

They stood holding each other for a while. "Jackson," she said. "I have to tell Reggie first."

Jackson began nibbling her on her neck. "I understand that. Tell him."

"Jackson?"

"Umm . . ." He was still nibbling.

"Reggie's coming to town this weekend."

Christina met Reggie at the airport. "We need to talk," she told him as soon as he greeted her. "Let's go to the lounge."

When they were seated in the lounge, Reggie said, "This has to be bad news."

Christina reached over and touched his hands. She felt the tears puddling in her eyes. "You're the best friend a girl could have, Reggie. I love you for all you've done for me and the baby, but I can't marry you."

"Has something happened?"

She nodded. "Jackson came to town a few days ago." She knew this would hurt, but she had to tell him. "I still love him, Reggie, and he loves me."

She was surprised to see a half smile form on Reggie's face. "I half expected this," he said. "I knew you loved him, I just hoped you'd get over it."

She smiled through her tears. "You don't get over love, Reggie. I hope you find someone and learn that for yourself some-day. You deserve more than I could have given you."

"Is Jackson still here?"

She nodded. "He's waiting in the car. I wanted to talk with you alone."

"I'm not ready to congratulate him yet. Do you understand that?"

She did. "And so does Jackson. Neither of us wanted to hurt you."

"I know. Why don't you leave now? I could use the time alone before I take the next flight back to Oklahoma City."

"Are you sure that's what you want?"

"I'm sure," he said, and then he smiled. "You'd better get back to Jackson. He's probably thinking I've convinced you that I'm the better man. Any minute now he'll come storming through the door."

There was so much Christina wanted to say. She wanted to tell him how much he had helped her. She wanted to tell him that if it were not for Jackson she could have loved him. Instead, without saying anything, she stood up, squeezed his hand again, and left.

Tears began to fall when she thought of Reggie and Angela, two innocent people who had been hurt because they had cared for her and Jackson. She wished they could find a love like the one she and Jackson shared.

Jackson met her at the exit door. "What happened? You were gone so long I thought something happened. Why are you crying?"

"Everything's all right, Jackson," she said through her tears. "Let's go home."

CHAPTER 26

"Remind me never to marry a pregnant woman," Jackson teased. They were in his hotel room following their wedding.

Christina chuckled. "It's your fault. This would never have happened if we hadn't had the honeymoon before the wedding."

"I'm dying here, Mrs. Duncan, and you're making jokes."

Christina was undressing in the oversized closet. "It's funny, Jackson."

Jackson stood and began to undress. "I haven't made love to you in over seven months. That's not what I call funny."

"It is when you think about it. Just think, you only have about seven more months to go."

Jackson stopped unbuckling his pants to stare at her. "Seven more months! You must be kidding."

"Doctors don't recommend sex for six months after the baby is born," Christina stated with authority. "We've still got one month till the birth."

"When is your next check-up? Your doctor and I need to have a talk. I'm not waiting six months. Is this a woman doctor?"

Christina walked out of the closet and sat on the bed to remove her hose. She thanked God for knee-highs. "What difference does that make?"

"Big difference. Is the doctor a woman?"

"She's a woman, but . . ."

"But nothing. That explains it. I'll have a little talk with Madam Doctor. Six weeks maybe, but not six months."

She looked at him. "Poor Jackson. Having such a hard time dealing with marriage."

"You'd better show some more under-standing, woman," he teased. "Since we haven't consummated this union, I could have this marriage annulled."

"I doubt that, once they see the pregnant wife. Maybe even a baby."

"I'm talking legal here, not moral. Treat me right, or you'll find yourself a single woman again. For starters, why don't you waddle over here and give me a kiss?"

The first time he'd said "waddle" she'd taken offense, but his continued sexual interest in her took away her concern. "I guess I can be generous with kisses, since that's all you're going to get."

When she was standing in his arms, he said, "Make it good, too."

She did. "You have to stop now, Christina. I can only take so much."

She smiled deceptively. "I have to make sure you don't lose interest in your wife who waddles, who's so big your arms won't go around her."

"I'm interested. All right. More than interested. Now, let's talk about something else before I have to take a shower."

Christina gave a quick glance and saw his problem. "Stop looking at me like that," Jackson commanded. "You're only making it worse. Now, think of something else to talk about."

Christina went to the bathroom to remove her makeup. "I'm glad your dad came to the wedding."

"Me, too." He laughed lightly. "He still thinks you tricked me into this marriage."

"Why does he think that?"

Jackson stood by the bathroom door and watched his wife. Love filled his heart. It pained him to think that they could have lost each other. "Remnants from his past, Christina. He'll come around."

"I hope so. He didn't bring up Sarah once."

Christina touched Jackson's arm. "Did you think a lot about her today?"

Jackson answered honestly. "I thought about her. A couple of times I wished she were here. Strange, huh?"

Christina shook her head. "Not strange at all." She was glad Jackson was allowing his loving feeling for Sarah to surface. Maybe one day she could be a part of their lives.

"How do you feel about your parents getting back together?" he asked.

"I'm happy for them, but I'm still getting used to my father being alive. To his being white. To his loving me. To his loving Mom. To Mom loving him."

"Don't think about it too much," Jackson said. "Consider yourself and your parents fortunate. Not many people get a second chance."

She knew he was right. She shuddered to think that they could have missed their chance. "We did."

"We were lucky, too. We came too close to losing each other."

"I like to think that we would have found our way back to each other somehow," she said.

"I'm glad we did, and I'm glad it didn't take us years. Thirty years! That's a long time to be separated from the one you love."

"I know."

Christina's thoughts went to Rosalind and Walter. She had been happy they'd made it to the wedding. Rosalind and Louise had cried buckets of tears. Christina knew Rosalind's tears were tears of sorrow as well as tears of happiness. Tears of sorrow because Rosalind knew she would never give Walter a child. Tears of happiness because Christina and Jackson had been blessed to find each other before too much time had passed. After her talk with Rosalind at the reception, Christina had sworn she would never again take her family or her family's love for granted.

Jackson came up behind her then and she shook off all thoughts that didn't include him. When she finished removing her makeup, they walked back to their bed. They lay together, she in his arms.

"I think the soccer player is acting up again," Jackson said.

"You can feel him, too?"

"How could I not? He kicks like a veteran."

"He *has* been pretty active lately. The doctor says it's normal."

"Does it bother you much?"

She shook her head. "It's reassuring to know he's moving around in there."

"We haven't thought of a name for him."

"I have. We could name him Junior."

Jackson frowned. "I don't like that. Let him have his own name."

"I'm glad you feel that way."

"You didn't want to name him Junior?"

"That wasn't my first choice. How about Marcus James?"

"For my dad?"

Christina nodded. "I know it would mean a lot to him."

He leaned down and kissed her. "Thank you. You don't think your dad will feel left out, do you?"

Christina shook her head and smiled impishly. "Christian's middle name is Marcus."

Christina went into labor exactly three weeks after her marriage. She was in labor twenty-four hours. Jackson knew she did most of the work, but he was pretty tired himself. He wouldn't have missed going through it with her for anything in the world. It was more than worth all the time he'd taken away from his work. He felt that he and Christina had brought their baby into the world together.

As Jackson looked at his wife, her parents, and their baby boy, his heart overflowed with love. His and Christina's love grew every day. He was confident their love had finally overcome all the childhood fears they had carried into adulthood.

He knew Christina's love for him was constant. She would always be there for him. He expected they would have problems, but he was confident they would meet each one head-on. He knew Christina's feelings had changed, too. She expected him to be there when she needed him, and she let him know it. That was a big move for a woman who practiced not expressing her needs for fear they wouldn't be met. Yes, he and Christina were on their way.

They still didn't know who sent the roses, but it didn't matter now. They had their new baby. All was right with the world.

Louise's baby talk ended his musing. "Isn't he the cutest baby?" she was asking.

"I've never seen a cuter one," Christian agreed.

Jackson looked at Christina. "If I didn't know they were exactly right, I'd say they were biased."

Christina laughed. "He's ours, and he *is* a cute baby. I'll agree with that."

"Have you called Jim yet, Jackson?" Christian asked. He and Louise stood on one side of Christina's bed. Jackson stood on the other.

Jackson touched his son's cheek. "Right after this little fellow was born. He got choked up when I told him the name. He's flying in tomorrow."

"I was a bit surprised at the name myself," Christian said. "You two will never know how much it means to me."

"It means a lot to us that you're here, Christian," Jackson said. "Marcus J. is going to need all his grandparents."

"We'd better get out of here and give you two some time alone," Louise said. She looked at Christian. "Buy me lunch, Grandpa?"

"I guess I can do that, Grandma." He turned to Jackson and Christina. "We'll be back later this afternoon."

Jackson watched them leave hand in hand. "We may have another wedding soon," he said to Christina. "How would you feel about that?"

"It'd be great. I think you're right. They're probably waiting for the right time to tell us."

Jackson looked at his son and then at his wife. "You've made me the happiest man in the world, Christina. I'll be good to you and the baby."

"I know you will, Jackson."

"Are you sure about moving to Boston?"

She nodded. "I'm not ready to go back to work yet. I want to spend some time with this little guy."

"You're not worried about your career?" he asked, to be sure.

She reached out and touched his chin. "Before you and," she looked down at Marcus J., "this little guy, work was all I had. That made it very important to me. It's not that important now."

"You're going to be content staying home with the baby?"

"I think so. I'll consider it my second career. If I find I'm not happy with it, I can always go back to work." At his look of uncertainty, she added, "Relax. I'm sure."

"I want you to be happy. Now that I'm sure of your love, I can handle your career. I don't want your concern for my feelings to keep you home."

His words endeared him to her even more. "That's not it," she said. "I want to stay home. I've waited all my life for what I have now. Let me enjoy it."

"If you're sure."

"I'm sure," she said. "Don't you see that everything is working out perfectly for us? We don't even have to worry about the house in Atlanta."

"Robert and Liza's offer was a great wedding gift. They love the place."

Christina nodded in agreement. "Oh, Jackson, I hope they can be happy as we are. But it looks like they're moving in different directions."

"I know. Robert wants to start a family and Liza doesn't. It's causing a strain in their relationship, because he thinks she's too wrapped up in her career."

Christina had feared that would happen. She didn't know how they were going to work it out. "I wish there was something we could do for them."

Jackson leaned down and kissed her. "There's nothing we can do. They have to work it out themselves."

Christina just nodded. More than anything, she wanted Liza and Robert to work it out. She wanted everyone to be as happy as she and Jackson were.

"What are you thinking about?" Jackson asked.

"Rosalind and Walter. Their generous donation to the radio-thon was a welcome surprise. Now, I'll be able to give a substantial donation even though I won't be able to participate."

"You're right, Mrs. Duncan, everything is working out for us."

"I'm glad you see it. Now I have a surprise for you."

"Now you're talking. I love surprises."

"I'd like to have more babies. At least two more."

Jackson leered at her. "We can start on that sooner than you thought. I talked with Dr. Gray the other day."

Christina laughed while her husband nibbled on her ear.

Jackson arrived at the hospital early the next morning. Christina and Louise had volunteered to pick up his dad at the airport so he, Christina, and the baby could have some time alone. He stopped by the nursery first. When the crib for Baby Duncan was empty, Jackson smiled and headed for Christina's room. He saw the roses when he first opened the door. He looked at the bed and saw that Christina was still asleep. The baby wasn't in the room. Fear bubbled in his stomach as he walked toward the roses.

Please, God, no. Not again.

He took the card and turned it over in his hand before opening it. *You lose, Bitch,* he read silently. He closed the card. Inside he screamed. He looked at Christina sleeping peacefully. He knew he had to wake her and tell her, but he couldn't. Not yet. Maybe he was wrong. He left the room and headed for the nurse's desk.

"The Duncan baby is not in the nursery or my wife's room. Is he taking tests or something?"

Jackson went to hell and back during the time the nurse checked. When she told him that one of the nurses had the baby, his knees buckled in relief and he had to hold on to the counter for support.

"Did you see a man take flowers to my wife's room?"

The nurse nodded. "After he delivered the flowers, he asked for directions to the nursery."

Jackson's heartbeat raced as he turned to run to the nursery. When he got there, a nurse holding a baby was arguing with an older, well-dressed man. The man's back was turned to him.

"What's going on here?" Jackson asked.

"He wants to hold your baby, Mr. Duncan," the nurse said. "I've told him it's against the rules."

The man turned then and the hate-filled look in his eyes told Jackson that this was the man who had sent the roses. "Did you leave the flowers in Mrs. Duncan's room?" Jackson asked.

"Sure I did," the man said. "There's no

law against it."

Jackson drew back to hit the man, but he stopped himself. What was the point? They had the man now and the incidents would stop. He didn't want revenge. He just wanted his family safe. "Call the police," he told the nurse. "We have a criminal here."

They held a celebration in Christina's room that night. "How do you like your grandson, Jim?" Louise asked.

"Fine-looking boy," Jim said proudly.

"Good set of lungs, too," Jackson added.

"Wait until we get him home and he needs to be fed at three o'clock in the morning," Christina said. "I'll see what you think of his lungs then."

"I can hardly wait," Jackson said. He added for Christina's ears only, "I'll be able to watch my beloved wife feed our beloved son from her beloved breasts."

"If you're good, I may let you watch. Now stop being bad," Christina whispered back to him.

"They've started whispering to each other," Louise announced. "That's our cue to leave. They need their privacy."

"Don't go, Mom," Christina said, "the party's just starting. Jackson and I have the next fifty years to be together. We want you all to stay."

"If you're sure?" Louise questioned.

"We're sure," Christina said.

Jim was still holding Marcus J. "Tell us what happened with that guy and the police."

"You'd never believe it," Christina told them. Thinking about it made her shiver. "Paul Bechtel sent the roses and the notes."

"Who's Paul Bechtel?" Christian asked.

"Paul is the guy I replaced when I came to Atlanta. He couldn't find another job, and that caused him to have a nervous breakdown. In his mind, I was responsible for his problems."

"We're lucky," Louise said. "There are many stories of people losing their jobs and doing much worse."

"I had the same thought," Christina said. "I'm grateful nothing happened to us or to Marcus J. Can you believe he was actually here in the hospital? Just thinking about it gives me chills."

"How did he know when to send them?" Christian asked. "Wasn't he trying to make it look like you were sending them, Jackson?"

Jackson nodded. "He was working with Doris, my secretary. She had been his secretary when he worked at CL."

"Was she in on it, too?" Jim asked.

Jackson shook his head. "He used her to get information about Christina and me."

"Poor Doris," Christina said. "She's probably never going to gossip again. That just might kill her."

They all laughed at that. Jackson looked around the room and saw all the smiles. He was happy, happier than he'd ever thought he could be.

He saw Christian whisper something in Louise's ear.

"We have an announcement," Christian said.

Jackson looked at Christina. His eyes said, "I told you so."

"Louise and I are getting married next week."

"That's great! I'm happy for both of you," Christina said. "Come over here so I can give you a kiss."

They did just that and Christina kissed them. Jackson shook hands with Christian and gave Louis a kiss, and Jim did the same.

"Does this mean I can call you Dad now?" Christina asked Christian.

Jackson saw the tears that quickly formed in Christian's eyes.

"I think that's exactly what it means, daughter."

CHAPTER 27

Six months later, Christina sat on the floor of their townhouse in Boston. Marcus J. was asleep, and Jackson was at work. The house was quiet, a welcome sound to her ears. She looked at the stack of boxes before her. She opened the one closest to her and pulled out a small black notebook. She smiled when she saw it. She took it out of the box, opened it, and turned to the page entitled "Personal Goals." She read:

1. Move to Atlanta
2. Get established in job
3. Buy house
4. Get established in community
5. Make friends
6. Fall in love
7. Get married
8. Have 3 children

Christina looked at the list. She had accomplished all the items on the list but one, number eight. She didn't have three children. Yet. She was working on it, though. All her dreams were about to come true. She closed the notebook with a smile on her face. She got up and went over to her dresser. She opened the third drawer and pulled out the purple teddy with black lace. "Who knows?" She asked aloud. "Maybe tonight we'll get lucky."